FREE AIR

FREE AIR

BY

SINCLAIR LEWIS

Introduction to the Bison Book Edition
by Robert E. Fleming

University of Nebraska Press
Lincoln and London

Copyright 1919, 1947 by Sinclair Lewis
Introduction to the Bison Book Edition copyright © 1993 by the University
of Nebraska Press
Manufactured in the United States of America

First Bison Book printing: 1993
Most recent printing indicated by the last digit below:
10   9   8   7   6   5   4   3   2   1

Library of Congress Cataloging-in-Publication Data
Lewis, Sinclair, 1885–1951.
Free air / by Sinclair Lewis: introduction to the Bison book edition by Robert
E. Fleming.
p.   cm.
Originally published: New York: Harcourt, Brace & Howe, 1919.
"Bison."
ISBN 0-8032-7943-4 (pbk.)
PS3523.E94F7   1993
813'.52—dc20
92-37702   CIP

Reprinted by arrangement with the Estate of Sinclair Lewis

∞

INTRODUCTION
by Robert E. Fleming

Sinclair Lewis is best remembered for his great novels of the 1920s: *Main Street* (1920), *Babbitt* (1922), *Arrowsmith* (1925), *Elmer Gantry* (1927), and *Dodsworth* (1929). During that incredibly successful decade, Lewis appeared regularly on the best-seller lists, won—and refused—the Pulitzer Prize, and became the first American ever to win the Nobel Prize for Literature, which was awarded to him in 1930 in spite of considerable controversy.

To much of the American public, *Main Street* appeared to be Lewis's first novel, but as Emerson said of Whitman's *Leaves of Grass, Main Street* had had a long foreground. Between 1912 and 1920, Lewis had learned to tell short stories well enough to crack the tough but high-paying *Saturday Evening Post* market. He had also published one boys' book (which appeared under the pseudonym Tom Graham) and five modestly successful novels. *Free Air* (1919) is the last of that series of early novels, and Lewis believed enough in its merits to suggest to his publisher that it should be submitted to the Pulitzer Prize Committee for consideration.

As a realist Lewis, writing about the Great Plains, knew his territory well. *Free Air* grew out of an automobile trip Lewis took with his new wife, Grace Hegger Lewis, in 1916. Lewis had returned to Sauk Centre, Minnesota, to introduce his wife to his family and to complete his third novel, *The Job* (1917). Afterwards, he and Grace bought a Model T Ford—modified to convert into a simple camper by the attachment of a tent—and set out for Seattle. Never one to waste material, Lewis turned out nonfiction articles such as "Adventures in Autobumming" based on the expedition.

However, Lewis realized that his material was too good to waste on mere low-paying journalism and soon turned his hand to a serial called "Free Air," which ran in the *Saturday Evening Post* from May 31 through June 21, 1919. The serial so pleased editor George Horace Lorimer that he urged Lewis to write a sequel, offering him $2,500 for two additional episodes. Lewis, who had already been thinking of expanding his work to legitimate book length, produced "Danger—Run Slow," which appeared in the *Post* on October 18 and 25, 1919. On October 23, Harcourt, Brace and Howe published the novel.

In spite of its having appeared first in a high-circulation magazine, *Free Air* sold respectably for an early Lewis novel—over eight thousand copies in prepublication sales. Reviewers for *Dial,* the *New York Times Review of Books,* and *New Republic* praised the novel for its various strengths: its accurate transcription of American speech patterns, its photographic reproduction of the western landscape, and in particular, its emphasis on the merit of the individual rather than his or her social class or family background.

By the time he wrote *Free Air* Lewis had grown confident about his ability to tell a good story laced with humor and was moving toward the role of social critic. Lewis honed the skills he would need and explored some of the themes he would treat in *Main Street.* Thus, there are many satirical passages, and, as he would in his more famous novel, Lewis directs his satire in both directions, toward his city heroine, Claire Boltwood, as well as toward the rural characters and settings with which she comes in contact. But one positive feature of her western trip across the plains is the western hero she encounters on her travels.

Milt Daggett lacks many of the social graces that would have made him welcome in polite society of his time. The son of a country doctor, Milt points with pride to the New England origins of his family and to a grandfather who was a judge. Milt, however, is only the proprietor of a two-man auto repair shop in Schoenstrom. He is a provincial westerner who has never in his life been out of Minnesota before he sees Claire Boltwood, falls in love, and decides to follow her cross-country to Seattle.

When easterner Claire Boltwood first encounters him, he seems to her the antithesis of all she has been told to admire in a man. He has grease under his fingernails and speaks a rough and ready English that betrays his lack of formal education. but although he lacks schooling, Milt displays both intelligence and adaptability. He is equal to any road emergency, from fouled spark plugs to a mistimed distributor. While rescuing Claire and her father from a farmer who is overcharging them for pulling their car out of the mud, Milt displays a working knowledge of human nature, broken but serviceable German, and the fine art of beating a bully at his own game. In addition, he is enough of a natural gentleman to refuse the tip which Claire's grateful father offers him after the rescue. Like Carl Ericson, of Lewis's 1915 novel *The Trail of the Hawk,* Milt anticipates later Lewis heroes such as medical researcher Martin Arrowsmith and automobile designer Sam Dodsworth, who will combine twentieth-century scientific and technical expertise with midwestern common sense and morality.

To complement his western hero, Lewis creates one of his finest examples of the new American woman, a character he had just experimented with in Una Golden, the feminist heroine of *The Job.* Much like Grace Lewis, her real-life source, Claire Boltwood is too intellectual, too independent, to be content with a role as charming hostess for a man and as housebound mother of his children. The man she marries will find that he has taken on a full partner. Claire anticipates not only Carol Kennicott of *Main Street* but later characters such as the protagonist of *Ann Vickers* (1933). Reared in luxury in a New York suburb, Claire seems destined to become the wife of Geoffrey Saxton, a man of her own social set. Sixteen years older than Claire, Saxton understands all about high finance—and nothing about women. While Claire's excuse for her western vacation is to cure her father of nervous prostration brought on by overwork, a better reason is to postpone the inevitability of marriage to Saxton. Yet for all her admirable qualities, Claire can be comically quixotic, refusing to allow Milt to accompany her and her father when both her self-interest and her romantic interest in Milt make her want him to stay with them.

In *Free Air* Lewis sounds a positive note that would also be present in *Main Street*—an appreciation for the free western spirit, the democratic atmosphere of the American frontier and its continuing importance even in the twentieth century. Sparsely settled by eastern standards, the West challenges its inhabitants. Rough, raw, and energetic new towns bear little resemblance to the conventional, cultured, long-established cities of the East. Although the West is no longer as wild as it once was, it still offers a vast natural setting where the individual is largely on his or her own and where people are judged by what they do rather than by who their parents are or where they went to school. The dominance of unpredictable nature and the absence of eastern amenities allow—or force—individuals into tests of character. As Claire gains more self-reliance than she could ever have developed in Brooklyn Heights, she also learns more about her own values and character.

The sights the Boltwoods see as they travel west are predictable in a novel named *Free Air*: they are exposed to a part of the country and a way of life of which they have been completely ignorant. Symbolic of this different world are modern-day reminders of the prairie schooners that once traveled the Oregon Trail, mechanized Conestogas driven by twentieth-century travelers:

> "Sagebrush Tourists" these camping adventurers were called. Claire became used to small cars, with curtain-lights broken, bearing wash-boilers or refrigerators on the back, pastboard [sic] suitcases lashed by rope to the running-board, frying pans and canvas water bottles dangling. . . . In each car was what looked like a crowd at a large farm-auction—grandfather, father, mother, a couple of sons and two or three daughters . . . all jammed into two seats already filled with trunks and baby-carriages. (119–20)

Such passages not only look back to James Fenimore Cooper's *The Prairie* but forward to John Steinbeck's *The Grapes of Wrath*.

Restaurants and hotels available to early tourists allow Lewis some of his best opportunities for satirical humor. A romantically named culinary establishment, the "Eats Garden" of Reaper, North Dakota, greets the hungry travelers with "a belch of smoke" from its overheated grill. A single table is graced with a utilitarian oilcloth "decorated with venerable spots of dried egg yolk," and the waiter-cook wears a filthy apron. The menus are fly-specked, steaks are like leather, and the cook can't even make toast successfully. In Gopher Prairie, a town soon to become familiar to many readers, Claire and her father find a single "tolerable" hotel, the decor of its unappealing lobby dominated by "poison-green" paint, brass cuspidors, and insurance company calendars. Claire's room in this "up-to-date place" is furnished with a bed so tilted that she is afraid to fall asleep lest she roll out. Lewis's experience and imagination furnish a comic variety of similarly unsavory accommodations and restaurants.

Travelers crossing the nation in the early twentieth century also faced a host of problems with their cars: fragile tube-type tires required frequent patching, brakes needed multiple overhauls between Minneapolis and Seattle, and engines suffered badly when cars climbed the intervening mountains. With enthusiasm, Lewis documents these early years of America's growing love affair with the automobile, a time when it was considered the height of adventure for a woman to attempt a cross-country drive. Just a few years earlier, in 1909, the Maxwell-Briscoe company had sought publicity by commissioning Alice Huyler Ramsey to drive one of its cars from New York to San Francisco, and in 1915 Paramount had sponsored actress Anita King's "solo" drive from Los Angeles to New York—accompanied by the press corps. The reader learns to admire Claire not only for her adventurous spirit in challenging the road west but also for her plucky willingness to patch inner tubes and change tires. And what modern reader can fail to sympathize when she falls into the hands of unscrupulous repairmen?

As the Boltwoods progress down the road, they continue to encounter Milt, whose skills as a traveler, a pathfinder, and a mechanic overshadow his lack of social acceptability. His skillful handling of the automobile epitomized the spirit of America in an era when the empty miles of the West could at long last be traversed in a relatively short time by automobile. Through Milt Daggett, Lewis speaks both for and to his age, an age when technology will replace bravery and physical force even in times of war. Milt is called upon to protect his charges from few melodramatic dangers, although a tramp attempts to commandeer the Boltwoods' car and a "highwayman" points a revolver at Milt. In keeping with Lewis's realistic and satirical view of America, the twentieth-century automobile pioneer contends not with highwaymen or Indians but with dishonest or incompetent garage mechanics and sloppy hotel-keepers. Not risk but extreme inconvenience besets the tourist who drives the vulnerable automobiles of the day.

If Milt is an expert at overcoming technological problems, he is less adept at overcoming social barriers. The outcome of his pursuit is by no means certain as he tries to woo Claire not only on the road but in Washington state, where she stays with her socially prominent relatives. Invited to the home of these pretentious relatives, Milt feels that his dress, table manners, and speech mark him as an ill-mannered lout, completely unworthy of such a refined woman as Claire. Lewis's skills at building suspense, honed by his years of writing for the popular magazines, keep his readers guessing about Milt's fate in this unlikely romance right up to the final chapter.

Free Air displays Sinclair Lewis's skills in development and anticipates the spectacularly successful career he was to enjoy during the next decade. He rapidly delineates characters, both sketching in unforgettable minor characters in the manner of Charles Dickens and depicting his protagonists first with the broad strokes of the caricaturist and then with a more subtle exploration of their complex feelings. He shows a linguist's ear for the American language—its regional dialects and its ability to cut through hypocrisy and get at the truth. He describes and analyzes the natural landscape, small-town peculiarities, and the haphazard "development" of larger cities with a deftness that prefigures his creation of the Gopher Prairies and Zeniths of his later career. His two principle characters look ahead to Carol and Will Kennicott, Leora and Martin Arrowsmith, Sam Dodsworth, and Ann Vickers. In *Free Air* Lewis depicts his country in all its strengths and weaknesses during an exciting period in its cultural history, a period that requires the fresh, free spirits of adventurous young Americans like Milt Daggett and Claire Boltwood.

CONTENTS

CONTENTS

FREE AIR

FREE AIR

CHAPTER I

MISS BOLTWOOD OF BROOKLYN IS LOST IN THE MUD

WHEN the windshield was closed it became so filmed with rain that Claire fancied she was piloting a drowned car in dim spaces under the sea. When it was open, drops jabbed into her eyes and chilled her cheeks. She was excited and thoroughly miserable. She realized that these Minnesota country roads had no respect for her polite experience on Long Island parkways. She felt like a woman, not like a driver.

But the Gomez-Dep roadster had seventy horse-power, and sang songs. Since she had left Minneapolis nothing had passed her. Back yonder a truck had tried to crowd her, and she had dropped into a ditch, climbed a bank, returned to the road, and after that the truck was not. Now she was regarding a view more splendid than mountains above a garden by the sea—a stretch of good road. To her passenger, her father, Claire chanted:

"Heavenly! There's some gravel. We can make time. We'll hustle on to the next town and get dry."

"Yes. But don't mind me. You're doing very well," her father sighed.

Instantly, the dismay of it rushing at her, she saw the end of the patch of gravel. The road ahead was a wet black smear, criss-crossed with ruts. The car shot into a morass of prairie gumbo—which is mud mixed with tar, fly-paper, fish glue, and well-chewed, chocolate-covered caramels. When cattle get into gumbo, the farmers send for the stump-dynamite and try blasting.

It was her first really bad stretch of road. She was frightened. Then she was too appallingly busy to be frightened, or to be Miss Claire Boltwood, or to comfort her uneasy father. She had to drive. Her frail graceful arms put into it a vicious vigor that was genius.

When the wheels struck the slime, they slid, they wallowed. The car skidded. It was terrifyingly out of control. It began majestically to turn toward the ditch. She fought the steering wheel as though she were shadow-boxing, but the car kept contemptuously staggering till it was sideways, straight across the road. Somehow, it was back again, eating into a rut, going ahead. She didn't know how she had done it, but she had got it back. She longed to take time to retrace her own cleverness in steering. She didn't. She kept going.

The car backfired, slowed. She yanked the gear

from third into first. She sped up. The motor ran
like a terrified pounding heart, while the car crept
on by inches through filthy mud that stretched ahead
of her without relief.

She was battling to hold the car in the principal
rut. She snatched the windshield open, and concentrated on that left rut. She felt that she was keeping
the wheel from climbing those high sides of the rut,
those six-inch walls of mud, sparkling with tiny grits.
Her mind snarled at her arms, " Let the ruts do the
steering. You're just fighting against them." It
worked. Once she let the wheels alone they comfortably followed the furrows, and for three seconds
she had that delightful belief of every motorist after
every mishap, " Now that this particular disagreeable-
ness is over, I'll never, never have any trouble again! "

But suppose the engine overheated, ran out of
water? Anxiety twanged at her nerves. And the deep
distinctive ruts were changing to a complex pattern,
like the rails in a city switchyard. She picked out
the track of the one motor car that had been through
here recently. It was marked with the swastika tread
of the rear tires. That track was her friend; she
knew and loved the driver of a car she had never seen
in her life.

She was very tired. She wondered if she might
not stop for a moment. Then she came to an up-slope.
The car faltered; felt indecisive beneath her. She

jabbed down the accelerator. Her hands pushed at the steering wheel as though she were pushing the car. The engine picked up, sulkily kept going. To the eye, there was merely a rise in the rolling ground, but to her anxiety it was a mountain up which she— not the engine, but herself—pulled this bulky mass, till she had reached the top, and was safe again—for a second. Still there was no visible end of the mud.

In alarm she thought, " How long does it last? I can't keep this up. I—Oh! "

The guiding tread of the previous car was suddenly lost in a mass of heaving, bubble-scattered mud, like a batter of black dough. She fairly picked up the car, and flung it into that welter, through it, and back into the reappearing swastika-marked trail.

Her father spoke: " You're biting your lips. They'll bleed, if you don't look out. Better stop and rest."

" Can't! No bottom to this mud. Once stop and lose momentum—stuck for keeps! "

She had ten more minutes of it before she reached a combination of bridge and culvert, with a plank platform above a big tile drain. With this solid plank bottom, she could stop. Silence came roaring down as she turned the switch. The bubbling water in the radiator steamed about the cap. Claire was conscious of tautness of the cords of her neck in front; of a pain at the base of her brain. Her father glanced at her curiously. " I must be a wreck. I'm sure my hair is frightful," she thought, but forgot it as she looked at him. His face was unusually pale. In the tumult of activity he had been betrayed into letting the old despondent look blur his eyes and sag his mouth. "Must get on," she determined.

Claire was dainty of habit. She detested untwisted hair, ripped gloves, muddy shoes. Hesitant as a cat by a puddle, she stepped down on the bridge. Even on these planks, the mud was three inches thick. It squidged about her low, spatted shoes. "Eeh!" she squeaked.

She tiptoed to the tool-box and took out a folding canvas bucket. She edged down to the trickling stream below. She was miserably conscious of a pastoral scene all gone to mildew—cows beneath willows by the creek, milkweeds dripping, dried mullein weed stalks no longer dry. The bank of the stream was so slippery that she shot down two feet, and nearly went sprawling. Her knee did touch the bank, and the skirt of her gray sports-suit showed a smear of yellow earth.

In less than two miles the racing motor had used up so much water that she had to make four trips to the creek before she had filled the radiator. When she had climbed back on the running-board she glared down at spats and shoes turned into gray lumps. She was not tearful. She was angry.

"Idiot! Ought to have put on my rubbers. Well

—too late now," she observed, as she started the engine.

She again followed the swastika tread. To avoid a hole in the road ahead, the unknown driver had swung over to the side of the road, and taken to the intensely black earth of the edge of an unfenced corn-field. Flashing at Claire came the sight of a deep, water-filled hole, scattered straw and brush, débris of a battlefield, which made her gaspingly realize that her swastikad leader had been stuck and—

And instantly her own car was stuck.

She had had to put the car at that hole. It dropped, far down, and it stayed down. The engine stalled. She started it, but the back wheels spun merrily round and round, without traction. She did not make one inch. When she again killed the blatting motor, she let it stay dead. She peered at her father.

He was not a father, just now, but a passenger try-ing not to irritate the driver. He smiled in a waxy way, and said, " Hard luck! Well, you did the best you could. The other hole, there in the road, would have been just as bad. You're a fine driver, dolly."

Her smile was warm and real. " No. I'm a fool. You told me to put on chains. I didn't. I deserve it."

" Well, anyway, most men would be cussing. You acquire merit by not beating me. I believe that's done, in moments like this. If you'd like, I'll get out and crawl around in the mud, and play turtle for you."

" No. I'm quite all right. I did feel frightfully strong-minded as long as there was any use of it. It kept me going. But now I might just as well be cheerful, because we're stuck, and we're probably going to stay stuck for the rest of this care-free summer day."

The weariness of the long strain caught her, all at once. She slipped forward, sat huddled, her knees crossed under the edge of the steering wheel, her hands falling beside her, one of them making a faint brushing sound as it slid down the upholstery. Her eyes closed; as her head drooped farther, she fancied she could hear the vertebræ click in her tense neck.

Her father was silent, a misty figure in a lap-robe. The rain streaked the mica lights in the side-curtains. A distant train whistled desolately across the sodden fields. The inside of the car smelled musty. The quiet was like a blanket over the ears. Claire was in a hazy drowse. She felt that she could never drive again.

CHAPTER II

CLAIRE ESCAPES FROM RESPECTABILITY

CLAIRE BOLTWOOD lived on the Heights, Brooklyn. Persons from New York and other parts of the Middlewest have been known to believe that Brooklyn is somehow humorous. In newspaper jokes and vaudeville it is so presented that people who are willing to take their philosophy from those sources believe that the leading citizens of Brooklyn are all deacons, undertakers, and obstetricians. The fact is that North Washington Square, at its reddest and whitest and fanlightedest, Gramercy Park at its most ivied, are not so aristocratic as the section of Brooklyn called the Heights. Here preached Henry Ward Beecher. Here, in mansions like mausoleums, on the ridge above docks where the good ships came sailing in from Sourabaya and Singapore, ruled the lords of a thousand sails. And still is it a place of wealth too solid to emulate the nimble self-advertising of Fifth Avenue. Here dwell the fifth-generation possessors of blocks of foundries and shipyards. Here, in a big brick house of much dignity, much ugliness, and much conservatory, lived Claire Boltwood, with her widower father.

Henry B. Boltwood was vice-president of a firm

dealing in railway supplies. He was neither wealthy
nor at all poor. Every summer, despite Claire's delicate hints, they took the same cottage on the Jersey
Coast, and Mr. Boltwood came down for Sunday.
Claire had gone to a good school out of Philadelphia,
on the Main Line. She was used to gracious leisure,
attractive uselessness, nut-center chocolates, and a
certain wonder as to why she was alive.

She wanted to travel, but her father could not get
away. He consistently spent his days in overworking, and his evenings in wishing he hadn't overworked.
He was attractive, fresh, pink-cheeked, white-mus-
tached, and nerve-twitching with years of detail.

Claire's ambition had once been babies and a solid
husband, but as various young males of the species
appeared before her, sang their mating songs and
preened their newly dry-cleaned plumage, she found
that the trouble with solid young men was that they
were solid. Though she liked to dance, the " dancing
men " bored her. And she did not understand the
district's quota of intellectuals very well; she was
good at listening to symphony concerts, but she never
had much luck in discussing the cleverness of the
wood winds in taking up the main motif. It is history
that she refused a master of arts with an old violin,
a good taste in ties, and an income of eight thousand.

The only man who disturbed her was Geoffrey
Saxton, known throughout the interwoven sets of

Brooklyn Heights as "Jeff." Jeff Saxton was thirty-nine to Claire's twenty-three. He was clean and busy; he had no signs of vice or humor. Especially for Jeff must have been invented the symbolic morning coat, the unwrinkable gray trousers, and the moral rimless spectacles. He was a graduate of a nice college, and he had a nice tenor and a nice family and nice hands and he was nicely successful in New York copper dealing. When he was asked questions by people who were impertinent, clever, or poor, Jeff looked them over coldly before he answered, and often they felt so uncomfortable that he didn't have to answer.

The boys of Claire's own age, not long out of Yale and Princeton, doing well in business and jumping for their evening clothes daily at six-thirty, light o' loves and admirers of athletic heroes, these lads Claire found pleasant, but hard to tell apart. She didn't have to tell Jeff Saxton apart. He did his own telling. Jeff called—not too often. He sang—not too sentimentally. He took her father and herself to the theater—not too lavishly. He told Claire—in a voice not too serious—that she was his helmed Athena, his rose of all the world. He informed her of his substantial position—not too obviously. And he was so everlastingly, firmly, quietly, politely, immovably always there.

She watched the hulk of marriage drifting down

on her frail speed-boat of aspiration, and steered in desperate circles.

Then her father got the nervous prostration he had richly earned. The doctor ordered rest. Claire took him in charge. He didn't want to travel. Certainly he didn't want the shore or the Adirondacks. As there was a branch of his company in Minneapolis, she lured him that far away.

Being rootedly of Brooklyn Heights, Claire didn't know much about the West. She thought that Milwaukee was the capital of Minnesota. She was not so uninformed as some of her friends, however. She had heard that in Dakota wheat was to be viewed in vast tracts—maybe a hundred acres.

Mr. Boltwood could not be coaxed to play with the people to whom his Minneapolis representative introduced him. He was overworking again, and perfectly happy. He was hoping to find something wrong with the branch house. Claire tried to tempt him out to the lakes. She failed. His nerve-fuse burnt out the second time, with much fireworks.

Claire had often managed her circle of girls, but it had never occurred to her to manage her executive father save by indirect and pretty teasing. Now, in conspiracy with the doctor, she bullied her father. He saw gray death waiting as alternative, and he was meek. He agreed to everything. He consented to drive with her across two thousand miles of plains and mountains to Seattle, to drop in for a call on their cousins, the Eugene Gilsons.

Back East they had a chauffeur and two cars—the limousine, and the Gomez-Deperdussin roadster, Claire's beloved. It would, she believed, be more of a change from everything that might whisper to Mr. Boltwood of the control of men, not to take a chauffeur. Her father never drove, but she could, she insisted. His easy agreeing was pathetic. He watched her with spaniel eyes. They had the Gomez roadster shipped to them from New York.

On a July morning, they started out of Minneapolis in a mist, and as it has been hinted, they stopped sixty miles northward, in a rain, also in much gumbo. Apparently their nearest approach to the Pacific Ocean would be this oceanically moist edge of a cornfield, between Schoenstrom and Gopher Prairie, Minnesota.

Claire roused from her damp doze and sighed, " Well, I must get busy and get the car out of this."

" Don't you think you'd better get somebody to help us? "

" But get who? "

" Whom! "

" No! It's just 'who,' when you're in the mud. No. One of the good things about an adventure like this is that I must do things for myself. I've always had people to do things for me. Maids and nice teachers and you, old darling! I suppose it's made me soft. Soft—I would like a soft davenport and a novel and a pound of almond-brittle, and get all sick, and not feel so beastly virile as I do just now. But——"

She turned up the collar of her gray tweed coat, painfully climbed out—the muscles of her back racking—and examined the state of the rear wheels. They were buried to the axle; in front of them the mud bulked in solid, shiny blackness. She took out her jack and chains. It was too late. There was no room to get the jack under the axle. She remembered from the narratives of motoring friends that brush in mud gave a firmer surface for the wheels to climb upon.

She also remembered how jolly and agreeably heroic the accounts of their mishaps had sounded—a week after they were over.

She waded down the road toward an old wood-lot. At first she tried to keep dry, but she gave it up, and there was pleasure in being defiantly dirty. She tramped straight through puddles; she wallowed in mud. In the wood-lot was long grass which soaked her stockings till her ankles felt itchy. Claire had never expected to be so very intimate with a brush-pile. She became so. As though she were a pioneer woman who had been toiling here for years, she came to know the brush stick by stick—the long valuable branch that she could never quite get out from under the others; the thorny bough that pricked her hands every time she tried to reach the curious bundle of switches.

Seven trips she made, carrying armfuls of twigs and solemnly dragging large boughs behind her. She patted them down in front of all four wheels. Her crisp hands looked like the paws of a three-year-old boy making a mud fort. Her nails hurt from the mud wedged beneath them. Her mud-caked shoes were heavy to lift. It was with exquisite self-approval that she sat on the running-board, scraped a car-load of lignite off her soles, climbed back into the car, punched the starter.

The car stirred, crept forward one inch, and settled back—one inch. The second time it heaved encouragingly but did not make quite so much headway. Then Claire did sob.

She rubbed her cheek against the comfortable, rough, heather-smelling shoulder of her father's coat, while he patted her and smiled, " Good girl! I better get out and help."

She sat straight, shook her head. " Nope. I'll do it. And I'm not going to insist on being heroic any longer. I'll get a farmer to pull us out."

As she let herself down into the ooze, she reflected that all farmers have hearts of gold, anatomical phenomena never found among the snobs and hirelings of New York. The nearest heart of gold was presumably beating warmly in the house a quarter of a mile ahead.

She came up a muddy lane to a muddy farmyard, with a muddy cur yapping at her wet legs, and geese hissing in a pool of purest mud serene. The house was small and rather old. It may have been painted once. The barn was large and new. It had been painted very much, and in a blinding red with white trimmings. There was no brass plate on the house, but on the barn, in huge white letters, was the legend, " Adolph Zolzac, 1913."

She climbed by log steps to a narrow frame back porch littered with parts of a broken cream-separator. She told herself that she was simple and friendly in going to the back door instead of the front, and it was with gaiety that she knocked on the ill-jointed screen door, which flapped dismally in response.

" *Ja?* " from within.

She rapped again.

" *Hinein!* "

She opened the door on a kitchen, the highlight of which was a table heaped with dishes of dumplings and salt pork. A shirt-sleeved man, all covered with mustache and calm, sat by the table, and he kept right on sitting as he inquired:

" Vell? "

" My car—my automobile—has been stuck in the

mud. A bad driver, I'm afraid! I wonder if you would be so good as to——"

"I usually get t'ree dollars, but I dunno as I vant to do it for less than four. Today I ain'd feelin' very goot," grumbled the golden-hearted.

Claire was aware that a woman whom she had not noticed—so much smaller than the dumplings, so much less vigorous than the salt pork was she—was speaking: "*Aber*, papa, dot's a shame you sharge de poor young lady dot, when she drive by *sei* self. Vot she t'ink of de Sherman people?"

The farmer merely grunted. To Claire, "Yuh, four dollars. Dot's what I usually charge sometimes."

"Usually? Do you mean to say that you leave that hole there in the road right along—that people keep on trying to avoid it and get stuck as I was? Oh! If I were an official——"

"Vell, I dunno, I don't guess I run my place to suit you smart alecks——"

"Papa! How you talk on the young lady! Make shame!"

"—from the city. If you don't like it, you stay *bei* Mineapolis! I haul you out for t'ree dollars and a half. Everybody pay dot. Last mont' I make forty-five dollars. They vos all glad to pay. They say I help them fine. I don't see vot you're kickin' about! Oh, these vimmins!"

"It's blackmail! I wouldn't pay it, if it weren't

for my father sitting waiting out there. But—go ahead. Hurry!"

She sat tapping her toe while Zolzac completed the stertorous task of hogging the dumplings, then stretched, yawned, scratched, and covered his merely dirty garments with overalls that were apparently woven of processed mud. When he had gone to the barn for his team, his wife came to Claire. On her drained face were the easy tears of the slave women.

"Oh, miss, I don't know vot I should do. My boys go on the public school, and they speak American just so goot as you. Oh, I vant man lets me luff America. But papa he says it is an *Unsinn;* you got the money, he says, nobody should care if you are American or Old Country people. I should vish I could ride once in an automobile! But—I am so 'shamed, so 'shamed that I must sit and see my *Mann* make this. Forty years I been married to him, and pretty soon I die——"

Claire patted her hand. There was nothing to say to tragedy that had outlived hope.

Adolph Zolzac clumped out to the highroad behind his vast, rolling-flanked horses—so much cleaner and better fed than his wisp of a wife. Claire followed him, and in her heart she committed murder and was glad of it. While Mr. Boltwood looked out with mild wonder at Claire's new friend, Zolzac hitched his team to the axle. It did not seem possible that two horses could pull out the car where seventy horsepower had fainted. But, easily, yawning and thinking about dinner, the horses drew the wheels up on the mud-bank, out of the hole and——

The harness broke, with a flying mess of straps and rope, and the car plumped with perfect exactness back into its bed.

CHAPTER III

A YOUNG MAN IN A RAINCOAT

"HUH! Such an auto! Look, it break my harness a'ready! Two dollar that cost you to mend it. De auto iss too heavy!" stormed Zolzac.

"All right! All right! Only for heaven's sake—go get another harness!" Claire shrieked.

"Fife-fifty dot will be, in all." Zolzac grinned.

Claire was standing in front of him. She was thinking of other drivers, poor people, in old cars, who had been at the mercy of this golden-hearted one. She stared past him, in the direction from which she had come. Another motor was in sight.

It was a tin beetle of a car; that agile, cheerful, rut-jumping model known as a "bug"; with a home-tacked, home-painted tin cowl and tail covering the stripped chassis of a little cheap Teal car. The lone driver wore an old black raincoat with an atrocious corduroy collar, and a new plaid cap in the Harry Lauder tartan. The bug skipped through mud where the Boltwoods' Gomez had slogged and rolled. Its pilot drove up behind her car, and leaped out. He trotted forward to Claire and Zolzac. His eyes were twenty-seven or eight, but his pink cheeks were twenty, and when he smiled—shyly, radiantly—he was no age at all, but eternal boy. Claire had a blurred impression that she had seen him before, some place along the road.

"Stuck?" he inquired, not very intelligently. "How much is Adolph charging you?"

"He wants three-fifty, and his harness broke, and he wants two dollars——"

"Oh! So he's still working that old gag! I've heard all about Adolph. He keeps that harness for pulling out cars, and it always busts. The last time, though, he only charged six bits to get it mended. Now let me reason with him."

The young man turned with vicious quickness, and for the first time Claire heard pidgin German— German as it is spoken between Americans who have never learned it, and Germans who have forgotten it:

"*Schon sex* hundred times *Ich höre* all about the way you been doing autos, Zolzac, you *verfluchter Schweinhund,* and I'll set the sheriff on you——"

"Dot ain'd true, maybe *einmal die Woche kommt* somebody and *Ich muss die Arbeit immer lassen und in die Regen ausgehen, und seh' mal* how *die* boots *sint mit* mud covered, two dollars it don't pay for dis boots——"

"Now that's enough-plenty out of you, *seien die* boots *verdammt,* and *mach' dass du fort gehst*— muddy boots, hell!—put *mal ein* egg in *die* boots and beat it, *verleicht* maybe I'll by golly arrest you my-self, *weiss du!* I'm a special deputy sheriff."

The young man stood stockily. He seemed to swell as his somewhat muddy hand was shaken directly at, under, and about the circumference of, Adolph Zolzac's hairy nose. The farmer was stronger, but he retreated. He took up the reins. He whined, " Don't I get nothing I break de harness? "

" Sure. You get ten—years! And you get out!"

From thirty yards up the road, Zolzac flung back, "You t'ink you're pretty damn smart!" That was his last serious reprisal.

Clumsily, as one not used to it, the young man lifted his cap to Claire, showing straight, wiry, rope-colored hair, brushed straight back from a rather fine forehead. "Gee, I was sorry to have to swear and holler like that, but it's all Adolph understands. Please don't think there's many of the folks around here like him. They say he's the meanest man in the county."

" I'm immensely grateful to you, but—do you know much about motors? How can I get out of this mud? "

She was surprised to see the youngster blush. His clear skin flooded. His engaging smile came again, and he hesitated, "Let me pull you out."

She looked from her hulking car to his mechanical flea.

He answered the look: " I can do it all right. I'm used to the gumbo—regular mud-hen. Just add my power to yours. Have you a tow-rope? "

" No. I never thought of bringing one."

" I'll get mine."

She walked with him back toward his bug. It lacked not only top and side-curtains, but even wind-shield and running-board. It was a toy—a card-board box on tooth-pick axles. Strapped to the bulging back was a wicker suitcase partly covered by tarpaulin. From the seat peered a little furry face.

" A cat? " she exclaimed, as he came up with a wire rope, extracted from the tin back.

" Yes. She's the captain of the boat. I'm just the engineer."

" What is her name? "

Before he answered the young man strode ahead to the front of her car, Claire obediently trotting after him. He stooped to look at her front axle. He raised his head, glanced at her, and he was blushing again.

" Her name is Vere de Vere ! " he confessed. Then he fled back to his bug. He drove it in front of the Gomez-Dep. The hole in the road itself was as deep as the one on the edge of the cornfield, where she was stuck, but he charged it. She was fascinated by his skill. Where she would for a tenth of a second have hesitated while choosing the best course, he hurled the bug straight at the hole, plunged through with sheets of glassy black water arching on either side, then viciously twisted the car to the right, to the left, and straight again, as he followed the tracks with the solidest bottoms.

Strapped above the tiny angle-iron step which replaced his running-board was an old spade. He dug channels in front of the four wheels of her car, so that they might go up inclines, instead of pushing against the straight walls of mud they had thrown up. On these inclines he strewed the brush she had brought, halting to ask, with head alertly lifted from his stooped huddle in the mud, " Did you have to get this brush yourself? "

" Yes. Horrid wet! "

He merely shook his head in commiseration.

He fastened the tow-rope to the rear axle of his car, to the front of hers. " Now will you be ready to put on all your power as I begin to pull? " he said casually, rather respectfully.

When the struggling bug had pulled the wire rope taut, she opened the throttle. The rope trembled. Her car seemed to draw sullenly back. Then it came out— out—really out, which is the most joyous sensation any motorist shall ever know. In excitement over actually moving again, as fast as any healthy young snail, she drove on, on, the young man ahead grinning back at her. Nor did she stop, nor he, till both cars were safe on merely thick mud, a quarter of a mile away.

She switched off the power—and suddenly she was in a whirlwind of dizzy sickening tiredness. Even in her abandonment to exhaustion she noticed that the young man did not stare at her but, keeping his back to her, removed the tow-rope, and stowed it away in his bug. She wondered whether it was tact or yokelish indifference.

Her father spoke for the first time since the Galahad of the tin bug had come: " How much do you think we ought to give this fellow? "

Now of all the cosmic problems yet unsolved, not cancer nor the future of poverty are the flustering questions, but these twain: Which is worse, not to wear evening clothes at a party at which you find every one else dressed, or to come in evening clothes to a house where, it proves, they are never worn? And: Which is worse, not to tip when a tip has been expected; or to tip, when the tip is an insult?

In discomfort of spirit and wetness of ankles Claire shuddered, " Oh dear, I don't believe he expects us to pay him. He seems like an awfully independent person. Maybe we'd offend him if we offered——"

" The only reasonable thing to be offended at in this vale of tears is not being offered money! "

" Just the same—— Oh dear, I'm so tired. But good little Claire will climb out and be diplomatic."

She pinched her forehead, to hold in her cracking brain, and wabbled out into new scenes of mud and wetness, but she came up to the young man with the most rain-washed and careless of smiles. "Won't you come back and meet my father? He's terribly grateful to you—as I am. And may we—— You've worked so hard, and about saved our lives. May I pay you for that labor? We're really much indebted——"

"Oh, it wasn't anything. Tickled to death if I could help you."

He heartily shook hands with her father, and he droned, "Pleased to meet you, Mr. Uh."

"Boltwood."

"Mr. Boltwood. My name is Milt—Milton Daggett. See you have a New York license on your car. We don't see but mighty few of those through here. Glad I could help you."

"Ah yes, Mr. Daggett." Mr. Boltwood was uninterestedly fumbling in his money pocket. Behind Milt Daggett, Claire shook her head wildly, rattling her hands as though she were playing castanets. Mr. Boltwood shrugged. He did not understand. His relations with young men in cheap raincoats were entirely monetary. They did something for you, and you paid them—preferably not too much—and they ceased to be. Whereas Milt Daggett respectfully but stolidly continued to be, and Mr. Henry Boltwood's

own daughter was halting the march of affairs by asking irrelevant questions:

"Didn't we see you back in—what was that village
we came through back about twelve miles?"

"Schoenstrom?" suggested Milt.

"Yes, I think that was it. Didn't we pass you or
something? We stopped at a garage there, to change
a tire."

"I don't think so. I was in town, though, this
morning. Say, uh, did you and your father grab any
eats——"

"A——"

"I mean, did you get dinner there?"

"No. I wish we had!"

"Well say, I didn't either, and—I'd be awfully glad
if you folks would have something to eat with me
now."

Claire tried to give him a smile, but the best she
could do was to lend him one. She could not associate
interesting food with Milt and his mud-slobbered, tin-
covered, dun-painted Teal bug. He seemed satisfied
with her dubious grimace. By his suggestion they
drove ahead to a spot where the cars could be parked
on firm grass beneath oaks. On the way, Mr. Boltwood lifted his voice in dismay. His touch of nervous
prostration had not made him queer or violent; he
retained a touching faith in good food.

"We might find some good little hotel and have

some chops and just some mushrooms and peas,"
insisted the man from Brooklyn Heights.

"Oh, I don't suppose the country hotels are really
so awfully good," she speculated. "And look—that
nice funny boy. We couldn't hurt his feelings. He's
having so much fun out of being a Good Samaritan."

From the mysterious rounded back of his car Milt
Daggett drew a tiny stove, to be heated by a can of
solidified alcohol, a frying pan that was rather large
for dolls but rather small for square-fingered hands,
a jar of bacon, eggs in a bag, a coffee pot, a can of
condensed milk, and a litter of unsorted tin plates
and china cups. While, by his request, Claire scoured
the plates and cups, he made bacon and eggs and coffee, the little stove in the bottom of his car sheltered
by the cook's bending over it. The smell of food made
Claire forgiving toward the fact that she was wet
through; that the rain continued to drizzle down her
neck.

He lifted his hand and demanded, "Take your
shoes off!"

"Uh?"

He gulped. He stammered, "I mean—I mean your
shoes are soaked through. If you'll sit in the car, I'll
put your shoes up by the engine. It's pretty well
heated from racing it in the mud. You can get your
stockings dry under the cowl."

She was amused by the elaborateness with which he

didn't glance at her while she took off her low shoes and slipped her quite too thin black stockings under the protecting tin cowl. She reflected, " He has such a nice, awkward gentleness. But such bad taste! They're really quite good ankles. Apparently ankles are not done, in Teal bug circles. His sisters don't even have limbs. But do fairies have sisters? He is a fairy. When I'm out of the mud he'll turn his rain-coat into a pair of lordly white wings, and vanish. But what will become of the cat?"

Thus her tired brain, like a squirrel in a revolving cage, while she sat primly and scraped at a clot of rust on a tin plate and watched him put on the bacon and eggs. Wondering if cats were used for this purpose in the Daggett family, she put soaked, unhappy Vere de Vere on her feet, to her own great comfort and the cat's delight. It was an open car, and the rain still rained, and a strange young man was a foot from her tending the not very crackly fire, but rarely had Claire felt so domestic.

Milt was apparently struggling to say something. After several bobs of his head he ventured, " You're so wet! I'd like for you to take my raincoat."

" No! Really! I'm already soaked through. You keep dry."

He was unhappy about it. He plucked at a button of the coat. She turned him from the subject. " I hope Lady Vere de Vere is getting warm, too."

"Seems to be. She's kind of demanding. She wanted a little car of her own, but I didn't think she could keep up with me, not on a long hike."

"A little car? With her paws on the tiny wheel? Oh—sweet! Are you going far, Mr. Daggett?"

"Yes, quite a ways. To Seattle, Washington."

"Oh, really? Extraordinary. We're going there, too."

"Honest? You driving all the way? Oh, no, of course your father——"

"No, he doesn't drive. By the way, I hope he isn't too miserable back there."

"I'll be darned. Both of us going to Seattle. That's what they call a coincidence, isn't it! Hope I'll see you on the road, some time. But I don't suppose I will. Once you're out of the mud, your Gomez will simply lose my Teal."

"Not necessarily. You're the better driver. And I shall take it easy. Are you going to stay long in Seattle?" It was not merely a polite dinner-payment question. She wondered; she could not place this fresh-cheeked, unworldly young man so far from his home.

"Why, I kind of hope—— Government railroad, Alaska. I'm going to try to get in on that, somehow. I've never been out of Minnesota in my life, but there's couple mountains and oceans and things I thought I'd

like to see, so I just put my suitcase and Vere de Vere
in the machine, and started out. I burn distillate
instead of gas, so it doesn't cost much. If I ever happen to have five whole dollars, why, I might go on to
Japan!"

"That would be jolly."

"Though I s'pose I'd have to eat—what is it?—
pickled fish? There's a woman from near my town
went to the Orient as a missionary. From what she
says, I guess all you need in Japan to make a house
is a bottle of mucilage and a couple of old newspapers
and some two-by-fours. And you can have the house
on a purple mountain, with cherry trees down below,
and——" He put his clenched hand to his lips. His
head was bowed. "And the ocean! Lord! The
ocean! And we'll see it at Seattle. Bay, anyway.
And steamers there—just come from India! Huh!
Getting pretty darn poetic here! Eggs are done."

The young man did not again wander into visions.
He was all briskness as he served her bacon and eggs,
took a plate of them to Mr. Boltwood in the Gomez,
gouged into his own. Having herself scoured the tin
plates, Claire was not repulsed by their naked tinni-
ness; and the coffee in the broken-handled china cup
was tolerable. Milt drank from the top of a vacuum
bottle. He was silent. Immediately after the lunch
he stowed the things away. Claire expected a drawn-
out, tact-demanding farewell, but he climbed into his

bug, said " Good-by, Miss Boltwood.   Good luck! "
and was gone.

The rainy road was bleakly empty without him.

It did not seem possible that Claire's body could be
nagged into going on any longer.   Her muscles were
relaxed, her nerves frayed.   But the moment the
Gomez started, she discovered that magic change
which every long-distance motorist knows.   Instantly
she was alert, seemingly able to drive forever.   The
pilot's instinct ruled her; gave her tireless eyes and
sturdy hands.   Surely she had never been weary;
never would be, so long as it was hers to keep the car
going.

She had driven perhaps six miles when she reached
a hamlet called St. Klopstock.   On the bedraggled
mud-and-shanty main street a man was loading
crushed rock into a truck.   By him was a large person
in a prosperous raincoat, who stepped out, held up his
hand.   Claire stopped.

" You the young lady that got stuck in that hole by
Adolph Zolzac's? "

" Yes.   And Mr. Zolzac wasn't very nice about it."

" He's going to be just elegant about it, now, and
there ain't going to be any more hole.   I think Adolph
has been keeping it muddy—throwing in soft dirt—
and he made a good and plenty lot out of pulling out
tourists.   Bill and I are going down right now and
fill it up with stone.   Milt Daggett come through here

—he's got a nerve, that fellow, but I did have to laugh
—he says to me, ' Barney——' This was just now.
He hasn't more than just drove out of town. He
said to me, ' Barney,' he says, 'you're the richest
man in this township, and the banker, and you got
a big car y'self, and you think you're one whale of
a political boss,' he says, ' and yet you let that Zolzac
maintain a private ocean, against the peace and damn
horrible inconvenience of the Commonwealth of Minnesota——' He's got a great line of talk, that fellow.
He told me how you got stuck—made me so ashamed
—I been to New York myself—and right away I got
Bill, and we're going down and hold a donation and
surprise party on Adolph and fill that hole."

"But won't Adolph dig it out again?"

The banker was puffy, but his eyes were of stone.
From the truck he took a shotgun. He drawled, " In
that case, the surprise party will include an elegant
wake."

"But how did—— Who is this extraordinary Milt
Daggett?"

"Him? Oh, nobody 'specially. He's just a fellow
down here at Schoenstrom. But we all know him.
Goes to all the dances, thirty miles around. Thing
about him is: if he sees something wrong, he picks out
some poor fellow like me, and says what he thinks."

Claire drove on. She was aware that she was looking for Milt's bug. It was not in sight.

"Father," she exclaimed, "do you realize that this lad didn't tell us he was going to have the hole filled? Just did it. He frightens me. I'm afraid that when we reach Gopher Prairie for the night, we'll find he has engaged for us the suite that Prince Collars and Cuffs once slept in."

"Hhhhmm," yawned her father.

"Curious young man. He said, 'Pleased to meet you.'"

"Huuuuhhm! Fresh air makes me so sleepy."

"And— Fooled you! Got through that mudhole, anyway! And he said——Look! Fields stretch out so here, and not a tree except the willow-groves round those farmhouses. And he said 'Gee' so many times, and 'dinner' for the noon meal. And his nails—— No, I suppose he really is just a farm youngster."

Mr. Boltwood did not answer. His machine-finish smile indicated an enormous lack of interest in young men in Teal bugs.

CHAPTER IV

A ROOM WITHOUT

GOPHER PRAIRIE has all of five thousand people. Its commercial club asserts that it has at least a thousand more population and an infinitely better band than the ridiculously envious neighboring town of Joralemon. But there were few signs that a suite had been engaged for the Boltwoods, or that Prince Collars and Cuffs had on his royal tour of America spent much time in Gopher Prairie. Claire reached it somewhat before seven. She gaped at it in a hazy way. Though this was her first prairie town for a considerable stay, she could not pump up interest.

The state of mind of the touring motorist entering a strange place at night is as peculiar and definite as that of a prospector. It is compounded of gratitude at having got safely in; of perception of a new town, yet with all eagerness about new things dulled by weariness; of hope that there is going to be a good hotel, but small expectation—and absolutely no probability—that there really will be one.

Claire had only a blotched impression of peaked wooden buildings and squatty brick stores with faded awnings; of a red grain elevator and a crouching station and a lumberyard; then of the hopelessly muddy road leading on again into the country. She felt that if she didn't stop at once, she would miss the town entirely. The driving-instinct sustained her, made her take corners sharply, spot a garage, send the Gomez whirling in on the cement floor.

The garage attendant looked at her and yawned.

"Where do you want the car?" Claire asked sharply.

"Oh, stick it in that stall," grunted the man, and turned his back.

Claire glowered at him. She thought of a good line about rudeness. But—oh, she was too tired to fuss. She tried to run the car into the empty stall, which was not a stall, but a space, like a missing tooth, between two cars, and so narrow that she was afraid of crumpling the lordly fenders of the Gomez. She ran down the floor, returned with a flourish, thought she was going to back straight into the stall— and found she wasn't. While her nerves shrieked, and it did not seem possible that she could change gears, she managed to get the Gomez behind a truck and side-on to the stall.

"Go forward again, and cramp your wheel— sharp!" ordered the garage man.

Claire wanted to outline what she thought of him, but she merely demanded, "Will you kindly drive it in?"

"Why, sure. You bet," said the man casually.

His readiness ruined her inspired fury. She was somewhat disappointed.

As she climbed out of the car and put a hand on the smart bags strapped on a running-board, the accumulated weariness struck her in a shock. She could have driven on for hours, but the instant the car was safe for the night, she went to pieces. Her ears rang, her eyes were soaked in fire, her mouth was dry, the back of her neck pinched. It was her father who took the lead as they rambled to the one tolerable hotel in the town.

In the hotel Claire was conscious of the ugliness of the poison-green walls and brass cuspidors and insurance calendars and bare floor of the office; conscious of the interesting scientific fact that all air had been replaced by the essence of cigar smoke and cooking cabbage; of the stares of the traveling men lounging in bored lines; and of the lack of welcome on the part of the night clerk, an oldish, bleached man with whiskers instead of a collar.

She tried to be important: " Two rooms with bath, please."

The bleached man stared at her, and shoved forward the register and a pen clotted with ink. She signed. He took the bags, led the way to the stairs. Anxiously she asked, " Both rooms are with bath?"

From the second step the night clerk looked down at her as though she were a specimen that ought to

be pinned on the corks at once, and he said loudly,
" No, ma'am. Neither of 'em. Got no rooms vacant
with bawth, or bath either! N̂ot but what we got 'em
in the house. This is an up-to-date place. But one of
'm's took, and the other has kind of been out of order,
the last three-four months."

From the audience of drummers below, a delicate
giggle.

Claire was too angry to answer. And too tired.
When, after miles of stairs, leagues of stuffy hall, she
reached her coop, with its iron bed so loose-jointed
that it rattled to a breath, its bureau with a list to
port, and its anemic rocking-chair, she dropped on the
bed, panting, her eyes closed but still brimming with
fire. It did not seem that she could ever move again.
She felt chloroformed. She couldn't even coax herself off the bed, to see if her father was any better off
in the next room.

She was certain that she was not going to drive to
Seattle. She wasn't going to drive anywhere! She
was going to freight the car back to Minneapolis, and
herself go back by train—Pullman!—drawing-room!

But for the thought of her father she would have
fallen asleep, in her drenched tweeds. When she did
force the energy to rise, she had to support herself
by the bureau, by the foot of the bed, as she moved
about the room, hanging up the wet suit, rubbing
herself with a slippery towel, putting on a dark silk

frock and pumps. She found her father sitting motionless in his room, staring at the wall. She made herself laugh at him for his gloomy emptiness. She paraded down the hall with him.

As they reached the foot of the stairs, the old one, the night clerk leaned across the desk and, in a voice that took the whole office into the conversation, quizzed, " Come from New York, eh? Well, you're quite a ways from home."

Claire nodded. She felt shyer before these solemnly staring traveling men than she ever had in a box at the opera. At the double door of the dining-room, from which the cabbage smell steamed with a lustiness undiminished by the sad passing of its youth, a man, one of the average-sized, average-mustached, average business-suited, average-brown-haired men who can never be remembered, stopped the Boltwoods and hawed, " Saw you coming into town. You've got a New York license?"

She couldn't deny it.

" Quite a ways from home, aren't you? "

She had to admit it.

She was escorted by a bouncing, black-eyed waitress to a table for four. The next table was a long one, at which seven traveling men, or local business men whose wives were at the lake for the summer, ceased trying to get nourishment out of the food, and gawped at her. Before the Boltwoods were seated, the waitress dabbed at non-existent spots on their napkins, ignored a genuine crumb on the cloth in front of Claire's plate, made motions at a cup and a formerly plated fork, and bubbled, "Autoing through?"

Claire fumbled for her chair, oozed into it, and breathed, "Yes."

"Going far?"

"Yes."

"Where do you live?"

"New York."

"My! You're quite a ways from home, aren't you?"

"Apparently."

"Hamnegs roasbeef roaspork thapplesauce frypickerel springlamintsauce."

"I—I beg your pardon."

The waitress repeated.

"I—oh—oh, bring us ham and eggs. Is that all right, father?"

"Oh—no—well——"

"You wanted same?" the waitress inquired of Mr. Boltwood.

He was intimidated. He said, "If you please," and feebly pawed at a fork.

The waitress was instantly back with soup, and a collection of china gathered by a man of much travel, catholic interests, and no taste. One of the plates alleged itself to belong to a hotel in Omaha.

She pushed a pitcher of condensed milk to the exact spot where it would catch Mr. Boltwood's sleeve, brushed the crumb from in front of Claire to a shelter beneath the pink and warty sugar bowl, recovered a toothpick which had been concealed behind her glowing lips, picked for a while, gave it up, put her hands on her hips, and addressed Claire:

" How far you going? "

" To Seattle."

" Got any folks there? "

" Any—— Oh, yes, I suppose so."

" Going to stay there long? "

" Really—— We haven't decided."

" Come from New York, eh? Quite a ways from home, all right. Father in business there? "

" Yes."

" What's his line? "

" I beg pardon? "

" What's his line? Ouch! Jiminy, these shoes pinch my feet. I used to could dance all night, but I'm getting fat, I guess, ha! ha! Put on seven pounds last month. Ouch! Gee, they certainly do pinch my toes. What business you say your father's in? "

" I didn't say, but—— Oh, railroad."

" G. N. or N. P.? "

" I don't think I quite understand——"

Mr. Boltwood interposed, " Are the ham and eggs ready? "

" I'll beat it out and see." When she brought them, she put a spoon in Claire's saucer of peas, and demanded, " Say, you don't wear that silk dress in the auto, do you? "

" No."

" I should think you'd put a pink sash on it. Seems like it's kind of plain—it's a real pretty piece of goods, though. A pink sash would be real pretty. You dark-complected ladies always looks better for a touch of color."

Then was Claire certain that the waitress was baiting her, for the amusement of the men at the long table. She exploded. Probably the waitress did not know there had been an explosion when Claire looked coldly up, raised her brows, looked down, and poked the cold and salty slab of ham, for she was continuing:

" A light-complected lady like me don't need so much color, you notice my hair is black, but I'm light, really, Pete Liverquist says I'm a blonde brunette, gee, he certainly is killing that fellow, oh, he's a case, he sure does like to hear himself talk, my! there's Old Man Walters, he runs the telephone exchange here, I heard he went down to St. Cloud on Number 2, but I guess he couldn't of, he'll be yodeling for friend soup and a couple slabs of moo, I better beat it, I'll say so, so long."

Claire's comment was as acid as the pale beets

before her, as bitter as the peas, as hard as the lumps in the watery mashed potatoes:

"I don't know whether the woman is insane or ignorant. I wish I could tell whether she was trying to make me angry for the benefit of those horrid unshaven men, or merely for her private edification."

"By me, dolly. So is this pie. Let's get some medium to levitate us up to bed. Uh—uh—— I think perhaps we'd better not try to drive clear to Seattle. If we just went through to Montana?—or even just to Bismarck?"

"Drive through with the hotels like this? My dear man, if we have one more such day, we stop right there. I hope we get by the man at the desk. I have a feeling he's lurking there, trying to think up something insulting to say to us. Oh, my dear, I hope you aren't as beastly tired as I am. My bones are hot pokers."

The man at the desk got in only one cynical question, "Driving far?" before Claire seized her father's arm and started him upstairs.

For the first time since she had been ten—and in a state of naughtiness immediately following a pronounced state of grace induced by the pulpit oratory of the new rector of St. Chrysostom's—she permitted herself the luxury of not stopping to brush her teeth before she went to bed. Her sleep was drugged—it was not sleep, but an aching exhaustion of the body which did not prevent her mind from revisualizing the road, going stupidly over the muddy stretches and sharp corners, then becoming conscious of that bed, the lump under her shoulder blades, the slope to westward, and the creak that rose every time she tossed. For at least fifteen minutes she lay awake for hours.

Thus Claire Boltwood's first voyage into democracy.

It was not so much that the sun was shining, in the morning, as that a ripple of fresh breeze came through the window. She discovered that she again longed to go on—keep going on—see new places, conquer new roads. She didn't want all good road. She wanted something to struggle against. She'd try it for one more day. She was stiff as she crawled out of bed, but a rub with cold water left her feeling that she was stronger than she ever had been; that she was a woman, not a dependent girl. Already, in the beating prairie sun-glare, the wide main street of Gopher Prairie was drying; the mud ruts flattening out. Beyond the town hovered the note of a meadow lark—sunlight in sound.

"Oh, it's a sweet morning! Sweet! We will go on! I'm terribly excited!" she laughed.

She found her father dressed. He did not know whether or not he wanted to go on. " I seem to have lost my grip on things. I used to be rather decisive. But we'll try it one more day, if you like," he said.

When she had gaily marched him downstairs, she suddenly and unhappily remembered the people she would have to face, the gibing questions she would have to answer.

The night clerk was still at the desk, as though he had slept standing. He hailed them. "Well, well! Up bright and early! Hope you folks slept well. Beds aren't so good as they might be, but we're kind of planning to get some new mattresses. But you get pretty good air to sleep in. Hope you have a fine hike today."

His voice was cordial; he was their old friend; faithful watcher of their progress. Claire found herself dimpling at him.

In the dining-room their inquisitional acquaintance, the waitress, fairly ran to them. "Sit down, folks. Waffles this morning. You want to stock up for your drive. My, ain't it an elegant morning! I hope you have a swell drive today!"

"Why!" Claire gasped, "why, they aren't rude. They care—about people they never saw before. That's why they ask questions! I never thought—I never thought! There's people in the world who want to know us without having looked us up in the Social Register! I'm so ashamed! Not that the sunshine changes my impression of this coffee. It's frightful! But that will improve. And the people—they were being friendly, all the time. Oh, Henry B., young

Henry Boltwood, you and your godmother Claire have a lot to learn about the world!"

As they came into the garage, their surly acquaintance of the night before looked just as surly, but Claire tried a boisterous " Good morning!"

" Mornin'! Going north? Better take the left-hand road at Wakamin. Easier going. Drive your car out for you?"

As the car stood outside taking on gas, a man flapped up, spelled out the New York license, looked at Claire and her father, and inquired, " Quite a ways from home, aren't you?"

This time Claire did not say " Yes!" She experimented with, " Yes, quite a ways."

" Well, hope you have a good trip. Good luck!"

Claire leaned her head on her hand, thought hard. " It's I who wasn't friendly," she propounded to her father. " How much I've been losing. Though I still refuse to like that coffee!"

She noticed the sign on the air-hose of the garage—" Free Air."

" There's our motto for the pilgrimage!" she cried.

She knew the exaltation of starting out in the fresh morning for places she had never seen, without the bond of having to return at night.

Thus Claire's second voyage into democracy.

While she was starting the young man who had pulled her out of the mud and given her lunch was folding up the tarpaulin and blankets on which he had slept beside his Teal bug, in the woods three miles north of Gopher Prairie. To the high-well-born cat, Vere de Vere, Milt Daggett mused aloud, " Your ladyship, as Shakespeare says, the man that gets cold feet never wins the girl. And I'm scared, cat, clean scared."

CHAPTER V

RELEASE BRAKES—SHIFT TO THIRD

MILT DAGGETT had not been accurate in his implication that he had not noticed Claire at a garage in Schoenstrom. For one thing, he owned the garage.

Milt was the most prosperous young man in the village of Schoenstrom. Neither the village itself nor the nearby *Strom* is really *schoen*. The entire business district of Schoenstrom consists of Heinie Rauskukle's general store, which is brick; the Leipzig House, which is frame; the Old Home Poolroom and Restaurant, which is of old logs concealed by a frame sheathing; the farm-machinery agency, which is galvanized iron, its roof like an enlarged washboard; the church; the three saloons; and the Red Trail Garage, which is also, according to various signs, the Agency for Teal Car Best at the Test, Stonewall Tire Service Station, Sewing Machines and Binders Repaired, Dr. Hostrum the Veterinarian every Thursday, Gas Today 27c.

The Red Trail Garage is of cement and tapestry brick. In the office is a clean hardwood floor, a typewriter, and a picture of Elsie Ferguson. The establishment has an automatic rim-stretcher, a wheel jack, and a reputation for honesty.

The father of Milt Daggett was the Old Doctor, born in Maine, coming to this frontier in the day when Chippewas camped in your dooryard, and came in to help themselves to coffee, which you made of roasted corn. The Old Doctor bucked northwest blizzards, read Dickens and Byron, pulled people through typhoid, and left to Milt his shabby old medicine case and thousands of dollars—in uncollectible accounts. Mrs. Daggett had long since folded her crinkly hands in quiet death.

Milt had covered the first two years of high school by studying with the priest, and been sent to the city of St. Cloud for the last two years. His father had meant to send him to the state university. But Milt had been born to a talent for machinery. At twelve he had made a telephone that worked. At eighteen he was engineer in the tiny flour mill in Schoenstrom. At twenty-five, when Claire Boltwood chose to come tearing through his life in a Gomez-Dep, Milt was the owner, manager, bookkeeper, wrecking crew, ignition expert, thoroughly competent bill-collector, and all but one of the working force of the Red Trail Garage.

There were two factions in Schoenstrom: the retired farmers who said that German was a good enough language for anybody, and that taxes for schools and sidewalks were yes something crazy; and the group who stated that a pig-pen is a fine place, but only for pigs. To this second, revolutionary wing belonged a few of the first generation, most of the second, and all of the third; and its leader was Milt Daggett. He did not talk much, normally, but when he thought things ought to be done, he was as annoying as a machine-gun test in the lot next to a Quaker meeting.

If there had been a war, Milt would probably have been in it—rather casual, clearing his throat, reckoning and guessing that maybe his men might try going over and taking that hill . . . then taking it. But all of this history concerns the year just before America spoke to Germany; and in this town buried among the cornfields and the wheat, men still thought more about the price of grain than about the souls of nations.

On the evening before Claire Boltwood left Minneapolis and adventured into democracy, Milt was in the garage. He wore union overalls that were tan where they were not grease-black; a faded blue cotton shirt; and the crown of a derby, with the rim not too neatly hacked off with a dull toad-stabber jack-knife.

Milt smiled at his assistant, Ben Sittka, and suggested, " Well, *wie geht 's mit* the work, eh? Like to stay and get the prof's flivver out, so he can have it in the morning? "

" You bet, boss."

" Getting to be quite a mechanic, Ben."

" I'll say so! "

" If you get stuck, come yank me out of the Old Home."

" Aw rats, boss. I'll finish it. You beat it." Ben grinned at Milt adoringly.

Milt stripped off his overalls and derby-crown, and washed his big, firm hands with gritty soft soap. He cleaned his nails with a file which he carried in his upper vest pocket in a red imitation morocco case which contained a comb, a mirror, an indelible pencil, and a note-book with the smudged pencil addresses of five girls in St. Cloud, and a memorandum about Rauskukle's car.

He put on a twisted brown tie, an old blue serge suit, and a hat which, being old and shabby, had become graceful. He ambled up the street. He couldn't have ambled more than three blocks and have remained on the street. Schoenstrom tended to leak off into jungles of tall corn.

Two men waved at him, and one demanded, " Say, Milt, is whisky good for the toothache? What d' you think! The doc said it didn't do any good. But then, gosh, he's only just out of college."

" I guess he's right."

" Is that a fact! Well, I'll keep off it then."

Two stores farther on, a bulky farmer hailed, " Say, Milt, should I get an ensilage cutter yet? "

" Yuh," in the manner of a man who knows too

much to be cocksure about anything, " I don't know but what I would, Julius."

" I guess I vill then."

Minnie Rauskukle, plump, hearty Minnie, heiress to the general store, gave evidence by bridling and straightening her pigeon-like body that she was aware of Milt behind her. He did not speak to her. He ducked into the door of the Old Home Poolroom and Restaurant.

Milt ranged up to the short lunch counter, in front of the pool table where two brick-necked farm youngsters were furiously slamming balls and attacking cigarettes. Loose-jointedly Milt climbed a loose-jointed high stool and to the proprietor, Bill McGolwey, his best friend, he yawned, " You might poison me with a hamburger and a slab of apple, Mac."

" I'll just do that little thing. Look kind of grouchy tonight, Milt."

" Too much excitement in this burg. Saw three people on the streets all simultaneously to-once."

" What's been eatin' you lately? "

" Me? Nothing. Only I do get tired of this metropolis. One of these days I'm going to buck some bigger place."

" Try Gopher Prairie maybe? " suggested Mac, through the hiss and steam of the frying hamburger sandwich.

" Rats. Too small."

"Small? Why, there's darn near five thousand people there!"

"I know, but—I want to tackle some sure-nuff city. Like Duluth or New York."

"But what'd you do?"

"That's the devil of it. I don't know just what I do want to do. I could always land soft in a garage, but that's nothing new. Might hit Detroit, and learn the motor-factory end."

"Aw, you're the limit, Milt. Always looking for something new."

"That's the way to get on. The rest of this town is afraid of new things. 'Member when I suggested we all chip in on a dynamo with a gas engine and have electric lights? The hicks almost died of nervousness."

"Yuh, that's true, but—— You stick here, Milt. You and me will just nachly run this burg."

"I'll say! Only—— Gosh, Mac, I would like to go to a real show, once. And find out how radio works. And see 'em put in a big suspension bridge!"

Milt left the Old Home rather aimlessly. He told himself that he positively would not go back and help Ben Sittka get out the prof's car. So he went back and helped Ben get out the prof's car, and drove the same to the prof's. The prof, otherwise professor, otherwise mister, James Martin Jones, B.A., and Mrs. James Martin Jones welcomed him almost as noisily as had Mac. They begged him to come in. With Mr. Jones he discussed—no, ye Claires of Brooklyn Heights, this garage man and this threadbare young superintendent of a paintbare school, talking in a town that was only a comma on the line, did not discuss corn-growing, nor did they reckon to guess that by heck the constabule was carryin' on with the Widdy Perkins. They spoke of fish-culture, Elihu Root, the spiritualistic evidences of immortality, government ownership, self-starters for flivvers, and the stories of Irvin Cobb.

Milt went home earlier than he wanted to. Because Mr. Jones was the only man in town besides the priest who read books, because Mrs. Jones was the only woman who laughed about any topics other than children and family sickness, because he wanted to go to their house every night, Milt treasured his welcome as a sacred thing, and kept himself from calling on them more than once a week.

He stopped on his way to the garage to pet Emil Baumschweiger's large gray cat, publicly known as Rags, but to Milt and to the lady herself recognized as the unfortunate Countess Vere de Vere—perhaps the only person of noble ancestry and mysterious past in Milt's acquaintance. The Baumschweigers did not treat their animals well; Emil kicked the bay mare, and threw pitchforks at Vere de Vere. Milt saluted her and sympathized:

" You have a punk time, don't you, countess?
Like to beat it to Minneapolis with me? "

The countess said that she did indeed have an ex-
traordinarily punk time, and she sang to Milt the
hymn of the little gods of the warm hearth. Then
Milt's evening dissipations were over. Schoenstrom
has movies only once a week. He sat in the office of
his garage ruffling through a weekly digest of events.
Milt read much, though not too easily. He had no
desire to be a poet, an Indo-Iranian etymologist, a lec-
turer to women's clubs, or the secretary of state. But
he did rouse to the marvels hinted in books and magazines; to large crowds, the mechanism of submarines,
palm trees, gracious women.

He laid down the magazine. He stared at the wall.
He thought about nothing. He seemed to be fumbling
for something about which he could deliciously think
if he could but grasp it. Without quite visualizing
either wall or sea, he was yet recalling old dreams of a
moonlit wall by a warm stirring southern sea. If
there was a girl in the dream she was intangible as
the scent of the night. Presently he was asleep, a
not at all romantic figure, rather ludicrously tipped
to one side in his office chair, his large solid shoes up
on the desk.

He half woke, and filtered to what he called home—
one room in the cottage of an oldish woman who had
prejudices against the perilous night air. He was too

sleepy to go through any toilet save pulling off his shoes, and achieving an unconvincing wash at the little stand, whose crackly varnish was marked with white rings from the toothbrush mug.

" I feel about due to pull off some fool stunt. Wonder what it will be? " he complained, as he flopped on the bed.

He was up at six, and at a quarter to seven was at work in the garage. He spent a large part of the morning in trying to prove to a customer that even a Teal car, best at the test, would not give perfect service if the customer persisted in forgetting to fill the oil-well, the grease-cups, and the battery.

At three minutes after twelve Milt left the garage to go to dinner. The fog of the morning had turned to rain. McGolwey was not at the Old Home. Sometimes Mac got tired of serving meals, and for a day or two he took to a pocket flask, and among his former customers the cans of prepared meat at Rauskukle's became popular. Milt found him standing under the tin awning of the general store. He had a troubled hope of keeping Mac from too long a vacation with the pocket flask. But Mac was already red-eyed. He seemed only half to recognize Milt.

" Swell day! " said Milt.

" Y' bet."

" Road darn muddy."

" I should worry. Yea, bo', I'm feelin' good! "

At eleven minutes past twelve a Gomez-Dep roadster appeared down the road, stopped at the garage. To Milt it was as exciting as the appearance of a comet to a watching astronomer.

"What kind of a car do you call that, Milt?" asked a loafer.

"Gomez-Deperdussin."

"Never heard of it. Looks too heavy."

This was sacrilege. Milt stormed, "Why, you poor floof, it's one of the best cars in the world. Imported from France. That looks like a special-made American body, though. Trouble with you fellows is, you're always scared of anything that's new. Too—heavy! Huh! Always wanted to see a Gomez—never have, except in pictures. And I believe that's a New York license. Let me at it!"

He forgot noon-hunger, and clumped through the rain to the garage. He saw a girl step from the car. He stopped, in the doorway of the Old Home, in uneasy shyness. He told himself he didn't "know just what it is about her—she isn't so darn unusually pretty and yet—gee—— Certainly isn't a girl to get fresh with. Let Ben take care of her. Like to talk to her, and yet I'd be afraid if I opened my mouth, I'd put my foot in it."

He was for the first time seeing a smart woman. This dark, slender, fine-nerved girl, in her plain, rough, closely-belted, gray suit, her small black Glengarry

cocked on one side of her smooth hair, her little kid
gloves, her veil, was as delicately adjusted as an aeroplane engine.

Milt wanted to trumpet her exquisiteness to the
world, so he growled to a man standing beside him,
" Swell car. Nice-lookin' girl, kind of."

" Kind of skinny, though. I like 'em with some
meat on 'em," yawned the man.

No, Milt did not strike him to earth. He insisted
feebly, " Nice clothes she's got, though."

" Oh, not so muchamuch. I seen a woman come
through here yesterday that was swell, though—had
on a purple dress and white shoes and a hat big 's a
bushel."

" Well, I don't know, I kind of like those simple
things," apologized Milt.

He crept toward the garage. The girl was inside.
He inspected the slope-topped, patent-leather motoring trunk on the rack at the rear of the Gomez-Dep.
He noticed a middle-aged man waiting in the car.
" Must be her father. Probably—maybe she isn't
married then." He could not get himself to shout at
the man, as he usually did. He entered the garage
office; from the inner door he peeped at the girl, who
was talking to his assistant about changing an inner
tube.

That Ben Sittka whom an hour ago he had cajoled
as a promising child he now admired for the sniffing

calmness with which he was demanding, " Want a red or gray tube?"

" Really, I don't know. Which is the better?" The girl's voice was curiously clear.

Milt passed Claire Boltwood as though he did not see her; stood at the rear of the garage kicking at the tires of a car, his back to her. Over and over he was grumbling, "If I just knew one girl like that—— Like a picture. Like—like a silver vase on a blue cloth!"

Ben Sittka did not talk to the girl while he inserted the tube in the spare casing. Only, in the triumphant moment when the parted ends of the steel rim snapped back together, he piped, " Going far?"

" Yes, rather. To Seattle."

Milt stared at the cobweb-grayed window. " Now I know what I was planning to do. I'm going to Seattle," he said.

The girl was gone at twenty-nine minutes after twelve. At twenty-nine and a half minutes after, Milt remarked to Ben Sittka, " I'm going to take a trip. Uh? Now don't ask questions. You take charge of the garage until you hear from me. Get somebody to help you. G'-by."

He drove his Teal bug out of the garage. At thirty-two minutes after twelve he was in his room, packing his wicker suitcase by the method of throwing things in and stamping on the case till it closed. In it he had absolutely all of his toilet refinements and wardrobe except the important portion already in use.

They consisted, according to faithful detailed report, of four extra pairs of thick yellow and white cotton socks; two shirts, five collars, five handkerchiefs; a pair of surprisingly vain dancing pumps; high tan laced boots; three suits of cheap cotton underclothes; his Sunday suit, which was dead black in color, and unimaginative in cut; four ties; a fagged toothbrush, a comb and hairbrush, a razor, a strop, shaving soap in a mug; a not very clean towel; and nothing else whatever.

To this he added his entire library and private picture gallery, consisting of Ivanhoe, Ben-Hur, his father's copy of Byron, a wireless manual, and the 1916 edition of Motor Construction and Repairing: the art collection, one colored Sunday supplement picture of a princess lunching in a Provençe courtyard, and a half-tone of Colonel Paul Beck landing in an early military biplane. Under this last, in a pencil scrawl now blurred to grayness, Milt had once written, "This what Ill be aviator."

What he was to wear was a piercing trouble. Till eleven minutes past twelve that day he had not cared. People accepted his overalls at anything except a dance, and at the dances he was the only one who wore pumps. But in his discovery of Claire Bolt-wood he had perceived that dressing is an art. Before

he had packed, he had unhappily pawed at the prized
black suit. It had become stupid. "Undertaker!"
he growled.

With a shrug which indicated that he had nothing
else, he had exchanged his overalls for a tan flannel
shirt, black bow tie, thick pigskin shoes, and the suit
he had worn the evening before, his best suit of two
years ago—baggy blue serge coat and trousers. He
could not know it, but they were surprisingly graceful on his wiry, firm, white body.

In his pockets were a roll of bills and an unexpectedly good gold watch. For warmth he had a
winter ulster, an old-fashioned turtle-neck sweater,
and a raincoat heavy as tarpaulin. He plunged into
the raincoat, ran out, galloped to Rauskukle's store,
bought the most vehement cap in the place—a plaid
of cerise, orange, emerald green, ultramarine, and five
other guaranteed fashionable colors. He stocked up
with food for roadside camping.

In the humping tin-covered tail of the bug was a
good deal of room, and this he filled with motor
extras, a shotgun and shells, a pair of skates, and all
his camping kit as used on his annual duck-hunting
trip to Man Trap Lake.

"I'm a darned fool to take everything I own
but—— Might be gone a whole month," he reflected.

He had only one possession left—a check book, concealed from the interested eye of his too maternal

landlady by sticking it under the stair carpet. This he retrieved. It showed a balance of two hundred dollars. There was ten dollars in the cash register in the office, for Ben Sittka. The garage would, with the mortgage deducted, be worth nearly two thousand. This was his fortune.

He bolted into the kitchen and all in one shout he informed his landlady, "Called out of town, li'l trip, b'lieve I don't owe you an'thing, here's six dollars, two weeks' notice, dunno just when I be back."

Before she could issue a questionnaire he was out in the bug. He ran through town. At his friend McGolwey, now loose-lipped and wabbly, sitting in the rain on a pile of ties behind the railroad station, he yelled, "So long, Mac. Take care yourself, old hoss. Off on li'l trip."

He stopped in front of the "prof's," tooted till the heads of the Joneses appeared at the window, waved and shouted, "G'-by, folks. Goin' outa town."

Then, while freedom and the distant Pacific seemed to rush at him over the hood, he whirled out of town. It was two minutes to one—forty-seven minutes since Claire Boltwood had entered Shoenstrom.

He stopped only once. His friend Lady Vere de Vere was at the edge of town, on a scientific exploring trip in the matter of ethnology and field mice. She hailed him, "Mrwr? Me mrwr!"

"You don't say so!" Milt answered in surprise.

" Well, if I promised to take you, I'll keep my word."
He vaulted out, tucked Vere de Vere into the seat,
protecting her from the rain with the tarpaulin winter
radiator-cover.

His rut-skipping car overtook the mud-walloping
Gomez-Dep in an hour, and pulled it out of the mud.

Before Milt slept that night, in his camp three miles
from Gopher Prairie, he went through religious rites.

" Girl like her, she's darn particular about her looks.
I'm a sloppy hound. Used to be snappier about my
clothes when I was in high school. Getting lazy—
too much like Mac. Think of me sleeping in my
clothes last night! "

" Mrwr! " rebuked the cat.

" You're dead right. Fierce is the word. Nev'
will sleep in my duds again, puss. That is, when I
have a reg'lar human bed. Course camping, different.
But still—— Let's see all the funny things we can
do to us."

He shaved—two complete shaves, from lather to
towel. He brushed his hair. He sat down by a campfire sheltered between two rocks, and fought his nails,
though they were discouragingly crammed with motor
grease. Throughout this interesting but quite painful
ceremony Milt kept up a conversation between himself as the World's Champion Dude, and his cat
as Vallay. But when there was nothing more to do,
and the fire was low, and Vere de Vere asleep in the

sleeve of the winter ulster, his bumbling voice slackened; in something like agony he muttered:

" But oh, what's the use? I can't ever be anything but a dub! Cleaning my nails, to make a hit with a girl that's got hands like hers! It's a long trail to Seattle, but it's a darn sight longer one to being—being—well, sophisticated. Oh! And incidentally, what the deuce am I going to do in Seattle if I do get there? "

CHAPTER VI

THE LAND OF BILLOWING CLOUDS

NEVER a tawny-beached ocean has the sweetness of the prairie slew. Rippling and blue, with long grass up to its edge, a spot of dancing light set in the miles of rustling wheat, it retains even in July, on an afternoon of glare and brazen locusts, the freshness of a spring morning. A thousand slews, a hundred lakes bordered with rippling barley or tinkling bells of the flax, Claire passed. She had left the occasional groves of oak and poplar and silver birch, and come out on the treeless Great Plains.

She had learned to call the slews "pugholes," and to watch for ducks at twilight. She had learned that about the pugholes flutter choirs of crimson-winged blackbirds; that the ugly brown birds squatting on fence-rails were the divine-voiced meadow larks; that among the humble cowbird citizens of the pastures sometimes flaunted a scarlet tanager or an oriole; and that no rose garden has the quaint and hardy beauty of the Indian paint brushes and rag babies and orange milkweed in the prickly, burnt-over grass between roadside and railway line.

She had learned that what had seemed rudeness in garage men and hotel clerks was often a resentful reflection of her own Eastern attitude that she was necessarily superior to a race she had been trained to call "common people." If she spoke up frankly, they made her one of their own, and gave her companionable aid.

For two days of sunshine and drying mud she followed a road flung straight across flat wheatlands, then curving among low hills. Often there were no fences; she was so intimately in among the grain that the fenders of the car brushed wheat stalks, and she became no stranger, but a part of all this vast-horizoned land. She forgot that she was driving, as she let the car creep on, while she was transported by Armadas of clouds, prairie clouds, wisps of vapor like a ribbed beach, or mounts of cumulus swelling to gold-washed snowy peaks.

The friendliness of the bearing earth gave her a calm that took no heed of passing hours. Even her father, the abstracted man of affairs, nodded to dusty people along the road; to a jolly old man whose bulk rolled and shook in a tiny, rhythmically creaking buggy, to women in the small abrupt towns with their huge red elevators and their long, flat-roofed stores.

Claire had discovered America, and she felt stronger, and all her days were colored with the sun.

She had discovered, too, that she could adventure. No longer was she haunted by the apprehension that had whispered to her as she had left Minneapolis.

She knew a thrill when she hailed—as though it were a passing ship—an Illinois car across whose dust-caked back was a banner " Chicago to the Yellowstone." She experienced a new sensation of common humanness when, on a railway paralleling the wagon road for miles, the engineer of a freight waved his hand to her, and tooted the whistle in greeting.

Her father was easily tired, but he drowsed through the early afternoons when a none-too-digestible small-town lunch was as lead within him. Despite the beauty of the land and the joy of pushing on, they both had things to endure.

After lunch, it was sometimes an agony to Claire to keep awake. Her eyes felt greasy from the food, or smarted with the sun-glare. In the still air, after the morning breeze had been burnt out, the heat from the engine was a torment about her feet; and if there was another car ahead, the trail of dust sifted into her throat. Unless there was traffic to keep her awake, she nodded at the wheel; she was merely a part of a machine that ran on without seeming to make any impression on the prairie's endlessness.

Over and over there were the same manipulations: slow for down hill, careful of sand at the bottom, letting her out on a smooth stretch, waving to a lonely farmwife in her small, baked dooryard, slow to pass a hay-wagon, gas for up the next hill, and repeat the round all over again. But she was joyous till noon;

and with mid-afternoon a new strength came which, as rose crept above the golden haze of dust, deepened into serene meditation.

And she was finding the one secret of long-distance driving—namely, driving; keeping on, thinking by fifty-mile units, not by the ten-mile stretches of Long Island runs; and not fretting over anything whatever. She seemed charmed; if she had a puncture—why, she put on the spare. If she ran out of gas—why, any passing driver would lend her a gallon. Nothing, it seemed, could halt her level flight across the giant land.

She rarely lost her way. She was guided by the friendly trail signs—those big red R's and L's on fence post and telephone pole, magically telling the way from the Mississippi to the Pacific.

Her father's occasional musing talk kept her from loneliness. He was a good touring companion. Motoring is not the best occasion for epigrams, satire, and the Good One You Got Off at the Lambs' Club last night. Such verbiage on motor trips invariably results in the mysterious finding of the corpse of a strange man, well dressed, hidden beside the road. Claire and her father mumbled, "Good farmhouse —brick," or "Nice view," and smiled, and were for miles as silent as the companionable sky.

She thought of the people she knew, especially of Jeff Saxton. But she could not clearly remember his lean earnest face. Between her and Jeff were sweeping sunny leagues. But she was not lonely. Certainly she was not lonely for a young man with a raincoat, a cat, and an interest in Japan.

No singer after a first concert has felt more triumphant than Claire when she crossed her first state-line; rumbled over the bridge across the Red River into North Dakota. To see Dakota car licenses everywhere, instead of Minnesota, was like the sensation of street signs in a new language. And when she found a good hotel in Fargo and had a real bath, she felt that by her own efforts she had earned the right to enjoy it.

Mr. Boltwood caught her enthusiasm. Dinner was a festival, and in iced tea the peaceful conquistadores drank the toast of the new Spanish Main; and afterward, arm in arm, went chattering to the movies.

In front of the Royal Palace, Pictures, 4 Great Acts Vaudeville 4, was browsing a small, beetle-like, tin-covered car.

"Dad! Look! I'm sure—yes, of course, there's his suitcase—that's the car of that nice boy—don't you remember?—the one that pulled us out of the mud at—I don't remember the name of the place. Apparently he's keeping going. I remember; he's headed for Seattle, too. We'll look for him in the theater. Oh, the darling, there's his cat! What was the funny name he gave her—the Marchioness Montmorency or something?"

Lady Vere de Vere, afraid of Fargo and movie crowds, but trusting in her itinerent castle, the bug, was curled in Milt Daggett's ulster, in the bottom of the car. She twinkled her whiskers at Claire, and purred to a stroking hand.

With the excitement of one trying to find the address of a friend in a strange land Claire looked over the audience when the lights came on before the vaudeville. In the second row she saw Milt's stiffish, rope-colored hair—surprisingly smooth above an astoundingly clean new tan shirt of mercerized silk.

He laughed furiously at the dialogue between Pete-Rosenheim & Larose-Bettina, though it contained the cheese joke, the mother-in-law joke, and the joke about the wife rifling her husband's pockets.

" Our young friend seems to have enviable youthful spirits," commented Mr. Boltwood.

" Now, no superiority! He's probably never seen a real vaudeville show. Wouldn't it be fun to take him to the Winter Garden or the Follies for the first time! . . . Instead of being taken by Jeff Saxton, and having the humor, oh! so articulately explained!"

The pictures were resumed; the film which, under ten or twelve different titles, Claire had already seen, even though Brooklyn Heights does not devote Saturday evening to the movies. The badman, the sheriff —an aged party with whiskers and boots—the holdup, the sad eyes of the sheriff's daughter—also an aged party, but with a sunbonnet and the most expensive rouge—the crook's reformation, and his violent adherence to law and order; this libel upon the portions of these United States lying west of longitude 101° Claire had seen too often. She dragged her father back to the hotel, sent him to bed, and entered her room—to find a telegram upon the bureau.

She had sent her friends a list of the places at which she would be likely to stop. The message was from Jeff Saxton, in Brooklyn. It brought to her mind the steady shine of his glasses—the most expensive glasses, with the very best curved lenses—as it demanded:

" Received letter about trip surprised anxious will tire you out fatigue prairie roads bad for your father mountain roads dangerous strongly advise go only part way then take train.   GEOFFREY."

She held the telegram, flipping her fingers against one end of it as she debated. She remembered how the wide world had flowed toward her over the hood of the Gomez all day. She wrote in answer:

" Awful perils of road, two punctures, split infinitive, eggs at lunch questionable, but struggle on."

Before she sent it she held council with her father. She sat on the foot of his bed and tried to sound dutiful. "I don't want to do anything that's bad for you, daddy. But isn't it taking your mind away from business?"

"Ye-es, I think it is. Anyway, we'll try it a few days more."

"I fancy we can stand up under the strain and perils. I think we can persuade some of these big farmers to come to the rescue if we encounter any walruses or crocodiles among the wheat. And I have a feeling that if we ever get stuck, our friend of the Teal bug will help us."

"Probably never see him again. He'll skip on ahead of us."

"Of course. We haven't laid an eye on him, along the road. He must have gotten into Fargo long before we did. Now tomorrow I think——"

CHAPTER VII

THE GREAT AMERICAN FRYING PAN

IT was Claire's first bad day since the hole in the mud. She had started gallantly, scooting along the level road that flies straight west of Fargo. But at noon she encountered a restaurant which made eating seem an evil.

That they might have fair fame among motorists the commercial club of Reaper had set at the edge of town a sign "Welcome to Reaper, a Live Town—Speed Limit 8 Miles perhr." Being interpreted, that sign meant that if you went much over twenty miles an hour on the main street, people might glance at you; and that the real welcome, the only impression of Reaper that tourists were likely to carry away, was the welcome in the one restaurant. It was called the Eats Garden. As Claire and her father entered, they were stifled by a belch of smoke from the frying pan in the kitchen. The room was blocked by a huge lunch counter; there was only one table, covered with oil cloth decorated with venerable spots of dried egg yolk.

The waiter-cook, whose apron was gravy-patterned, with a border and stomacher of plain gray dirt, grumbled, "Whadyuhwant?"

Claire sufficiently recovered to pick out the type

74

from the fly specks on the menu, and she ordered a small steak and coffee for her father; for herself tea, boiled eggs, toast.

" Toast? We ain't got any toast! "

" Well, can't you make it? "

" Oh, I suppose I could—— "

When they came, the slices of toast were an inch thick, burnt on one side and raw on the other. The tea was bitter and the eggs watery. Her father reported that his steak was high-test rawhide, and his coffee—well, he wasn't sure just what substitute had been used for chicory, but he thought it was luke-warm quinine.

Claire raged: " You know, this town really has aspirations. They're beginning to build such nice little bungalows, and there's a fine clean bank—— Then they permit this scoundrel to advertise the town among strangers, influential strangers, in motors, by serving food like this! I suppose they think that they arrest criminals here, yet this restaurant man is a thief, to charge real money for food like this—— Yes, and he's a murderer! "

" Oh, come now, dolly! "

" Yes he is, literally. He must in his glorious career have given chronic indigestion to thousands of people —shortened their lives by years. That's wholesale murder. If I were the authorities here, I'd be indulgent to the people who only murder one or two

people, but imprison this cook for life. Really! **I**
mean it!"

"Well, he probably does the best he———"

"He does not! These eggs and this bread were
perfectly good, before he did black magic over them.
And did you see the contemptuous look he gave me
when I was so eccentric as to order toast? Oh, Reaper,
Reaper, you desire a modern town, yet I wonder if you
know how many thousands of tourists go from coast
to coast, cursing you? If I could only hang that
restaurant man—and the others like him—in a rope
of his own hempen griddle cakes! The Great American Frying Pan! I don't expect men building a new
town to have time to read Hugh Walpole and James
Branch Cabell, but I do expect them to afford a cook
who can fry eggs!"

As she paid the check, Claire tried to think of some
protest which would have any effect on the obese wits
of the restaurant man. In face of his pink puffiness
she gave it up. Her failure as a Citizeness Fixit sent
her out of the place in a fury, carried her on in a dusty
whirl till the engine spat, sounded tired and reflective,
and said it guessed it wouldn't go any farther that
day.

Now that she had something to do, Claire became
patient. "Run out of gas. Isn't it lucky I got that
can for an extra gallon?"

But there was plenty of gas. There was no discernible reason why the car should not go. She started the engine. It ran for half a minute and quit. All the plugs showed sparks. No wires were detached in the distributor. There was plenty of water, and the oil was not clogged. And that ended Claire's knowledge of the inside of a motor.

She stopped two motorists. The first was sure that there was dirt on the point of the needle valve, in the carburetor. While Claire shuddered lest he never get it back, he took out the needle valve, wiped it, put it back—and the engine was again started, and again, with great promptness, it stopped.

The second Good Samaritan knew that one of the wires in the distributor must be detached and, though she assured him that she had inspected them, he looked pityingly at her smart sports-suit, said, " Well, I'll just take a look," and removed the distributor cover. He also scratched his head, felt of the fuses under the cowl, scratched his cheek, poked a finger at the carburetor, rubbed his ear, said, " Well, uh——" looked to see if there was water and gas, sighed, " Can't just seem to find out what's the trouble," shot at his own car, and escaped.

Claire had been highly grateful and laudatory to both of them—but she remained here, ten miles from nowhere. It was a beautiful place. Down a hill the wheat swam toward a village whose elevator was a glistening tower. Mud-hens gabbled in a slew, alfalfa shone with unearthly green, and bees went junketing toward a field of red clover. But she had the motorist's fever to go on. The road behind and in front was very long, very white—and very empty.

Her father, out of much thought and a solid ignorance about all of motoring beyond the hiring of chauffeurs and the payment of bills, suggested, " Uh, dolly, have you looked to see if these, uh—— Is the carburetor all right? "

" Yes, dear; I've looked at it three times, so far," she said, just a little too smoothly.

On the hill five miles to eastward, a line of dust, then a small car. As it approached, the driver must have sighted her and increased speed. He came up at thirty-five miles an hour.

" Now we'll get something done! Look! It's a bug—a flivver or a Teal or something. I believe it's the young man that got us out of the mud."

Milt Daggett stopped, casually greeted them: " Why, hello, Miss Boltwood. Thought you'd be way ahead of me some place! "

" Mrwr," said Vere de Vere. What this meant the historian does not know.

" No; I've been taking it easy. Mr., Uh—I can't quite remember your name——"

" Milt Daggett."

" There's something mysterious the matter with my car. The engine will start, after it's left alone a while, but then it stalls. Do you suppose you could tell what it is?"

"I don't know. I'll see if I can find out."

"Then you probably will. The other two men knew everything. One of them was the inventor of wheels, and the other discovered skidding. So of course they couldn't help me."

Milt added nothing to her frivolity, but his smile was friendly. He lifted the round rubber cap of the distributor. Then Claire's faith tumbled in the dust. Twice had the wires been tested. Milt tested them again. She was too tired of botching to tell him he was wasting time.

"Got an oil can?" he hesitated.

Through a tiny hole in the plate of the distributor he dripped two drops of oil—only two drops. "I guess maybe that's what it needed. You might try her now, and see how she runs," he said mildly.

Dubiously Claire started the engine. It sang jubilantly, and it did not stop. Again was the road open to her. Again was the settlement over there, to which it would have taken her an hour to walk, only six minutes away.

She stopped the engine, beamed at him—there in the dust, on the quiet hilltop. He said as apologetically as though he had been at fault, "Distributor got dry. Might give it a little oil about once in six months."

"We are so grateful to you! Twice now you've saved our lives."

"Oh, I guess you'd have gone on living! And if drivers can't help each other, who can?"

"That's a good start toward world-fellowship, I suppose. I wish we could do—— Return your lunch or—— Mr. Daggett! Do you read books? I mean——"

"Yes I do, when I run across them."

"Mayn't I gi—lend you these two that I happen to have along? I've finished them, and so has father, I think."

From the folds of the strapped-down top she pulled out Compton Mackenzie's *Youth's Encounter,* and Vachel Lindsay's *Congo.* With a curious faint excitement she watched him turn the leaves. His blunt fingers flapped through them as though he was used to books. As he looked at *Congo,* he exclaimed, "Poetry! That's fine! Like it, but I don't hardly ever run across it. I—— Say—— I'm terribly obliged!"

His clear face lifted, sun-brown and young and adoring. She had not often seen men look at her thus. Certainly Jeff Saxton's painless worship did not turn him into the likeness of a knight among banners. Yet the good Geoffrey loved her, while to Milt Daggett she could be nothing more than a strange young woman in a car with a New York license. If

her tiny gift could so please him, how poor he must
be. " He probably lives on some barren farm," she
thought, " or he's a penniless mechanic hoping for a
good job in Seattle. How white his forehead is! "

But aloud she was saying, " I hope you're enjoying
your trip."

" Oh yes. I like it fine. You having a good time?
Well—— Well, thanks for the books."

She was off before him. Presently she exclaimed
to Mr. Boltwood: " You know—just occurs to me—
it's rather curious that our young friend should be so
coincidental as to come along just when we needed
him."

" Oh, he just happened to, I suppose," hemmed her
father.

" I'm not so sure," she meditated, while she absently watched another member of the Poultry Suicide
Club rush out of a safe ditch, prepare to take leave
for immortality, change her fowlish mind, flutter up
over the hood of the car, and come down squawking
her indignities to the barnyard. " I'm not so sure
about his happening—— No. I wonder if he could
possibly—— Oh no. I hope not. Flattering, but——
You don't suppose he could be deliberately following
us? "

" Nonsense! He's a perfectly decent young chap."

" I know. Of course. He probably works hard in
a garage, and is terribly nice to his mother and sisters

at home. I mean—— I wouldn't want the dear lamb
to be a devoted knight, though. Too thankless a job."

She slowed the car down to fifteen an hour. For
the first time she began to watch the road behind her.
In a few minutes a moving spot showed in the dust
three miles back. Oh, naturally; he would still be
behind her. Only—— If she stopped, just to look at
the scenery, he would go on ahead of her. She
stopped for a moment—for a time too brief to indicate
that anything had gone wrong with her car. Staring
back she saw that the bug stopped also, and she fancied
that Milt was out standing beside it, peering with his
palm over his eyes—a spy, unnatural and disturbing
in the wide peace.

She drove on a mile and halted again; again halted
her attendant. He was keeping a consistent two to
four miles behind, she estimated.

" This won't do at all," she worried. " Flattering,
but somehow—— Whatever sort of a cocoon-
wrapped hussy I am, I don't collect scalps. I won't
have young men serving me—graft on them—get
amusement out of their struggles. Besides—suppose
he became just a little more friendly, each time he
came up, all the way from here to Seattle? . . . Fresh.
. . . No, it won't do."

She ran the car to the side of the road.

" More trouble? " groaned her father.

" No. Just want to see scenery."

"But—— There's a good deal of scenery on all sides, without stopping, seems to me!"

"Yes, but——" She looked back. Milt had come into sight; had paused to take observations. Her father caught it:

"Oh, I see. Pardon me. Our squire still following? Let him go on ahead? Wise lass."

"Yes. I think perhaps it's better to avoid complications."

"Of course." Mr. Boltwood's manner did not merely avoid Milt; it abolished him.

She saw Milt, after five minutes of stationary watching, start forward. He came dustily rattling up with a hail of "Distributor on strike again?" so cheerful that it hurt her to dismiss him. But she had managed a household. She was able to say suavely:

"No, everything is fine. I'm sure it will be, now. I'm afraid we are holding you back. You mustn't worry about us."

"Oh, that's all right," breezily. "Something might go wrong. Say, is this poetry book——"

"No, I'm sure nothing will go wrong now. You mustn't feel responsible for us. But, uh, you understand we're very grateful for what you have done and, uh, perhaps we shall see each other in Seattle?" She made it brightly interrogatory.

"Oh, I see." His hands gripped the wheel. His cheeks had been too ruddily tinted by the Dakota sun to show a blush, but his teeth caught his lower lip. He had no starter on his bug; he had in his embarrassment to get out and crank. He did it quietly, not looking at her. She could see that his hand trembled on the crank. When he did glance at her, as he drove off, it was apologetically, miserably. His foot was shaking on the clutch pedal.

The dust behind his car concealed him. For twenty miles she was silent, save when she burst out to her father, " I do hope you're enjoying the trip. It's so easy to make people unhappy. I wonder—— No. Had to be done."

CHAPTER VIII

THE DISCOVERY OF CANNED SHRIMPS AND HESPERIDES

ON the morning when Milt Daggett had awakened to sunshine in the woods north of Gopher Prairie, he had discovered the golden age. As mile on mile he jogged over new hills, without having to worry about getting back to his garage in time to repair somebody's car, he realized that for the past two years he had forced himself to find contentment in building up a business that had no future.

Now he laughed and whooped; he drove with one foot inelegantly and enchantingly up on the edge of the cowl; he made Lady Vere de Vere bow to astounded farmers; he went to the movies every evening—twice, in Fargo; and when the chariot of the young prince swept to the brow of a hill, he murmured, not in the manner of a bug-driver but with a stinging awe, "All that big country! Ours to see, puss! We'll settle down some day and be solid citizens and raise families and wheeze when we walk, but—— All those hills to sail over and—— Come on! Lez sail!"

Milt attended the motion pictures every evening, and he saw them in a new way. As recently as one week before he had preferred those earnest depictions in which hard-working, moral ctors shoot one another, or ride the most uncomfortable horses up mountain-sides. But now, with a mental apology to that propagandist of lowbrowism, the absent Mac, he chose the films in which the leading men wore evening clothes, and no one ever did anything without being assisted by a "man." Aside from the pictures Milt's best tutors were traveling men. Though he measured every cent, and for his campfire dinners bought modest chuck steaks, he had at least one meal a day at a hotel, to watch the traveling men.

To Claire, traveling men were merely commercial persons in hard-boiled suits. She identified them with the writing-up of order-slips on long littered writing-tables, and with hotels that reduced the delicate arts of dining and sleeping to gray greasiness. But Milt knew traveling men. He knew that not only were they the missionaries of business, supplementing the taking of orders by telling merchants how to build up trade, how to trim windows and treat customers like human beings; but also that they, as much as the local ministers and doctors and teachers and newspaper-men, were the agents in spreading knowledge and justice. It was they who showed the young men how to have their hair cut—and to wash behind the ears and shave daily; they who encouraged villagers to rise from scandal and gossip to a perception of the Great World, of politics and sports, and some measure of art and science.

Claire, and indeed her father and Mr. Jeff Saxton as
well, had vaguely concluded that because drummers
were always to be seen in soggy hotels and badly con-
necting trains and the headachy waiting-rooms of
stations, they must like these places. Milt knew that
the drummers were martyrs; that for months of a
trip, all the while thinking of the children back home,
they suffered from landlords and train schedules; that
they were Claire's best allies in fighting the Great
American Frying Pan; that they knew good things,
and fought against the laziness and impositions of
people who " kept hotel " because they had failed as
farmers; and that when they did find a landlord who
was cordial and efficient, they went forth mightily
advertising that glorious man. The traveling men, he
knew, were pioneers in spats.

Hence it was to the traveling men, not to supercilious tourists in limousines, that Milt turned for
suggestions as to how to perform the miracle of changing from an ambitious boy into what Claire would
recognize as a charming man. He had not met enough
traveling men at Schoenstrom. They scooped up what
little business there was, and escaped from the Leipzig
House to spend the night at St. Cloud or Sauk Centre.

In the larger towns in Minnesota and Dakota, after
evening movies, before slipping out to his roadside
camp Milt inserted himself into a circle of traveling
men in large leather chairs, and ventured, " Saw a

Gomez-Dep with a New York license down the line today."

"Oh. You driving through?"

"Yes. Going to Seattle."

That distinguished Milt from the ordinary young-men-loafers, and he was admitted as one of the assembly of men who traveled and saw thir s and wondered about the ways of men. It was gc d talk he heard; too much of hotels, and too many tight banal little phrases suggesting the solution of all economic complexities by hanging "agitators," but with this, an exciting accumulation of impressions of Vancouver and San Diego, Florida and K. C.

"That's a wonderful work farm they have at Duluth," said one, and the next, "speaking of that, I was in Chicago last week, and I saw a play——"

Milt had, in his two years of high school in St. Cloud, and in his boyhood under the genial but abstracted eye of the Old Doctor, learned that it was not well thought of to use the knife as a hod and to plaster mashed potatoes upon it, as was the custom in Mac's Old Home Lunch at Schoenstrom. But the arts of courteously approaching oysters, salad, and peas were rather unfamiliar to him. Now he studied forks as he had once studied carburetors, and he gave spiritual devotion to the nice eating of a canned-shrimp cocktail—a lost legion of shrimps, now two thousand miles and two years away from their ocean home.

He peeped with equal earnestness at the socks and the shirts of the traveling men. Socks had been to him not an article of faith but a detail of economy. His attitude to socks had lacked in reverence and technique. He had not perceived that socks may be as sound a symbol of culture as the 'cello or even demountable rims. He had been able to think with respect of ties and damp piqué collars secured by gold safety-pins; and to the belted fawn overcoat that the St. Klopstock banker's son had brought back from St. Paul, he had given jealous attention. But now he graduated into differential socks.

By his campfire, sighing to the rather somnolent Vere de Vere, he scornfully yanked his extra pairs of thick, white-streaked, yellow cotton socks from the wicker suitcase, and uttered anathema:

"Begone, ye unworthy and punk-looking raiment. I know ye! Ye werst a bargain and two pairs for two bits. But even as Adolph Zolzac and an agent for flivver accessories are ye become in my eyes, ye generation of vipers, ye clumsy, bag-footed, wrinkle-sided gunny-sacking ye!"

Next day, in the woods, a happy hobo found that the manna-bringing ravens had left him four pairs of good socks.

Five quite expensive pairs of silk and lisle socks Milt purchased—all that the general merchant at Jeppe had in stock. What they lost in suitability to touring and to private laundering at creeks, they gained as symbols. Milt felt less shut out from the life of leisure. Now, in Seattle, say, he could go into a good hotel with less fear of the clerks.

He added attractive outing shirts, ties neither too blackly dull nor too flashily crimson, and a vicious nail-brush which simply tore out the motor grease that had grown into the lines of his hands. Also he added a book.

The book was a rhetoric. Milt knew perfectly that there was an impertinence called grammar, but it had never annoyed him much. He knew that many persons preferred " They were " to " They was," and were nervous in the presence of " ain't." One teacher in St. Cloud had buzzed frightfully about these minutiæ. But Milt discovered that grammar was only the beginning of woes. He learned that there were such mental mortgages as figures of speech and the choice of synonyms. He had always known, but he had never passionately felt that the invariable use of "hell," "doggone," and "You bet!" left certain subtleties unexpressed. Now he was finding subtleties which he had to express.

As joyously adventurous as going on day after day was his experimentation in voicing his new observations. He gave far more eagerness to it than Claire Boltwood had. Gustily intoning to Vere de Vere, who was the perfect audience, inasmuch as she never had anything to say but "Mrwr," and didn't mind being interrupted in that, he clamored, "The prairies are the sea. In the distance they are kind of silvery— no—they are dim silver; and way off on the skyline are the Islands of the—of the—— Now what the devil was them, were those, islands in the mythology book in high school? Of the—Blessed? Great snakes' boots, you're an ignorant cat, Vere! Hesperyds? No! Hesperides! Yea, 'bo! Now that man in the hotel: 'May I trouble you for the train guide? Thanks so much!' But how much is so much?"

As Claire's days were set free by her consciousness of sun and brown earth, so Milt's odyssey was only the more valorous in his endeavor to criticize life. He saw that Mac's lunch room had not been an altogether satisfactory home; that Mac's habit of saying to dissatisfied customers, "If you don't like it, get out," had lacked something of courtesy. Staring at towns along the way, Milt saw that houses were not merely large and comfortable, or small and stingy; but that there was an interesting thing he remembered hearing his teachers call "good taste."

He was not the preoccupied Milt of the garage but a gay-eyed gallant, the evening when he gave a lift to the school-teacher and drove her from the district school among the wild roses and the corn to her home in the next town. She was a neat, tripping, trim-sided school-teacher of nineteen or twenty.

"You're going out to Seattle? My! That's a wonderful trip. Don't you get tired?" she adored.

"Oh, no. And I'm seeing things. I used to think everything worth while was right near my own town."

"You're so wise to go places. Most of the boys I know don't think there is any world beyond Jimtown and Fargo."

She glowed at him. Milt was saying to himself, "Am I a fool? I probably could make this girl fall in love with me. And she's better than I am; so darn neat and clean and gentle. We'd be happy. She's a nice comfy fire, and here I go like a boob, chasing after a lone, cold star like Miss Boltwood, and probably I'll fall into all the slews from hell to breakfast on the way. But—— I'd get sleepy by a comfy fire."

"Are you thinking hard? You're frowning so," ventured the school-teacher.

"Didn't mean to. 'Scuse!" he laughed. One hand off the steering wheel, he took her hand—a fresh, cool, virginal hand, snuggling into his, suddenly stirring him. He wanted to hold it tighter. The lamenting historian of love's pilgrimage must set down the fact that the pilgrim for at least a second forgot the divine tread of the goddess Claire, and made rapid calculation that he could, in a pinch, drive from Schoenstrom to the teacher's town in two days and a night; that therefore courtship, and this sweet white hand resting in his, were not impossible. Milt himself did not know what it was that made him lay down the hand and say, so softly that he was but half audible through the rattle of the engine:

"Isn't this a slick, mean to say glorious evening? Sky rose and then that funny lavender. And that new moon—— Makes me think of—the girl I'm in love with."

"You're engaged?" wistfully.

"Not exactly but——Say, did you study rhetoric in Normal School? I have a rhetoric that's got all kind of poetic extracts, you know, and quotations and everything, from the big writers, Stevenson and all. Always been so practical, making a garage pay, never thought much about how I said things as long as I could say 'No!' and say it quick. 'Cept maybe when I was talking to the prof there. But it's great sport to see how musical you can make a thing sound. Words. Like Shenandoah. Gol-lee! Isn't that a wonderful word? Makes you see old white mansion, and mocking birds—— Wonder if a fellow could be a big engineer, you know, build bridges and so on, and still talk about, oh, beautiful things? What d' you think, girlie?"

"Oh, I'm sure you could!"

Her admiration, the proximity of her fragrant slightness, was pleasant in the dusk, but he did not press her hand again, even when she whispered, "Good night, and thank you—oh, thank you."

If Milt had been driving at the rate at which he usually made his skipjack carom over the roads about Schoenstrom, he would by now have been through Dakota, into Montana. But he was deliberately holding down the speed. When he had been tempted by a smooth stretch to go too breathlessly, he halted, teased Vere de Vere, climbed out and, sitting on a hilltop, his hands about his knees, drenched his soul with the vision of amber distances.

He tried so to time his progress that he might always be from three to five miles behind Claire—distant enough to be unnoticed, near enough to help in case of need. For behind poetic expression and the use of forks was the fact that his purpose in life was to know Claire.

When he was caught, when Claire informed him that he " mustn't worry about her "; when, slowly, he understood that she wasn't being neighborly and interested in his making time, he wanted to escape, never to see her again.

For thirty miles his cheeks were fiery. He, most considerate of roadmen, crowded a woman in a flivver, passed a laboring car on an upgrade with such a burst that the uneasy driver bumped off into a ditch. He hadn't really seen them. Only mechanically had he got past them. He was muttering:

" She thought I was trying to butt in! Stung again! Like a small boy in love with teacher. And I thought I was so wise! Cussed out Mac—blamed Mac—no, damn all the fine words—cussed out Mac for being the village rumhound. Boozing is twice as sensible as me. See a girl, nice dress—start for Seattle! Two thousand miles away! Of course she bawled me out. She was dead right. Boob! Yahoo! Goat!"

He caught up Vere de Vere, rubbed her fur against his cheek while he mourned, " Oh, puss, you got to be nice to me. I thought I'd do big things. And then the alarm clock went off. I'm back in Schoenstrom. For keeps, I guess. I didn't know I had feelings that could get hurt like this. Thought I had a rhinoceros hide. But—— Oh, it isn't just feeling ashamed over being a fool. It's that—— Won't ever see her again. Not once. Way I saw her through the window, at that hotel, in that blue silky dress—that funny long line of buttons, and her throat. Never have dinner—lunch—with her by the road——"

In the reaction of anger he demanded of Vere de Vere, " What the deuce do I care? If she's chump enough to chase away a crack garage man that's gone batty and wants to work for nothing, let her go on and hit some crook garage and get stuck for an entire overhauling. What do I care? Had nice trip; that's all I wanted. Never did intend to go clear to Seattle, anyway. Go on to Butte, then back home. No more fussing about fool table-manners and books, and I cer-

tainly will cut out tagging behind her! No, sir!
Nev-er again!"

It was somewhat inconsistent to add, "There's a
bully place—sneak in and let her get past me again.
But she won't catch me following next time!"

While he tried to keep up his virtuous anger, he
was steering into an abandoned farmyard, parking
the car behind cottonwoods and neglected tall currant
bushes which would conceal it from the road.

The windows of the deserted house stared at him;
a splintered screen door banged in every breeze.
Lichens leered from the cracks of the porch. The
yard was filled with a litter of cottonwood twigs, and
over the flower garden hulked ragged weeds. In the
rank grass about the slimy green lip of the well,
crickets piped derisively. The barn-door was open.
Stray kernels of wheat had sprouted between the
spokes of a rusty binder-wheel. A rat slipped across
the edge of the shattered manger. As dusk came on,
gray things seemed to slither past the upper windows
of the house, and somewhere, under the roof, there
was a moaning. Milt was sure that it was the wind
in a knothole. He told himself that he was absolutely
sure about it. And every time it came he stroked
Vere de Vere carefully, and once, when the moaning
ended in the slamming of the screen door, he said,
"Jiminy!"

This boy of the unghostly cylinders and tangible

magnetos had never seen a haunted house. To toil of
the harvest field and machine shop and to trudging
the sun-beaten road he was accustomed, but he had
never crouched watching the slinking spirits of old
hopes and broken aspirations; feeble phantoms of the
first eager bridegroom who had come to this place, and
the mortgage-crushed, rust-wheat-ruined man who
had left it. He wanted to leap into the bug and go on.
Yet the haunt of murmurous memories dignified his
unhappiness. In the soft, tree-dimmed dooryard
among dry, blazing plains it seemed indecent to go on
growling " Gee," and " Can you beat it? " It was a
young poet, a poet rhymeless and inarticulate, who
huddled behind the shield of untrimmed currant
bushes, and thought of the girl he would never see
again.

He was hungry, but he did not eat. He was
cramped, but he did not move. He picked up the books
she had given him. He was quickened by the powdery
beauty of *Youth's Encounter;* by the vision of laughter
and dancing steps beneath a streaky gas-glow in the
London fog; of youth not " roughhousing " and wanting to "be a sport," yet in frail beauty and faded
crimson banners finding such exaltation as Schoenstrom had never known. But every page suggested
Claire, and he tucked the book away.

In Vachel Lindsay's *Congo,* in a poem called " The
Santa Fe Trail," he found his own modern pilgrimage

from another point of view. Here was the poet, disturbed by the honking hustle of passing cars. But Milt belonged to the honking and the hustle, and it was not the soul of the grass that he read in the poem, but his own sun-flickering flight:

> Swiftly the brazen car comes on.
> It burns in the East as the sunrise burns.
> I see great flashes where the far trail turns.
> Butting through the delicate mists of the morning,
> It comes like lightning, goes past roaring,
> It will hail all the windmills, taunting, ringing,
> On through the ranges the prairie-dog tills—
> Scooting past the cattle on the thousand hills.
> Ho for the tear-horn, scare-horn, dare-horn,
> Ho for the gay-horn, bark-horn, bay-horn.

Milt did not reflect that if the poet had watched the Teal bug go by, he would not have recorded a scarehorn, a dare-horn, or anything mightier than a yiphorn. Milt saw himself a cross-continent racer, with the envious poet, left behind as a dot on the hill, celebrating his passing.

"Lord!" he cried. "I didn't know there were books like these! Thought poetry was all like Longfellow and Byron. Old boys. Europe. And rhymed bellyachin' about hard luck. But these books—they're me." Very carefully: "No; they're I! And she gave 'em to me! I will see her again! But she won't know

it. Now be sensible, son! What do you expect? Oh
—nothing. I'll just go on, and sneak in one more
glimpse of her to take back with me where I belong."

Half an hour after Claire had innocently passed his
ambush, he began to follow her. But not for days was
he careless. If he saw her on the horizon he paused
until she was out of sight. That he might not fail her
in need, he bought a ridiculously expensive pair of
field glasses, and watched her when she stopped by the
road. Once, when both her right rear tire and the
spare were punctured before she could make a town,
Milt from afar saw her patch a tube, pump up the tire
in the dust. He ached to go to her aid—though it
cannot be said that hand-pumping was his favorite
July afternoon sport.

Lest he encounter her in the streets, he always
camped to the eastward of the town at which she spent
the night. After dusk, when she was likely to end the
day's drive in the first sizable place, he hid his bug in
an alley and, like a spy after the papers, sneaked into
each garage to see if her car was there.

He would stroll in, look about vacuously, and pipe
to the suspicious night attendant, " Seen a traveling
man named Smith? " Usually the garage man snarled,
" No, I ain't seen nobody named Smith. An'thing
else I can do for you? " But once he was so unlucky
as to find the long-missing Mr. Smith!

Mr. Smith was surprised and insistent. Milt had to

do some quick lying. During that interview the cement floor felt very hard under his fidgeting feet, and he thought he heard the garage man in the office telephoning, "Don't think he knows Smith at all. I got a hunch he's that auto thief that was through here last summer."

When Claire did not stop in the first town she reached after twilight, but drove on by dark, he had to do some perilous galloping to catch up. The lights of a Teal are excellent for adornment, but they have no relation to illumination. They are dependent upon a magneto which is dependent only upon faith.

Once, skittering along by dark, he realized that the halted car which he had just passed was the Gomez. He thought he heard a shout behind him, but in a panic he kept going.

To the burring motor he groaned, "Now I probably never will see her again. Except that she thinks I'm such a pest that I dassn't let her know I'm in the same state, I sure am one successful lover. As a Prince Charming I win the Vanderbilt Cup. I'm going ahead backwards so fast I'll probably drop off into the Atlantic over the next hill!"

CHAPTER IX

THE MAN WITH AGATE EYES

WHEN her car had crossed the Missouri River on the swing-ferry between Bismarck and Mandan, Claire had passed from Middle West to Far West. She came out on an upland of virgin prairie, so treeless and houseless, so divinely dipping, so rough of grass, that she could imagine buffaloes still roving. In a hollow a real prairie schooner was camped, and the wandering homestead-seekers were cooking dinner beside it. From a quilt on the hay in the wagon a baby peeped, and Claire's heart leaped.

Beyond was her first butte, its sharp-cut sides glittering yellow, and she fancied that on it the Sioux scout still sat sentinel, erect on his pony, the feather bonnet down his back.

Now she seemed to breathe deeper, see farther. Again she came from unbroken prairie into wheat country and large towns.

Her impression of the new land was not merely of sun-glaring breadth. Sometimes, on a cloudy day, the wash of wheatlands was as brown and lowering and mysterious as an English moor in the mist. It dwarfed the far-off houses by its giant enchantment; its brooding reaches changed her attitude of brisk, gas-driven efficiency into a melancholy that was full of hints of old dark beauty.

Even when the sun came out, and the land was brazenly optimistic, she saw more than just prosperity. In a new home, house and barn and windmill square-cornered and prosaic, plumped down in a field with wheat coming up to the unporticoed door, a habitation unshadowed, unsheltered, unsoftened, she found a frank cleanness, as though the inhabitants looked squarely out at life, unafraid. She felt that the keen winds ought to blow away from such a prairie-fronting post of civilization all mildew and cowardice, all the mummy dust of ancient fears.

These were not peasants, these farmers. Nor, she learned, were they the "hicks" of humor. She could never again encounter without fiery resentment the Broadway peddler's faith that farmers invariably say "Waal, by heck." For she had spent an hour talking to one Dakota farmer, genial-eyed, quiet of speech. He had explained the relation of alfalfa to soil-chemistry; had spoken of his daughter, who taught economics in a state university; and asked Mr. Boltwood how turbines were hitched up on liners.

In fact, Claire learned that there may be an almost tolerable state of existence without gardenias or the news about the latest Parisian imagists.

She dropped suddenly from the vast, smooth-swelling miles of wheatland into the tortured marvels of the Bad Lands, and the road twisted in the shadow of flying buttresses and the terraced tombs of maharajas. While she tried to pick her way through a herd of wild, arroyo-bred cattle, she forgot her maneuvering as she was startled by the stabbing scarlet of a column of rock marking the place where for months deep beds of lignite had burned.

Claire had often given lifts to tramping harvesters and even hoboes along the road; had enjoyed the sight of their duffle-bags stuck up between the sleek fenders and the hood, and their talk about people and crops along the road, as they hung on the running-board. In the country of long hillslopes and sentinel buttes between the Dakota Bad Lands and Miles City she stopped to shout to a man whose plodding heavy back looked fagged, " Want a ride? "

" Sure! You bet! "

Usually her guests stepped on the right-hand running-board, beside Mr. Boltwood, and this man was far over on the right side of the road. But, while she waited, he sauntered in front of the car, round to her side, mounted beside her. Before the car had started, she was sorry to have invited him. He looked her over grinningly, almost contemptuously. His unabashed eyes were as bright and hard as agates. Below them, his nose was twisted a little, his mouth bent insolently up at one corner, and his square long chin bristled.

Usually, too, her passengers waited for her to start the conversation, and talked at Mr. Boltwood rather than directly to her. But the bristly man spat at her as the car started, " Going far? "

" Ye-es, some distance."

" Expensive car? "

" Why——"

" 'Fraid of getting held up? "

" I hadn't thought about it."

" Pack a cannon, don't you? "

" I don't think I quite understand."

" Cannon! Gun! Revolver! Got a revolver, of course? "

" W-why, no." She spoke uncomfortably. She was aware that his twinkling eyes were on her throat. His look made her feel unclean. She tried to think of some question which would lead the conversation to the less exclamatory subject of crops. They were on a curving shelf road beside a shallow valley. The road was one side of a horseshoe ten miles long. The unprotected edge of it dropped sharply to fields forty or fifty feet below.

" Prosperous-looking wheat down there," she said.

" No. Not a bit!" His look seemed to add, " And you know it—unless you're a fool!"

" Well, I didn't——"

" Make Glendive tonight? "

" At least that far."

" Say, lady, how's the chance for borrowin' a couple of dollars? I was workin' for a Finnski back here a ways, and he did me dirt—holdin' out my wages on me till the end of the month."

" Why, uh——"

It was Claire, not the man, who was embarrassed.

He was snickering, " Come on, don't be a tightwad. Swell car—poor man with no eats, not even a two-bits flop for tonight. Could yuh loosen up and slip me just a couple bones? "

Mr. Boltwood intervened. He looked as uncomfortable as Claire. " We'll see. It's rather against my principles to give money to an able-bodied man like you, even though it is a pleasure to give you a ride——"

" Sure! Don't cost you one red cent! "

"—and if I could help you get a job, though of course—— Being a stranger out here—— Seems strange to me, though," Mr. Boltwood struggled on, " that a strong fellow like you should be utterly destitute, when I see all these farmers able to have cars——"

Their guest instantly abandoned his attitude of supplication for one of boasting: " Destitute? Who the hell said I was destitute, heh? " He was snarling across Claire at Mr. Boltwood. His wet face was five inches from hers. She drew her head as far back as she could. She was sure that the man completely

appreciated her distaste, for his eyes popped with
amusement before he roared on:

"I got plenty of money! Just 'cause I'm hoofin'
it—— I don't want no charity from nobody! I could
buy out half these Honyockers! I don't need none of
no man's money!" He was efficiently working himself into a rage. "Who you calling destitute? All I
wanted was an advance till pay day! Got a check
coming. You high-tone, kid-glove Eastern towerists
want to watch out who you go calling destitute. I bet
I make a lot more money than a lot of your four-
flushin' friends!"

Claire wondered if she couldn't stop the car now,
and tell him to get off. But—that snapping eye was
too vicious. Before he got off he would say things—
scarring, vile things, that would never heal in her
brain. Her father was murmuring, "Let's drop him,"
but she softly lied, "No. His impertinence amuses
me."

She drove on, and prayed that he would of himself
leave his uncharitable hosts at the next town.

The man was storming—with a very meek ending:
"I'm tellin' you! I can make money anywhere! I'm
a crack machinist. . . . Give me two-bits for a
meal, anyway."

Mr. Boltwood reached in his change pocket. He had
no quarter. He pulled out a plump bill-fold. Without looking at the man, Claire could vision his eyes

glistening and his chops dripping as he stared at the
hoard. Mr. Boltwood handed him a dollar bill.
" There, take that, and let's change the subject," said
Mr. Boltwood testily.

" All right, boss. Say, you haven't got a cartwheel
instead of this wrapping paper, have you? I like to
feel my money in my pocket."

" No, sir, I have not! "

" All right, boss. No bad feelin's! "

Then he ignored Mr. Boltwood. His eyes focused
on Claire's face. To steady himself on the running-
board he had placed his left hand on the side of the
car, his right on the back of the seat. That right
hand slid behind her. She could feel its warmth on
her back.

She burst out, flaring, " Kindly do not touch me! "

" Gee, did I touch you, girlie? Why, that's a
shame!" he drawled, his cracked broad lips turning
up in a grin.

An instant later, as they skipped round a bend of
the long, high-hung shelf road, he pretended to sway
dangerously on the running-board, and deliberately
laid his filthy hand on her shoulder. Before she could
say anything he yelped in mock-regret, " Love o'
Mike! 'Scuse me, lady. I almost fell off."

Quietly, seriously, Claire said, " No, that wasn't
accidental. If you touch me again, I'll stop the car
and ask you to walk."

"Better do it now, dolly!" snapped Mr. Boltwood.
The man hooked his left arm about the side-post of
the open window-shield. It was a strong arm, a firm
grip. He seized her left wrist with his free hand.
Though all the while his eyes grotesquely kept their
amused sparkle, and beside them writhed laughter-
wrinkles, he shouted hoarsely, "You'll stop hell!"
His hand slid from her wrist to the steering wheel. "I
can drive this boat 's well as you can. You make one
move to stop, and I steer her over—— Blooie! Down
the bank!"

He did twist the front wheels dangerously near to
the outer edge of the shelf road. Mr. Boltwood gazed
at the hand on the wheel. With a quick breath Claire
looked at the side of the road. If the car ran off, it
would shoot down forty feet . . . . turning over and
over.

"Y-you wouldn't dare, because you'd g-go, too!"
she panted.

"Well, dearuh, you just try any monkey-business
and you'll find out how much I'll ggggggo-too! I'll
start you down the joy-slope and jump off, savvy?
Take your foot off that clutch."

She obeyed.

"Pretty lil feet, ain't they, cutie! Shoes cost
about twelve bucks, I reckon. While a better man
than you or old moldy-face there has to hit the pike
in three-dollar brogans. Sit down, yuh fool!"

This last to Mr. Boltwood, who had stood up,
swaying with the car, and struck at him. With a
huge arm the man swept Mr. Boltwood back into the
seat, but without a word to her father, he continued
to Claire:

"And keep your hand where it belongs. Don't go
trying to touch that switch. Aw, be sensible! What
would you do if the car did stop? I could blackjack
you both before this swell-elegant vehickle lost momentum, savvy? I don't want to pay out my good
money to a lawyer on a charge of—murder. Get me?
Better take it easy and not worry." His hand was
constantly on the wheel. He had driven cars before.
He was steering as much as she. "When I get you up
the road a piece I'm going to drive all the cute lil
boys and girls up a side trail, and take all of papa's
gosh-what-a-wad in the cunnin' potet-book, and I guess
we'll kiss lil daughter, and drive on, a-wavin' our
hand politely, and let you suckers walk to the next
burg."

"You wouldn't dare! You wouldn't dare!"

"Dare? Huh! Don't make the driver laugh!"

"I'll get help!"

"Yep. Sure. Fact, there's a car comin' toward
us. 'Bout a mile away I'd make it, wouldn't you?
Well, dollface, if you make one peep—over the bank
you go, both of you dead as a couplin'-pin. Smeared
all over those rocks. Get me? And me—I'll be sorry

the regrettable accident was so naughty and went and
happened—and I just got off in time meself. And I'll
pinch papa's poke while I'm helping get out the
bodies!"

Till now she hadn't believed it. But she dared not
glance at the approaching car. It was their interesting
guest who steered the Gomez past the other; and he
ran rather too near the edge of the road . . . so
that she looked over, down.

Beaming, he went on, " I'd pull the rough stuff right
here, instead of wastin' my time as a cap'n of industry
by taking you up to see the scenery in that daisy little
gully off the road; but the whole world can see us
along here—the hicks in the valley and anybody that
happens to sneak along in a car behind us. Shame the
way this road curves—see too far along it. Fact,
you're giving me a lot of trouble. But you'll give me
a kiss, won't you, Gwendolyn? "

He bent down, chuckling. She could feel his bristly
chin touch her cheek. She sprang up, struck at him.
He raised his hand from the wheel. For a second the
car ran without control. He jabbed her back into the
seat with his elbow. " Don't try any more monkey-
shines, if you know what's good for you," he said,
quite peacefully, as he resumed steering.

She was in a haze, conscious only of her father's
hand fondling hers. She heard a quick pit-pit-pit-pit
behind them. Car going to pass? She'd have to let it

go by. She'd concentrate on finding something she could——

Then, " Hello, folks. Having a picnic? Who's your little friend in the rompers?" sang out a voice beside them. It was Milt Daggett—the Milt who must be scores of miles ahead. His bug had caught up with them, was running even with them on the broad road.

CHAPTER X

THE CURIOUS INCIDENT OF THE HILLSIDE ROAD

SO unexpectedly, so genially, that Claire wondered if he realized what was happening, Milt chuckled to the tough on the running-board, as the two cars ran side by side, "Bound for some place, brother?"

The unwelcome guest looked puzzled. For the first time his china eyes ceased twinkling; and he answered dubiously: "Just gettin' a lift." He sped up the car with the hand-throttle. Milt accelerated equally.

Claire roused; wanted to shout. She was palsied afraid that Milt would leave them. The last time she had seen him, she had suggested that leaving them would be a favor.

Her guest growled at her—the words coming through a slit at the corner of his rowdy mouth, "Sit still, or I'll run you over."

Milt innocently babbled on, "Better come ride with me, 'bo. More room in this-here handsome coupelet."

Then was the rough relieved in his uneasy tender little heart, and his eyes flickered again as he shouted back, not looking at Milt, "Thanks, bub, I'll stick by me friends."

"Oh no; can't lose pleasure of your company. I like your looks. You're a bloomin' little island way off on the dim silver skyline." Claire knitted her brows. She had not seen Milt's rhetoric. "You're an island of Hesperyds or Hesperides. Accent on the bezuzus. Oh, yes, moondream, I think you better come. Haven't decided "—Milt's tone was bland—" whether to kill you or just have you pinched. Miss Boltwood! Switch off your power!"

"If she does," the tough shouted, "I'll run 'em off the bank."

"No, you won't, sweetheart, 'cause why? 'Cause what'll I do to you afterwards?"

"You won't do nothin', Jack, 'cause I'd gouge your eyes out."

"Why, lovesoul, d' you suppose I'd be talking up as brash as this to a bid, stwong man like oo if I didn't have a gun handy?"

"Yuh, I guess so, lil sunbeam. And before you could shoot, I'd crowd your tin liz into the bank, and jam right into it! I may get killed, but you won't even be a grease-spot!"

He was turning the Gomez from its straight course, forcing Milt's bug toward the high bank of earth which walled in the road on the left.

While Claire was very sick with fear, then more sick with contempt, Milt squealed, "You win!" And he had dropped back. The Gomez was going on alone.

There was only one thing more for Claire—to jump. And that meant death.

The tough was storming, "Your friend's a crack shot—with his mouth!"

The thin pit-pit-pit was coming again. She looked back. She saw Milt's bug snap forward so fast that on a bump its light wheels were in the air. She saw Milt standing on the right side of the bug holding the wheel with one hand, and the other hand—firm, grim, broad-knuckled hand—outstretched toward the tough, then snatching at his collar.

The tough's grip was torn from the steering wheel. He was yanked from the running-board. He crunched down on the road.

She seized the wheel. She drove on at sixty miles an hour. She had gone a good mile before she got control of her fear and halted. She saw Milt turn his little car as though it were a prancing bronco. It seemed to paw the air with its front wheels. He shot back, pursuing the late guest. The man ran bobbing along the road. At this distance he was no longer formidable, but a comic, jerking, rabbity figure, humping himself over the back track.

As the bug whirled down on him, the tough was to be seen throwing up his hands, leaping from the high bank.

Milt turned again and came toward them, but slowly; and after he had drawn up even and switched

off the engine, he snatched off his violent plaid cap
and looked apologetic.

"Sorry I had to kid him along. I was afraid he
really would drive you off the bank. He was a bad
actor. And he was right; he could have licked me.
Thought maybe I could jolly him into getting off, and
have him pinched, next town."

"But you had a gun—a revolver—didn't you,
lad?" panted Mr. Boltwood.

"Um, wellllll—— I've got a shotgun. It wouldn't
take me more 'n five or ten minutes to dig it out, and
put it together. And there's some shells. They may
be all right. Haven't looked at 'em since last fall.
They didn't get so awful damp then."

"But suppose he'd had a revolver himself?" wailed
Claire.

"Gee, you know, I thought he probably did have
one. I was scared blue. I had a wrench to throw at
him though," confided Milt.

"How did you know we needed you?"

"Why back there, couple miles behind you, maybe
I saw your father get up and try to wrestle him, so I
suspected there was kind of a disagreement. Say,
Miss Boltwood, you know when you spoke to me—
way back there—I hadn't meant to butt in. Honest. I thought maybe as we were going——"

"Oh, I know!"

"—the same way, you wouldn't mind my trailing,

if I didn't sit in too often; and I thought maybe I could help you if——"

"Oh, I know! I'm so ashamed! So bitterly ashamed! I just meant—— Will you forgive me? You were so good, taking care of us——"

"Oh, sure, that's all right!"

"I fancy you do know how grateful father and I are that you were behind us, this time! Wasn't it a lucky accident that we'd slipped past you some place!"

"Yes," dryly, "quite an accident. Well, I'll skip on ahead again. May run into you again before we hit Seattle. Going to take the run through Yellowstone Park?"

"Yes, but——" began Claire. Her father interrupted:

"Uh, Mr., uh—Daggett, was it?—I wonder if you won't stay a little closer to us hereafter? I was getting rather a good change out of the trip, but I'm afraid that now—— If it wouldn't be an insult, I'd beg you to consider staying with us for a consideration, uh, you know, remuneration, and you could——"

"Thanks, uh, thank you, sir, but I wouldn't like to do it. You see, it's kind of my vacation. If I've done anything I'm tickled——"

"But perhaps," Mr. Boltwood ardently begged the young man recently so abysmally unimportant, "perhaps you would consent to being my guest, when you cared to—say at hotels in the Park."

" 'Fraid I couldn't. I'm kind of a lone wolf."

" Please! Pretty please!" besought Claire. Her smile was appealing, her eyes on his.

Milt bit his knuckles. He looked weak. But he persisted, " No, you'll get over this scrap with our friend. By the way, I'll put the deputy onto him, in the next town. He'll never get out of the county. When you forget him—— Oh no, you can go on fine. You're a good steady driver, and the road's perfectly safe—if you give people the once-over before you pick 'em up. Picking up badmen is no more dangerous here than it would be in New York. Fact, there's lot more hold-ups in any city than in the wildest country. I don't think you showed such awfully good taste in asking Terrible Tim, the two-gun man, right into the parlor. Gee, please don't do it again! Please!"

" No," meekly. " I was an idiot. I'll be good, next time. But won't you stay somewhere near us?"

" I'd like to, but I got to chase on. Don't want to wear out the welcome on the doormat, and I'm due in Seattle, and—— Say, Miss Boltwood." He swung out of the bug, cranked up, climbed back, went awkwardly on, " I read those books you gave me. They're slick—mean to say, interesting. Where that young fellow in *Youth's Encounter* wanted to be a bishop and a soldier and everything—— Just like me, except Schoenstrom is different, from London, some ways! I always wanted to be a brakie, and then a yeggman.

But I wasn't bright enough for either. I just became a garage man. And I—— Some day I'm going to stop using slang. But it'll take an operation!"

He was streaking down the road, and Claire was sobbing, "Oh, the lamb, the darling thing! Fretting about his slang, when he wasn't afraid in that horrible nightmare. If we could just do something for him!"

"Don't you worry about him, dolly. He's a very energetic chap. And—— Uh—— Mightn't we drive on a little farther, perhaps? I confess that the thought of our recent guest still in this vicinity——"

"Yes, and—— Oh, I'm shameless. If Mohammed Milton won't stay with our car mountain, we're going to tag after him."

But when she reached the next hill, with its far shining outlook, there was no Milt and no Teal bug on the road ahead.

CHAPTER XI

SAGEBRUSH TOURISTS OF THE GREAT HIGHWAY

SHE had rested for two days in Miles City; had seen the horse-market, with horse-wranglers in chaps; had taken dinner with army people at Fort Keogh, once the bulwark against the Sioux, now nodding over the dry grass on its parade ground.

By the Yellowstone River, past the Crow reservation, Claire had driven on through the Real West, along the Great Highway. The Red Trail and the Yellowstone Trail had joined now and she was one of the new Canterbury Pilgrims. Even Mr. Boltwood caught the trick of looking for licenses, and cried, " There's a Connecticut car! "

To the Easterner, a drive from New York to Cape Cod, over asphalt, is viewed as heroic, but here were cars that had casually started on thousand-mile vacations. She kept pace not only with large cars touring from St. Louis or Detroit to Glacier Park and Yellowstone, but also she found herself companionable with families of workmen, headed for a new town and a new job, and driving because a flivver, bought second-hand and soon to be sold again, was cheaper than trains.

" Sagebrush Tourists " these camping adventurers

were called. Claire became used to small cars, with curtain-lights broken, bearing wash-boilers or refrigerators on the back, pastboard suitcases lashed by rope to the running-board, frying pans and canvas water bottles dangling from top-rods. And once baby's personal laundry was seen flapping on a line across a tonneau!

In each car was what looked like the crowd at a large farm-auction—grandfather, father, mother, a couple of sons and two or three daughters, at least one baby in the arms of each grown-up, all jammed into two seats already filled with trunks and baby-carriages. And they were happy—incredibly happier than the smart people being conveyed in a bored way behind chauffeurs.

The Sagebrush Tourists made camp; covered the hood with a quilt from which the cotton was oozing; brought out the wash-boiler, did a washing, had dinner, sang about the fire; granther and the youngest baby gamboling together, while the limousinvalids, insulated from life by plate glass, preserved by their steady forty an hour from the commonness of seeing anything along the road, looked out at the campers for a second, sniffed, rolled on, wearily wondering whether they would find a good hotel that night—and why the deuce they hadn't come by train.

If Claire Boltwood had been protected by Jeff Saxton or by a chauffeur, she, too, would probably

have marveled at cars gray with dust, the unshaved
men in fleece-lined duck coats, and the women wind-
burnt beneath the boudoir caps they wore as motoring
bonnets. But Claire knew now that filling grease-cups
does not tend to delicacy of hands; that when you
wash with a cake of petrified pink soap and half a
pitcher of cold hard water, you never quite get the
stain off—you merely get through the dust stratum
to the Laurentian grease formation, and mutter, " a
nice clean grease doesn't hurt food," and go sleepily
down to dinner.

She saw a dozen camping devices unknown to the
East: trailers, which by day bobbed along behind the
car like coffins on two wheels, but at night opened into
tents with beds, an ice-box, a table; tents covering a
bed whose head rested on the running-board; beds
made-up in the car, with the cushions as mattresses.

The Great Transcontinental Highway was colored
not by motors alone. It is true that the Old West of
the stories is almost gone; that Billings, Miles City,
Bismarck, are more given to Doric banks than to
gambling hells. But still are there hints of frontier
days. Still trudge the prairie schooners; cowpunchers
in chaps still stand at the doors of log cabins—when
they are tired of playing the automatic piano; and
blanket Indians, Blackfeet and Crows, stare at five-
story buildings—when they are not driving modern
reapers on their farms.

They all waved to Claire. Telephone linemen, lolling with pipes and climber-strapped legs in big trucks,
sang out to her; traction engine crews shouted; and
these she found to be her own people. Only once did
she lose contentment—when, on the observation platform of a train bound for Seattle, she saw a Britisher
in flannels and a monocle, headed perhaps for the
Orient. As the train slipped silkenly away, the Gomez
seemed slow and clumsy, and the strain of driving
intolerable. And that Britisher must be charming——
Then a lonely, tight-haired woman in the doorway of
a tar-paper shack waved to her, and in that wistful
gesture Claire found friendship.

And sometimes in the "desert" of yet unbroken
land she paused by the Great Highway and forgot
the passion to keep going——

She sat on a rock, by a river so muddy that it was
like yellow milk. The only trees were a bunch of cottonwoods untidily scattering shreds of cotton, and
the only other vegetation left in the dead world was
dusty green sagebrush with lumps of gray yet preg-
nant earth between, or a few exquisite green and white
flashes of the herb called Snow-on-the-Mountain. The
inhabitants were jackrabbits, or American magpies in
sharp black and white livery, forever trying to balance
their huge tails against the wind, and yelling in low-
magpie their opinion of tourists.

She did not desire gardens, then, nor the pettiness

of plump terraced hills. She was in the Real West, and it was hers, since she had won to it by her own plodding. Her soul—if she hadn't had one, it would immediately have been provided, by special arrangement, the moment she sat there—sailed with the hawks in the high thin air, and when it came down it sang hallelujahs, because the sagebrush fragrance was more healing than piney woods, because the sharp-bitten edges of the buttes were coral and gold and basalt and turquoise, and because a real person, one Milt Daggett, though she would never see him again, had found her worthy of worship.

She did not often think of Milt; she did not know whether he was ahead of her, or had again dropped behind. When she did recall him, it was with respect quite different from the titillation that dancing men had sometimes aroused, or the impression of manicured agreeableness and efficiency which Jeff Saxton carried about.

She always supplicated the mythical Milt in moments of tight driving. Driving, just the actual getting on, was her purpose in life, and the routine of driving was her order of the day: Morning freshness, rolling up as many miles as possible before lunch, that she might loaf afterward. The invariable two P.M. discovery that her eyes ached, and the donning of huge amber glasses, which gave to her lithe smartness a counterfeit scholarliness. Toward night, the quarter-hour of level sun-glare which prevented her seeing the road. Dusk, and the discovery of how much light there was after all, once she remembered to take off her glasses. The worst quarter-hour when, though the roads were an amethyst rich to the artist, they were also a murkiness exasperating to the driver, yet still too light to be thrown into relief by the lamps. The mystic moment when night clicked tight, and the lamps made a fan of gold, and Claire and her father settled down to plodding content—and no longer had to take the trouble of admiring the scenery!

The morning out of Billings, she wondered why a low cloud so persistently held its shape, and realized that it was a far-off mountain, her first sight of the Rockies. Then she cried out, and wished for Milt to share her exultation. Rather earnestly she said to Mr. Boltwood:

"The mountains must be so wonderful to Mr. Daggett, after spending his life in a cornfield. Poor Milt! I hope——"

"I don't think you need to worry about that young man. I fancy he's quite able to run about by himself, as jolly as a sand-dog. And—— Of course I'm extremely grateful to him for his daily rescue of us from the jaws of death, but he was right; if he had stayed with us, it would have been inconvenient to keep considering him. He isn't accustomed to the comedy of manners——"

"He ought to be. He'd enjoy it so. He's the real American. He has imagination and adaptability. It's a shame: all the *petits fours* and Bach recitals wasted on Jeff Saxton, when a Milt Dag——"

"Yes, yes, quite so!"

"No, honest! The dear honey-lamb, so ingenious, and really, rather good-looking. But so lonely and gregarious—like a little woolly dog that begs you to come and play; and I slapped him when he patted his paws and gamboled—— It was horrible. I'll never forgive myself. Making him drive on ahead in that nasty, patronizing way—— I feel as if we'd spoiled his holiday. I wonder if he had intended to make the Yellowstone Park trip? He didn't——"

"Yes, yes. Let's forget the young man. Look! How very curious!"

They were crossing a high bridge over a railroad track along which a circus train was bending. Mr. Boltwood offered judicious remarks upon the migratory habits of circuses, and the vision of the Galahad of the Teal bug was thoroughly befogged by parental observations, till Claire returned from youthful romance to being a sensible Boltwood, and decided that after all, Milt was not a lord of the sky-painted mountains.

Before they bent south, at Livingston, Claire had her first mountain driving, and once she had to ford a stream, putting the car at it, watching the water curve up in a lovely silver veil. She felt that she was conquering the hills as she had the prairies.

She pulled up on a plateau to look at her battery. She noted the edge of a brake-band peeping beyond the drum, in a ragged line of fabric and copper wire. Then she knew that she didn't know enough to conquer. "Do you suppose it's dangerous?" she asked her father, who said a lot of comforting things that didn't mean anything.

She thought of Milt. She stopped a passing car. The driver "guessed" that the brake-band was all gone, and that it would be dangerous to continue with it along mountain roads. Claire dustily tramped two miles to a ranch house, and telephoned to the nearest garage, in a town called Saddle Back.

Whenever a motorist has delirium he mutters those lamentable words, " Telephoned to the nearest garage."

She had to wait a tedious hour before she saw a flivver rattling up with the garage man, who wasn't a man at all, but a fourteen-year-old boy. He snorted, " Rats, you didn't need to send for me. Could have made it perfectly safe. Come on."

Never has the greatest boy pianist received such awe as Claire gave to this contemptuous young god, with grease on his peachy cheeks. She did come on. But she rather hoped that she was in great danger. It was humiliating to telephone to a garage for nothing. When she came into the gas-smelling garage in Saddle

Back she said appealingly to the man in charge, a serious, lip-puffing person of forty-five, " Was it safe to come in with the brake-band like that? "

" No. Pretty risky. Wa'n't it, Mike? "

The Mike to whom he turned for authority was the same fourteen-year-old boy. He snapped, " Heh? That? Naw! Put in new band. Get busy. Bring me the jack. Hustle up, uncle."

While the older man stood about and vainly tried to impress people who came in and asked questions which invariably had to be referred to his repair boy, the precocious expert stripped the wheel down to something that looked to Claire distressingly like an empty milk-pan. Then the boy didn't seem to know exactly what to do. He scratched his ear a good deal, and thought deeply. The older man could only scratch.

So for two hours Claire and her father experienced that most distressing of motor experiences—waiting, while the afternoon that would have been so good for driving went by them. Every fifteen minutes they came in from sitting on a dry-goods box in front of the garage, and never did the repair appear to be any farther along. The boy seemed to be giving all his time to getting the wrong wrench, and scolding the older man for having hidden the right one.

When she had left Brooklyn Heights, Claire had not expected to have such authoritative knowledge of the Kalifornia Kandy Kitchen, Saddle Back, Montana,

across from Tubbs' Garage, that she could tell whether
they were selling more Atharva Cigarettes or Polu-
tropons. She prowled about the garage till she knew
every pool of dripped water in the tin pail of soft
soap in the iron sink.

She was worried by an overheard remark of the
boy wonder, "Gosh, we haven't any more of that
decent brake lining. Have to use this piece of mush."
But when the car was actually done, nothing like a
dubious brake could have kept her from the glory
of starting. The first miles seemed miracles of ease
and speed.

She came through the mountains into Livingston.

Kicking his heels on a fence near town, and
fondling a gray cat, sat Milt Daggett, and he yelped
at her with earnestness and much noise.

CHAPTER XII

THE WONDERS OF NATURE WITH ALL MODERN IMPROVEMENTS

"HELLO!" said Milt.

"Hel-lo!" said Claire.

"How dee do," said Mr. Boltwood.

"This is so nice! Where's your car? I hope nothing's happened," glowed Claire.

"No. It's back here from the road a piece. Camp there tonight. Reason I stopped—— Struck me you've never done any mountain driving, and there's some pretty good climbs in the Park; slick road, but we go up to almost nine thousand feet. And cold mornings. Thought I'd tip you off to some driving tricks—if you'd like me to."

"Oh, of course. Very grateful——"

"Then I'll tag after you tomorrow, and speak my piece."

"So jolly you're going through the Park."

"Yes, thought might as well. What the guide books call 'Wonders of Nature.' Only wonder of nature I ever saw in Schoenstrom was my friend Mac trying to think he was soused after a case of near-beer. Well—— See you tomorrow."

Not once had he smiled. His tone had been impersonal. He vaulted the fence and tramped away.

When they drove out of town, in the morning, they found Milt waiting by the road, and he followed them till noon. By urgent request, he shared a lunch, and lectured upon going down long grades in first or second speed, to save brakes; upon the use of the retarded spark and the slipped clutch in climbing. His bug was beside the Gomez in the line-up at the Park gate, when the United States Army came to seal one's firearms, and to inquire on which mountain one intended to be killed by defective brakes. He was just behind her all the climb up to Mammoth Hot Springs.

When she paused for water to cool the boiling radiator, the bug panted up, and with the first grin she had seen on his face since Dakota Milt chuckled, " The Teal is a grand car for mountains. Aside from over-heating, bum lights, thin upholstery, faulty ignition, tissue-paper brake-bands, and this-here special aviation engine, specially built for a bumble-bee, it's what the catalogues call a powerful brute! "

Claire and her father stayed at the chain of hotels through the Park. Milt was always near them, but not at the hotels. He patronized one of the chains of permanent camps.

The Boltwoods invited him to dinner at one hotel, but he refused and——

Because he was afraid that Claire would find him intrusive, Milt was grave in her presence. He couldn't respond either to her enthusiasm about canyon and colored pool—or to her rage about the tourists who, she alleged, preferred freak museum pieces to plain beauty; who never admired a view unless it was labeled by a signpost and megaphoned by a guide as something they ought to admire—and tell the Folks Back Home about.

When she tried to express this social rage to Milt he merely answered uneasily, " Yes, I guess there's something to that."

She was, he pondered, so darn particular. How could he ever figure out what he ought to do? No thanks; much obliged, but guessed he'd better not accept her invitation to dinner. Darn sorry couldn't come but—— Had promised a fellow down at the camp to have chow with him.

If in this Milt was veracious, he was rather fickle to his newly discovered friend; for while Claire was finishing dinner, a solemn young man was watching her through a window.

She was at a table for six. She was listening to a man of thirty in riding-breeches, a stock, and a pointed nose, who bowed to her every time he spoke, which was so frequently that his dining gave the impression of a man eating grape-fruit on a merry-go-round. Back in Schoenstrom, fortified by Mac and the bunch at the Old Home Lunch, Milt would have called the man a " dude," and—though less noisily than the others—would have yelped, " Get onto Percy's beer-bottle pants. What's he got his neck bandaged for? Bet he's got a boil."

But now Milt yearned, " He does look swell. Wish I could get away with those things. Wouldn't I look like a fool with my knees buttoned up, though! And there's two other fellows in dress suits. Wouldn't mind those so much. Gee, it must be awful where you've got so many suits of trick clothes you don't know which one to wear.

" That fellow and Claire are talking pretty swift. He doesn't need any piston rings, that lad. Wonder —wonder what they're talking about? Music, I guess, and books and pictures and scenery. He's saying that no tongue or pen can describe the glories of the Park, and then he's trying to describe 'em. And maybe they know the same folks in New York. Lord, how I'd be out of it. I wish——"

Milt made a toothpick out of a match, decided that toothpicks were inelegant in his tragic mood, and longed: " Never did see her among her own kind of folks till now. I wish I could jabber about music and stuff. I'll learn it. I will! I can! I picked up autos in three months. I—— Milt, you're a dub. I wonder can they be talking French, maybe, or Wop, or something? I could get onto the sedan styles in highbrow talk as long as it was in American.

" I could probably spring linen-collar stuff about,

'Really a delightful book, so full of delightful characters,' if I stuck by the rhetoric books long enough. But once they begin the *parlez-vous, oui, oui*, I'm a gone goose. Still, by golly, didn't I pick up Dutch —German—like a mice? Back off, son! You did not! You can talk Plattdeutsch something grand, as long as you keep the verbs and nouns in American. You got a nice character, Milt, but you haven't got any parts of speech.

"Now look at Percy! Taking a bath in a fingerbowl. I never could pull that finger-bowl stuff; pinning your ears back and jiu-jitsing the fried chicken, and then doing a high dive into a little dish that ain't —that isn't either a wash-bowl or real good lemonade. He's a perfect lady, Percy is. Dabs his mouth with his napkin like a watchmaker tinkering the carburetor in a wrist watch.

"Lookit him bow and scrape—asking her something—— Rats, he's going out in the lobby with her. Walks like a cat on a wet ash-pile. But—— Oh thunder, he's all right. Neat. I never could mingle with that bunch. I'd be web-footed and butter-fingered. And he seems to know all that bunch— bows to every maiden aunt in the shop. Now if I was following her, I'd never see anybody but her; rest of the folks could all bob their heads silly, and I'd never see one blame thing except that funny little soft spot at the back of her neck. Nope, you're kind to your cat, Milt, but you weren't cut out to be no parlor-organ duet."

This same meditative young man might have been discovered walking past the porch of the hotel, his hands in his pockets, his eyes presumably on the stars —certainly he gave no signs of watching Claire and the man in riding-breeches as they leaned over the rail, looked at mountain-tops filmy in starlight, while in the cologne-atomized mode, Breeches quoted:

> Ah, 'tis far heaven my awed heart seeks
> When I behold those mighty peaks.

Milt could hear him commenting, "Doesn't that just get the feeling of the great open, Miss Bolt-wood?"

Milt did not catch her answer. Himself, he grunted, "I never could get much het up about this poetry that's full of Ah's and 'tises."

Claire must have seen Milt just after he had sauntered past. She cried, "Oh, Mr. Daggett! Just a moment!" She left Breeches, ran down to Milt. He was frightened. Was he going to get what he deserved for eavesdropping?

She was almost whispering. "Save me from our friend up on the porch," she implored.

He couldn't believe it. But he took a chance. "Won't you have a little walk?" he roared.

"So nice of you—just a little way, perhaps?" she sang out.

They were silent till he got up the nerve to admire, " Glad you found some people you knew in the hotel."

" But I didn't."

" Oh, I thought your friend in the riding-pants was chummy."

" So did I ! " She rather snorted.

" Well, he's a nice-looking lad. I did admire those pants. I never could wear anything like that."

" I should hope not—at dinner ! The creepy jackass, I don't believe he's ever been on a horse in his life ! He thinks riding-breeches are the——"

" Oh, that's it. Breeches, not pants."

"—last word in smartness. Overdressing is just ten degrees worse than underdressing."

" Oh, I don't know. Take this sloppy old blue suit of mine——"

" It's perfectly nice and simple, and quite well cut. You probably had a clever tailor."

" I had. He lives in Chicago or New York, I believe."

" Really? How did he come to Schoenstrom? "

" Never been there. This tailor is a busy boy. He fitted about eleventeen thousand people, last year."

" I see. Ready mades. Cheer up. That's where Henry B. Boltwood gets most of his clothes. Mr. Daggett, if ever I catch you in the Aren't-I-beautiful frame of mind of our friend back on the porch, I'll give up my trip to struggle for your soul."

"He seemed to have soul in large chunks. He seemed to talk pretty painlessly. I had a hunch you and he were discussing sculpture, anyway. Maybe Rodin."

"What do you know about Rodin?"

"Articles in the magazines. Same place you learned about him!" But Milt did not sound rude. He said it chucklingly.

"You're perfectly right. And we've probably read the very same articles. Well, our friend back there said to me at dinner, 'It must be dreadful for you to have to encounter so many common people along the road.' I said, 'It is,' in the most insulting tone I could, and he just rolled his eyes, and hadn't an idea I meant him. Then he slickered his hair at me, and mooed, 'Is it not wonderful to see all these strange manifestations of the secrets of Nature!' and I said, 'Is it?' and he went on, 'One feels that if one could but meet a sympathetic lady here, one's cup of rejoicing in untrammeled nature——' Honest, Milt, Mr. Daggett, I mean, he did talk like that. Been reading books by optimistic lady authors. And one looked at me, one did, as if one would be willing to hold my hand, if I let one.

"He invited me to come out on the porch and give the double O. to handsome mountains as illuminated by terrestrial bodies, and I felt so weak in the presence of his conceit that I couldn't refuse. Then he insisted on introducing me to a woman from my own Brooklyn, who condoled with me for having to talk to Western persons while motoring. Oh, dear God, that such people should live . . . that the sniffy little Claire should once have been permitted to live! . . . And then I saw you!"

Through all her tirade they had stood close together, her face visibly eager in the glow from the hotel; and Milt had grown taller. But he responded, " I'm afraid I might have been just as bad. I haven't even reached the riding-breeches stage in evolution. Maybe never will."

" No. You won't. You'll go right through it. By and by, when you're so rich that father and I won't be allowed to associate with you, you'll wear riding-breeches—but for riding, not as a donation to the beauties of nature."

" Oh, I'm already rich. It shows. Waitress down at the camp asked me whose car I was driving through."

" I know what I wanted to say. Since you won't be our guest, will you be our host—I mean, as far as welcoming us? I think it would be fun for father and me to stop at your camp, tomorrow night, at the canyon, instead of at the hotel. Will you guide me to the canyon, if I do?"

" Oh—terribly—glad!"

CHAPTER XIII

ADVENTURERS BY FIRELIGHT

NEITHER of the Boltwoods had seen the Grand Canyon of the Colorado. The Canyon of the Yellowstone was their first revelation of intimidating depth and color gone mad. When their car and Milt's had been parked in the palisaded corral back of the camp at which they were to stay, they three set out for the canyon's edge chattering, and stopped dumb.

Mr. Boltwood declined to descend. He returned to the camp for a cigar. The boy and girl crept down seeming miles of damp steps to an outhanging pinnacle that still was miles of empty airy drop above the river bed. Claire had a quaking feeling that this rock pulpit was going to slide. She thrust out her hand, seized Milt's paw, and in its firm warmth found comfort. Clinging to its security she followed him by the crawling path to the river below. She looked up at columns of crimson and saffron and burning brown, up at the matronly falls, up at lone pines clinging to jutting rocks that must be already crashing toward her, and in the splendor she knew the Panic fear that is the deepest reaction to beauty.

Milt merely shook his head as he stared up. He had neither gossiped nor coyly squeezed her hand as he had guided her. She fell to thinking that she preferred this American boy in this American scene to a nimble gentleman saluting the Alps in a dinky green hat with a little feather.

It was Milt who, when they had labored back up again, when they had sat smiling at each other with comfortable weariness, made her see the canyon not as a freak, but as the miraculous work of a stream rolling grains of sand for millions of years, till it had cut this Jovian intaglio. He seemed to have read —whether in books, or in paragraphs in mechanical magazines—a good deal about geology. He made it real. Not that she paid much attention to what he actually said! She was too busy thinking of the fact that he should say it at all.

Not condescendingly but very companionably she accompanied Milt in the exploration of their camp for the night—the big dining tent, the city of individual bedroom tents, canvas-sided and wooden-floored, each with a tiny stove for the cold mornings of these high altitudes. She was awed that evening by hearing her waitress discussing the novels of Ibanez. Jeff Saxton knew the names of at least six Russian novelists, but Jeff was not highly authoritative regarding Spanish literature.

" I suppose she's a school-teacher, working here in

vacation," Claire whispered to Milt, beside her at the long, busy, scenically conversational table.

"Our waitress? Well, sort of. I understand she's professor of literature in some college," said Milt, in a matter of fact way. And he didn't at all see the sequence when she went on:

"There is an America! I'm glad I've found it!"

The camp's evening bonfire was made of logs on end about a stake of iron. As the logs blazed up, the guests on the circle of benches crooned "Suwanee River," and "Old Black Joe," and Claire crooned with them. She had been afraid that her father would be bored, but she saw that, above his carefully tended cigar, he was dreaming. She wondered if there had been a time when he had hummed old songs.

The fire sank to coals. The crowd wandered off to their tents. Mr. Boltwood followed them after an apologetic, "Good night. Don't stay up too late." With a scattering of only half a dozen people on the benches, this huge circle seemed deserted; and Claire and Milt, leaning forward, chins on hands, were alone —by their own campfire, among the mountains.

The stars stooped down to the hills; the pines were a wall of blackness; a coyote yammered to point the stillness; and the mighty pile of coals gave a warmth luxurious in the creeping mountain chill.

The silence of large places awes the brisk intruder, and Claire's voice was unconsciously lowered as she begged, " Tell me something about yourself, Mr. Daggett. I don't really know anything at all."

" Oh, you wouldn't be interested. Just Schoenstrom ! "

" But just Schoenstrom might be extremely interesting."

" But honest, you'd think I was—edging in on you ! "

" I know what you are thinking. The time I suggested, way back there in Dakota, that you were sticking too close. You've never got over it. I've tried to make up for it, but—— I really don't blame you. I was horrid. I deserve being beaten. But you do keep on punishing ra——"

" Punishing? Lord, I didn't mean to! No! Honest! It was nothing. You were right. Looked as though I was inviting myself—— But, oh, pleassssse, Miss Boltwood, don't ever think for a sec. that I meant to be a grouch——"

" Then do tell me—— Who is this Milton Daggett that you know so much better than I ever can? "

" Well," Milt crossed his kness, caught his chin in his hand, " I don't know as I really do know him so well. I thought I did. I was onto his evil ways. He was the son of the pioneer doctor, Maine folks."

" Really? My mother came from Maine."

Milt did not try to find out that they were cousins. He went on, " This kid, Milt, went to high school in

St. Cloud—town twenty times as big as Schoenstrom
—but he drifted back because his dad was old and
needed him, after his mother's death——"

"You have no brothers or sisters?"

"No. Nobody. 'Cept Lady Vere de Vere—which
animal she is going to get cuffed if she chews up any
more of my overcoat out in my tent tonight! . . .
Well, this kid worked 'round, machinery mostly, and
got interested in cars, and started a garage—— Wee,
that was an awful shop, first one I had! In
Rauskukle's barn. Six wrenches and a screw-driver
and a one-lung pump! And I didn't know a roller-
bearing from three-point suspension! But—— Well,
anyway, he worked along, and built a regular garage,
and paid off practically all the mortgage on it——"

"I remember stopping at a garage in Schoenstrom,
I'm almost sure it was, for something. I seem to re-
member it was a good place. Do you own it?
Really?"

"Ye-es, what there is of it."

"But there's a great deal of it. It's efficient.
You've done your job. That's more than most high-
born aides-de-camp could say."

"Honestly? Well—I don't know——"

"Who did you play with in Schoenstrom? Oh, I
wish I'd noticed that town. But I couldn't tell then
that—— What, uh, which girl did you fall in love
with?"

"None! Honest! None! Not one! Never fell in love——"

"You're unfortunate. I have, lots of times. I remember quite enjoying being kissed once, at a dance."

When he answered, his voice was strange: "I suppose you're engaged to somebody."

"No. And I don't know that I shall be. Once, I thought I liked a man, rather. He has nice eyes and the most correct spectacles, and he is polite to his mother at breakfast, and his name is Jeff, and he will undoubtedly be worth five or six hundred thousand dollars, some day, and his opinions on George Moore and commercial paper are equally sound and unoriginal—— Oh, I ought not to speak of him, and I certainly ought not to be spiteful. I'm not at all reticent and ladylike, am I! But—— Somehow I can't see him out here, against a mountain of jagged rock."

"Only you won't always be out here against mountains. Some day you'll be back in—where is it in New York State?"

"I confess it's Brooklyn—but not what you'd mean by Brooklyn. Your remark shows you to have subtlety. I must remember that, mustn't I! I won't always be driving through this big land. But—— Will I get all fussy and ribbon-tied again, when I go back?"

"No. You won't. You drive like a man."

"What has that——"

"It has a lot to do with it. A garage man can trail along behind another car and figger out, figure out, just about what kind of a person the driver is from the way he handles his boat. Now you bite into the job. You drive pretty neat—neatly. You don't either scoot too far out of the road in passing a car, or take corners too wide. You won't be fussy. But still, I suppose you'll be glad to be back among your own folks and you'll forget the wild Milt that tagged along——"

"Milt—or Mr. Daggett—no, Milt! I shall never, in my oldest grayest year, in a ducky cap by the fireplace, forget the half-second when your hand came flashing along, and caught that man on the running-board. But it wasn't just that melodrama. If that hadn't happened, something else would have, to symbolize you. It's that you—oh, you took me in, a stranger, and watched over me, and taught me the customs of the country, and were never impatient. No, I shan't forget that; neither of the Boltwoods will."

In the rose-haze of firelight he straightened up and stared at her, but he settled into shyness again as she added:

"Perhaps others would have done the same thing. I don't know. If they had, I should have remembered them too. But it happened that it was you, and I, uh, my father and I, will always be grateful. We both hope we may see you in Seattle. What are you planning to do there? What is your ambition? Or is that a rude question?"

" Why, uh——"

" What I mean—— I mean, how did you happen to want to go there, with a garage at home? You still control it?"

" Oh yes. Left my mechanic in charge. Why, I just kind of decided suddenly. I guess it was what they call an inspiration. Always wanted a long trip, anyway, and I thought maybe in Seattle I could hook up with something a little peppier than Schoenstrom. Maybe something in Alaska. Always wished I were a mechanical or civil engineer so——"

" Then why don't you become one? You're young—— How old are you?"

" Twenty-five."

" We're both children, compared with Je—compared with some men who are my friends. You're quite young enough to go to engineering school. And take some academic courses on the side—English, so on. Why don't you? Have you ever thought of it?"

" N-no, I hadn't thought of doing it, but—— All right. I will! In Seattle! B'lieve the University of Washington is there."

" You mean it?"

" Yes. I do. You're the boss."

" That's—that's flattering, but—— Do you always make up your mind as quickly as this?"

"When the boss gives orders!"

He smiled, and she smiled back, but this time it was she who was embarrassed. "You're rather overwhelming. You change your life—if you really do mean it—because a *jeune fille* from Brooklyn is so impertinent, from her Olympian height of finishing-school learning, as to suggest that you do so."

"I don't know what a *jeune fille* is, but I do know——" He sprang up. He did not look at her. He paraded back and forth, three steps to the right, three to the left, his hands in his pockets, his voice impersonal. "I know you're the finest person I ever met. You're the kind—I knew there must be people like you, because I knew the Joneses. They're the only friends I've got that have, oh, I suppose it's what they call culture."

In a long monologue, uninterrupted by Claire, he told of his affection for the Schoenstrom "prof" and his wife. The practical, slangy Milt of the garage was lost in the enthusiastic undergraduate adoring his instructor in the university that exists as veritably in a teacher's or a doctor's sitting-room in every Schoenstrom as it does in certain lugubrious stone hulks recognized by a state legislature as magically empowered to paste on sacred labels lettered "Bachelor of Arts."

He broke from his revelations to plump down on the bench beside her, to slap his palm with his fist,

and sigh, "Lord, I've been gassing on! Guess I bored
you!"

"Oh, please, Milt, please! I see it all so—— It
must have been wonderful, the evening when Mrs.
Jones read Noyes's 'Highwayman' aloud. Tell me
—long before that—were you terribly lonely as a little
boy?"

Now Milt had not been a terribly lonely little boy.
He had been a leader in a gang devoted to fighting,
swimming, pickerel-spearing, beggie-stealing, and
catching rides on freights.

But he believed that he was accurately presenting
every afternoon of his childhood, as he mused, "Yes,
I guess I was, pretty much. I remember I used to sit
on dad's doorstep, all those long sleepy summer afternoons, and I'd think, 'Aw, geeeeee, I—wisht—I—had
—some-body—to—play—with!' I always wanted to
make-b'lieve Robin Hood, but none of the other kids
—so many of them were German; they didn't know
about Robin Hood; so I used to scout off alone."

"If I could only have been there, to be Maid
Marian for you! We'd have learned archery! Lonely
little boy on the doorstep!" Her fingers just touched
his sleeve. In her gesture, the ember-light caught the
crystal of her wrist watch. She stooped to peer at it,
and her pitying tenderness broke off in an agitated:
"Heavings! Is it that late? To bed! Good night,
Milt."

"Good night, Cl—— Miss Boltwood."

"No. 'Claire,' of course. I'm not normally a first-name-snatcher, but I do seem to have fallen into saying 'Milt.' Night!"

As she undressed, in her tent, Claire reflected, "He won't take advantage of my being friendly, will he? Only thing is—— I sha'n't dare to look at Henry B. when Milt calls me 'Claire' in that sedate Brooklyn Heights presence. The dear lamb! Lonely afternoons——!"

CHAPTER XIV

THE BEAST OF THE CORRAL

THEY met in the frost-shimmering mountain morning, on their way to the corral, to get their cars ready before breakfast. They were shy, hence they were boisterous, and tremendously unreferential to campfire confidences, and informative about distilled water for batteries, and the price of gas in the Park. On Milt's shoulder rode Vere de Vere who, in her original way, relieved one pause by observing " Mrwr."

They came in through the corral gate before any of the other motor tourists had appeared—and they stupidly halted to watch a bear, a large, black, adipose and extremely unchained bear, stalk along the line of cars, sniff, cock an ear at the Gomez, lumber up on its running-board, and bundle into the seat. His stern filled the space between side ánd top, and he was to be heard snuffing.

" Oh! Look! Milt! Left box of candy on seat—— Oh, please drive him away! "

" Me? Drive—that? "

" Frighten him away. Aren't animals afraid human eye—— "

" Not in this park. Guns forbidden. Animals protected by U. S. Army, President, Congress, Supreme

Court, Department of Interior, Monroe Doctrine, W. C. T. U. But I'll try—cautiously."

"Don't you want me think you're hero?"

"Ye-es, providin' I don't have to go and be one."

They edged toward the car. The bear flapped his hind legs, looked out at the intruders, said "Oofflll!" and returned to the candy.

"Shoo!" Milt answered politely.

"Llooffll!"

From his own bug, beside the Gomez, Milt got a tool kit, and with considerable brilliance as a pitcher he sent a series of wrenches at the agitated stern of the bear. They offended the dignity of the ward of the Government. He finished the cover and ribbons of the candy box, and started for Milt . . . who proceeded with haste toward Claire . . . who was already at the gate.

Lady Vere de Vere, cat of a thousand battles, gave one frightful squawl, shot from Milt's shoulder and at the bear, claws out, fur electric. The bear carelessly batted once with its paw, and the cat sailed into the air. The satisfied bear strolled to the fence, shinned up it and over.

"Good old Vere! That wallop must of darn near stunned her, though!" Milt laughed to Claire, as they trotted back into the corral. The cat did not move, as they came up; did not give the gallant "Mrwr" with which she had saluted Milt on lonely morning after morning of forlorn driving behind the Gomez. He picked Vere up.

"She's—she's dead," he said. He was crying.

"Oh, Milt—— Last night you said Vere was all the family you had. You have the Boltwoods, now!"

She did not touch his hand, nor did they speak as they walked soberly to the far side of the corral, and buried Lady Vere de Vere. At breakfast they talked of the coming day's run, from the canyon out of the Park, and northward. But they had the queer, quick casualness of intimates.

It was at breakfast that her father heard one Milt Daggett address the daughter of the Boltwoods as "Claire." The father was surprised into clearing his throat, and attacking his oatmeal with a zealousness unnatural in a man who regarded breakfast-foods as moral rather than interesting.

While he was lighting a cigar, and Claire was paying the bill, Mr. Boltwood stalked Milt, cleared his throat all over again, and said, "Nice morning."

It was the first time the two men had talked unchaperoned by Claire.

"Yes. We ought to have a good run, sir." The "sir" came hard. The historian puts forth a theory that Milt had got it out of fiction. "We might go up over Mount Washburn. Take us up to ten thousand feet."

"Uh, you said—didn't Miss Boltwood tell me that you are going to Seattle, too?"

"Yes."

"Friends there, no doubt?"

Milt grinned irresistibly. "Not a friend. But I'm going to make 'em. I'm going to take up engineering, and some French, I guess, at the university there."

"Ah. Really?"

"Yes. Been too limited in my ambition. Don't see why I shouldn't get out and build railroads and power plants and roads—Siberia, Africa, all sorts of interesting places."

"Quite right. Quite right. Uh, ah, I, oh, I—— Have you seen Miss Boltwood?"

"I saw Miss Boltwood in the office."

"Oh yes. Quite so. Uh—ah, here she is."

When the Gomez had started, Mr. Boltwood skirmished, "This young man—— Do you think you better let him call you by your Christian name?"

"Why not? I call him 'Milt.' 'Mr. Daggett' is too long a handle to use when a man is constantly rescuing you from the perils of the deep or hoboes or bears or something. Oh, I haven't told you. Poor old Milt, his cat was killed——"

"Yes, yes, dolly, you may tell me about that in due time, but let's stick to this social problem for a moment. Do you think you ought to be too intimate with him?"

" He's only too self-respecting. He wouldn't take advantage——"

" I'm quite aware of that. I'm not speaking on your behalf, but on his. I'm sure he's a very amiable chap, and ambitious. In fact—— Did you know that he has saved up money to attend a university?"

" When did he tell you that? How long has he been planning—— I thought that I——"

" Just this morning; just now."

" Oh! I'm relieved."

" I don't quite follow you, dolly, but—— Where was I? Do you realize what a demure tyrant you are? If you can drag me from New York to the aboriginal wilds, and I did *not* like that oatmeal, what will you do to this innocent? I want to protect him!"

" You better! Because I'm going to carve him, and paint him, and possibly spoil him. The creating of a man—of one who knows how to handle life—is so much more wonderful than creating absurd pictures or statues or stories. I'll nag him into completing college. He'll learn dignity—or perhaps lose his simplicity and be ruined; and then I'll marry him off to some nice well-bred pink-face, like Jeff Saxton's pretty cousin—who may turn him into a beastly money-grubber; and I'm monkeying with destiny, and I ought to be slapped, and I realize it, and I can't help it, and all my latent instinct as a feminine meddler is aroused, and—golly, I almost went off that curve!"

CHAPTER XV

THE BLACK DAY OF THE VOYAGE

THAT was the one black day of her voyage—black stippled with crimson.

It began with the bear's invasion of the car, resulting in long claw-marks across the upholstery, the loss of some particularly good candy bought at a Park hotel, and genuine grief abiding after the sentimental tragedy of Vere de Vere's death. The next act was the ingenious loss of all power of her engine. She forgot that, before breakfast, Milt had filled the oil-well for her. When she stopped for gasoline, and the seller inquired, " Quart of oil? " she absently nodded. So the cylinders filled with surplus oil, the spark-plugs were fouled, and the engine had the power of a sewing machine.

She could not make Mount Washburn—she could not make even the slopes of the lower road. Now she knew the agony of the feeble car in the mountains—most shameful and anxious of a driver's dolors: the brisk start up the hill, the belief that you will keep on going this time; the feeling of weariness through all the car; the mad shifting of gears, the slipping of the clutch, and more gas, and less gas, and wondering whether more gas or less is the better, and the appalling knocking when you finally give her a lot too much gas; the remembrance, when it's too late, to retard the spark; the safe crawling up to the last sharp pitch, just fifteen feet from the summit; the car's halting; the yelp at your passenger, "Jump out and push!"; the painful next five feet; and the final death of the power just as the front wheels creep up over the pitch. Then the anxious putting on of brakes—holding the car with both foot-brake and emergency, lest it run down backward, slip off the road. The calf of your leg begins to ache from the pressure on the foot-brake, and with an unsuccessful effort to be courteous you bellow at the passenger, who has been standing beside the car looking deprecatory, "Will you please block the back wheels with a stone—hustle up, will you!"

All this routine Claire thoroughly learned. Always Milt bumbled up, said cheerful things, and either hauled the Gomez over the pitch by a towline to his bug, or getting out, pushing on a rear fender till his neck was red and bulgy, gave the extra impetus necessary to get the Gomez over.

"Would you mind shoving on that side, just a little bit?" he suggested to Mr. Boltwood, who ceased the elaborate smoking of cigars, dusted his hands, and gravely obeyed, while Claire was awaiting the new captain's command to throw on the power.

"I wish we weren't under so much obligation to this young man," said Mr. Boltwood, after one crisis.

"I know but—what can we do?"

"Don't you suppose we might pay him?"

"Henry B. Boltwood, if you tried to do that——
I'm not sure. Your being my parent might save you,
but even so, I think he'd probably chase you off the
road, clear down into that chasm."

"I suppose so. Shall we have to entertain him in
Seattle?"

"Have to? My dear parent, you can't keep me from
it! Any of the Seattle friends of Gene Gilson who
don't appreciate that straight, fine, aspiring boy may
go—— Not overdo it, you understand. But——
Oh, take him to the theater. By the way; shall we
try to climb Mount Rainier before——"

"See here, my good dolly; you stop steering me
away from my feeble parental efforts. Do you wish
to be under obligations——"

"Don't mind, with Milt. He wouldn't charge interest, as Jeff Saxton would. Milt is, oh, he's folks!"

"Quite true. But are we? Are you?"

"Learning to be!"

Between discussions and not making hills, Claire
cleaned the spark plugs as they accumulated carbon
from the surplus oil—or she pretended to help Milt
clean them. The plugs were always very hot, and
when you were unscrewing the jacket from the core,
you always burned your hand, and wished you could
swear . . . and sometimes you could.

After noon, when they had left the Park and entered Gardiner, Milt announced, " I've got to stick around a while. The key in my steering-gear seems to be worn. May have to put in a new one. Get the stuff at a garage here. If you wouldn't mind waiting, be awful glad to tag, and try to give a few helping hands till the oil cleans itself out."

" I'll just stroll on," she said, but she drove away as swiftly as she could. Her father's worry about obligations disturbed her, and she did not wish to seem too troublesome an amateur to Milt. She would see him in Livingston, and tell him how well she had driven. The spark plugs kept clean enough now so that she could command more power, but——

Between the Park and the transcontinental road there are many climbs short but severely steep; upshoots like the humps on a scenic railway. To tackle them with her uncertain motor was like charging a machine-gun nest. She spent her nerve-force lavishly, and after every wild rush to make a climb, she had to rest, to rub the suddenly aching back of her neck. Because she was so tired, she did not take the trouble to save her brakes by going down in gear. She let the brakes smoke while the river and railroad below rose up at her.

There was a long drop. How long it was she did not guess, because it was concealed by a curve at the top. She seemed to plane down forever. The brakes

squealed behind. She tried to shift to first but there
was a jarring snarl, and she could neither get into
first nor back into third. She was running in neutral,
the great car coasting, while she tried to slow it by
jamming down the foot-brake. The car halted—and
started on again. The brake-lining which had been
wished on her at Saddle Back was burnt out.

She had the feeling of the car bursting out from
under control . . . ready to leap off the road, into a
wash. She wanted to jump. It took all her courage to
stay in the seat. She got what pressure she could
from the remaining band. With one hand she kept
the accelerating car in the middle of the road; with
the other she tried to pull the handle of the emergency brake back farther. She couldn't. She was
not strong enough. Faster, faster, rushing at the
next curve so that she could scarce steer round it——

As quietly as she could, she demanded of her father,
" Pull back on this brake lever, far as you can. Take
both hands."

" I don't understand——"

" Heavens! Y' don't haft un'stand! Yank back!
Yank, I tell you! "

Again the car slowed. She was able to get into
second speed. Even that check did not keep the car
from darting down at thirty miles an hour—which
pace, to one who desires to saunter down at a dignified
rate of eighteen, is equivalent in terms of mileage on

level ground to seventy an hour, with a drunken driver on a foggy evening, amid traffic.

She got the car down and, in the midst of a valley of emptiness and quiet, she dropped her head on her father's knee and howled.

"I just can't face going down another hill! I just can't face it!" she sobbed.

"No, dolly. Mustn't. We better—— You're quite right. This young Daggett is a very gentlemanly fellow. I didn't think his table-manners—— But we'll sit here and regard the flora and fauna till he comes. He'll see us through."

"Yes! He will! Honestly, dad——" She said it with the first touch of hero-worship since she had seen an aviator loop loops. "Isn't he, oh, effective! Aren't you glad he's here to help us, instead of somebody like Jeff Saxton?"

"We-ul, you must remember that Geoffrey wouldn't have permitted the brake to burn out. He'd have foreseen it, and have had a branch office, with special leased wire, located back on that hill, ready to do business the instant the market broke. Enthusiasm is a nice quality, dolly, but don't misplace it. This lad, however trustworthy he may be, would scarcely even be allowed to work for a man like Geoffrey Saxton. It may be that later, with college——"

"No. He'd work for Jeff two hours. Then Jeff would give him that 'You poor fish!' look, and Milt

would hit him, and stroll out, and go to the North
Pole or some place, and discover an oil-well, and hire
Jeff as his nice, efficient general manager. And——
I do wish Milt would hurry, though!"

It was dusk before they heard the pit-pit-pit chuckling down the hill. Milt's casual grin changed to
bashfulness as Claire ran into the road, her arms wide
in a lovely gesture of supplication, and cried, "We
been waiting for you so long! One of my brake-
bands is burnt out, and the other is punk."

"Well, well. Let's try to figure out something
to do."

She waited reverently while the local prophet sat in
his bug, stared at the wheels of the Gomez, and
thought. The level-floored, sagebrush-sprinkled hollow had filled with mauve twilight and creeping stilly
sounds. The knowable world of yellow lights and
security was far away. Milt was her only means of
ever getting back to it.

"Tell you what we might try," he speculated. "I'll
hitch on behind you, and hold back in going down
hill."

She did not even try to help him while he again
cleaned the spark plugs and looked over brakes, oil,
gas, water. She sat on the running-board, and it was
pleasant to be relieved of responsibility. He said
nothing at all. While he worked he whistled that recent refined ballad:

I wanta go back to Oregon
And sit on the lawn, and look at the dawn.
Oh motheruh dear, don't leavuh me here,
The leaves are so sere, in the fallothe year,
I wanta go back to Oregugon,
To dearuh old Oregugon.

They started, shouting optimistically to each other, lights on, trouble seeming over—and they stopped after the next descent, and pools of tears were in the corners of Claire's eyes. The holdback had not succeeded. Her big car, with its quick-increasing momentum, had jerked at the bug as though it were a lard-can. The tow-rope had stretched, sung, snapped, and again, in fire-shot delirium, she had gone rocking down hill.

He drove up beside her, got out, stood at her elbow. His " I'm a bum inventor. We'll try somethin' else " was so careless that, in her nerve-twanging exhaustion she wailed, " Oh, don't be so beastly cheerful! You don't care a bit! "

In the dusk she could see him straighten, and his voice came sharp as he ignored the ever-present parental background and retorted, " Somebody has got to be cheerful. Matter fact, I worked out the right stunt, coming down."

Like a man in the dentist's chair, recovering between bouts, she drowsed and ignored the fact that in a few minutes she would again have to reassemble herself, become wakeful and calm, and go through quite impossible maneuvers of driving. Milt was, with a hatchet from his camping-kit, cutting down a large scrub pine. He dragged it to the Gomez and hitched it to the back axle. The knuckles of the branches would dig into the earth, the foliage catch at every pebble.

"There! That anchor would hold a truck!" he shouted.

It held. She went down the next two hills easily. But she was through. Her forearms and brain were equally numb. She appealed to Milt, "I can't seem to go on any more. It's so dark, and I'm so tired——"

"All right. No ranch houses anywheres near, so we'll camp here, if Mr. Boltwood doesn't mind."

Claire stirred herself to help him prepare dinner. It wasn't much of a dinner to prepare. Both cars had let provisions run low. They had bacon and petrified ends of a loaf and something like coffee—not much like it. Scientists may be interested in their discovery that as a substitute for both cream and sugar in beverages strawberry jam is a fallacy.

For Mr. Boltwood's bed Milt hauled out the springy seat-cushions of both cars. The Gomez cushion was three inches thicker than that of the bug, which resulted in a mattress two stories in front with a lean-to at the foot, and the entire edifice highly slippery. But with a blanket from Milt's kit, it was sufficient.

To Claire, Milt gave another blanket, his collection of antique overcoats, and good advice. He spoke vaguely of a third blanket for himself. And he had one. Its dimensions were thirteen by twenty inches, it was of white wool, he had bought it in Dakota for Vere de Vere, and many times that day he had patted it and whispered, " Poor old cat."

Under his blankets Mr. Boltwood thought of rattle-snakes, bears, rheumatism, Brooklyn, his debt to Milt, and the fact that—though he hadn't happened to mention it to Claire—he had expected to be killed when the brake had burned out.

Claire was drowsily happy. She had got through. She was conscious of rustling sagebrush, of the rapids of the Yellowstone beside her, of open sky and sweet air and a scorn for people in stuffy rooms, and comfortably ever conscious of Milt, ten feet away. She had in him the interest that a young physician would have in a new X-ray machine, a printer in a new font of type, any creator in a new outlet for his power. She would see to it that her Seattle cousins, the Gilsons, helped him to know the right people, during his university work. She herself would be back in Brooklyn, but perhaps he would write to her, write—write letters—Brooklyn—she was in Brooklyn—no, no, where was she?—oh, yes, camping—bad day—brakes—— No, she would not marry Jeff Saxton! Brooklyn—river singing—stars——

And when Milt wasn't unromantically thinking of his cold back, he exulted. "She won't be back among her own folks till Seattle. Probably forget me then. Don't blame her. But till we get there, she'll let me play in her yard. Gee! In the morning I'll be talking to her again, and she's right there, right now!"

In the morning they were all very stiff, but glad of the sun on sagebrush and river, and the boy and girl sang over breakfast. While Milt was gathering fuel he looked up at Claire standing against a background of rugged hills, her skirt and shoes still smug, but her jacket off, her blouse turned in at the throat, her hair blowing, her sleeves rolled up, one hand on her hip, erect, charged with vigor—the spirit of adventure.

When her brake had been relined, at Livingston, they sauntered companionably on to Butte. And the day after Butte, when Milt was half a mile behind the Gomez, a pink-haired man with a large, shiny revolver stepped out from certain bushes, and bowed politely, and at that point Milt stopped.

CHAPTER XVI

THE SPECTACLES OF AUTHORITY

OVER the transcontinental divide and into Butte, diamond-glittering on its hills in the dark; into Missoula, where there are trees and a university, with a mountain in everybody's backyard; through the Flathead Agency, where scarlet-blanketed Indians stalk out of tepees and the papoose rides on mother's back as in forgotten days; down to St. Ignatius, that Italian Alp town with its old mission at the foot of mountains like the wall of Heaven, Claire had driven west, then north. She was sailing past Flathead Lake, where fifty miles of mountain glory are reflected in bright waters. Everywhere were sections of flat wheat-plains, stirring with threshing, with clattering machinery and the flash of blown straw. But these miniature prairies were encircled by abrupt mountains.

Mr. Boltwood remarked, "I'd rather have one of these homesteads and look across my fields at those hills than be King of England." Not that he made any effort to buy one of the homesteads. But then, he made no appreciable effort to become King of England.

Claire had not seen Milt for a day and a half; not since the morning when both cars had left Butte. She wondered, and was piqued, and slightly lonely. Toward evening, when she was speculating as to whether she would make Kalispell—almost up to the Canadian border—she saw a woman run into the road from a house on the shore of Flathead Lake. The woman held out her hand. Claire pulled up.

" Are you. Miss Boltwood? "

It was as startling as the same question would have been in a Chinese village.

" W-why, yes."

" Somebody trying to get you on the long-distance 'phone."

" Me? 'Phone? "

She was trembling. " Something's happened to Milt. He needs me!" She could not manage her voice, as she got the operator on the farmers'-line wire, and croaked, " Was some one trying to get Miss Boltwood? "

" Yes. This Boltwood? Hotel in Kalispell trying to locate you, for two hours. Been telephoning all along the line, from Butte to Somers."

" W-well, w-will you g-get 'em for me? "

It was not Milt's placid and slightly twangy voice but one smoother, more decisive, perplexingly familiar, that finally vibrated, " Hello! Hello! Miss Boltwood! Operator, I can't hear. Get me a better connection. Miss Boltwood? "

" Yes! Yes! This is Miss Boltwood!" she kept

beseeching, during a long and not unheated controversy between the unknown and the crisp operator,
who knew nothing of the English language beyond,
" Here's your party. Why don't you talk? Speak
louder!"

Then came clearly, " Hear me now?"

"Yes! Yes!"

" Miss Boltwood?"

"Yes?"

"Oh. Oh, hello, Claire. This is Jeff."

" Jess who?"

"Not Jess. Jeff! Geoffrey! J-e-f-f! Jeff Saxton!"

"Oh!" It was like a sob. "Why—why—but
you're in New York."

" Not exactly, dear. I'm in Kalispell, Montana."

" But that's right near here."

"So am I!"

" B-but——"

" Out West to see copper interests. Traced you
from Yellowstone Park but missed you at Butte.
Thought I'd catch you on road. You talking from
Barmberry's?"

The woman who had hailed her was not missing a
word of a telephone conversation which might be rela-
tive to death, fire, elopement, or any other dramatic
event. Claire begged of her, " Where in the world
am I talking from, anyway?"

" This is Barmberry's Inn."

"Yes," Claire answered on the telephone, "I seem to be. Shall I start on and——"

"No. Got ripping plan. Stay right where you are. Got a fast car waiting. Be right down. We'll have dinner. By!"

A click. No answer to Claire's urgent hellos. She hung up the receiver very, very carefully. She hated to turn and face her audience of Mr. Henry B. Boltwood, Mr. James Barmberry, Mrs. James Barmberry, and four Barmberry buds averaging five and a quarter in age. She tried to ignore the Barmberrys, but their silence was noisy and interested while she informed her father, "It's Jeff Saxton! Out here to see copper mines. Telephoned along road to catch us. Says we're to wait dinner till he comes."

"Yessum," Mrs. Barmberry contributed, "he told me if I did catch you, I was to have some new-killed chickens ready to fry, and some whipped cream—— Jim Barmberry, you go right out and finish whipping that cream, and don't stand there gawping and gooping, and you children, you scat!"

Claire seized the moment of Mr. Boltwood's lordly though bewildered bow to their hostess, and escaped outdoors. Round the original settler's log-cabin were nests of shacks and tents, for bedrooms, and on a screened porch, looking on Flathead Lake, was the dining-room. The few other guests had finished supper and gone to their tents.

She ambled to the lake shore, feeling feebler, more slapped and sent back to be a good little girl, than she had when Milt had hitched a forest to the back axle, three days ago. A map of her thoughts about Jeff Saxton would have shown a labyrinth. Now, she was muttering, "Dear Jeff! So thoughtful! Clever of him to find me! So good to see him again!" Now: "It's still distinctly understood that I am not engaged to him, and I'm not going to be surprised into kissing him when he comes down like a wolf on the fold." Now: "Jeff Saxton! Here! Makes me homesick for the Heights. And nice shops in Manhattan, and a really good play—music just before the curtain goes up." Now: "Ohhhhhh geeeeee whizzzzzz! I wonder if he'll let us go any farther in the car? He's so managerial, and dad is sure to take his side. He tried to scare us off by that telegram to Fargo." Now: "He'd be horrified if he knew about that bum brake. Milt didn't mind. Milt likes his womenfolks to be daring. Jeff wants his harem admiring and very reliable."

She crouched on the shore, a rather forlorn figure. The peaks of the Mission Range, across the violet-shadowed mirror of Flathead Lake, were a sudden pure rose, in reflection of sunset, then stony, forbidding. Across the road, on the Barmberry porch, she could hear her father saying "Ah?" and "Indeed?" to James's stories.

Up the road, a blaring horn, great lights growing

momently more dazzling, a roar, a rush, the halting
car, and out of its blurred bulk, a trim figure darting—
Jeff Saxton—home and the people she loved, and the
ways and days she knew best of all. He had shouted
only " Is Miss——" before she had rushed to him,
into the comfort of his arms, and kissed him.

She backed off and tried to sound as if it hadn't
happened, but she was quavery: " I can't believe it!
It's too ridiculously wonderful to see you! " She
retreated toward the Barmberry porch, Jeff following,
his two hands out. They came within the range of
the house lights, and Mr. Boltwood hailed, " Ah!
Geoffrey! Never had such a surprise—nor a more
delightful one! "

" Mr. Boltwood! Looking splendid, sir! New
man! William Street better look to its laurels when
you come back and get into the game! "

Then, on the lamp-lighted porch, the two men
shook hands, and looked for some other cordial thing
to do. They thought about giving each other cigars.
They smiled, and backed away, and smiled, in the
foolish, indeterminate way males have, being unable
to take it out in kissing. Mr. Boltwood solved the
situation by hemming, " Must trot in and wash. See
you very soon." Mr. James Barmberry and the squad
of lesser Barmberrys regretfully followed. Claire
was alone with Jeff, and she was frightened. Yet she
was admitting that Jeff, in his English cap and flaring

London top-coat, his keen smile and his extreme shavedness, was more attractive than she had remembered.

"Glad to see me?" he demanded.

"Oh, rather!"

"You're looking——"

"You're so——"

"Nice trip? You know you've sent me nothing but postcards with 'Pretty town,' or something equally sentimental."

"Yes, it's really been bully. These mountains and big spaces simply inspire me." She said it rather defiantly.

"Of course they do! Trouble is, with you away, we've nothing to inspire us!"

"Do you need anything, with your office and your club?"

"Why, Claire!"

"I'm sorry. That was horrid of me."

"Yes, it was. Though I don't mind. I'm sure we've all become meek, missing you so. I'm quite willing to be bullied, and reminded that I'm a mere T.B.M."

She had got herself into it; she had to tell him that he wasn't just a business man; that she had "just meant" he was so practical.

"But Jeff is no longer the practical one," he declared. "Think of Claire driving over deserts and mountains. But—— Oh, it's been so lonely for us. Can you guess how much? A dozen times every evening, I've turned to the telephone to call you up and beg you to let me nip in and see you, and then realized you weren't there, and I've just sat looking at the 'phone—— Oh, other people are so dull!"

" You reall, miss——"

" I wish I were a poet, so I could tell you adequately. But you haven't said you missed me, Claire. Didn't you, a teeny bit? Wouldn't it have been tolerable to have poor old Jeff along, to drive down dangerous hills——"

" And fill grease-cups! Nasty and stickum on the fingers!"

" Yes, I'd have done that, too. And invented surprises along the way. I'm a fine surpriser! I've arranged for a motor-boat so we can explore the lake here tomorrow. That's why I had you wait here instead of coming on to Kalispell. Tomorrow morning, unfortunately, I have to hustle back and catch a train —called to California, and possibly a northern trip. But meantime—— By now, my driver must have sneaked my s'prises into the kitchen."

" What are they?"

" Guess."

" Food. Eats. Divine eats."

" Maybe."

" But what? Please, sir. Claire is so hungry."

"We shall see in time, my child. Uncle Jeff is not to be hurried."

"Ah—let—me—see—now! I'll kick and scream!"

From New York Jeff had brought a mammoth picnic basket. To the fried chicken ordered for dinner he added sealed jars of purée of wood pigeon, of stuffed artichokes prepared by his club chef; caviar and anchovies; a marvelous nightmare-creating fruit cake to go with the whipped cream; two quarts of a famous sherry; candied fruits in a silver box. Dinner was served not on the dining-porch but before the fire in the Barmberrys' living-room. Claire looked at the candied fruits, stared at Jeff rather queerly—as though she was really thinking of some one else—and mused:

"I didn't know I cared so much for these foolish luxuries. Tonight, I'd like a bath, just a tiny bit scented, and a real dressing-table with a triple mirror, and French talc, and come down in a dinner-gown—— Oh, I have enjoyed the trip, Jeff. But my poor body does get so tired and dusty, and then you treacherously come along with these things that you've magicked out of the mountains and—— I'm not a pioneer woman, after all. And Henry B. is not a caveman. See him act idolatrously toward his soup."

"I feel idolatrous. I'd forgotten the supreme ethical importance of the soup. I'll never let myself forget it again," said Mr. Boltwood, in the tone of one who has come home.

Claire was grateful to Jeff that he did not let her go on being grateful. He turned the talk to Brooklyn. He was neat and explicit—and almost funny—in his description of an outdoor presentation of *Midsummer Night's Dream,* in which a domestic and intellectual lady weighing a hundred and eighty-seven stageside had enacted Puck. As they sat after dinner, as Claire shivered, he produced a knitted robe, and pulled it about her shoulders, smiling at her in a lonely, hungry way. She caught his hand.

"Nice Jeff!" she whispered.

"Oh, my dear!" he implored. He shook his head in a wistful way that caught her heart, and dutifully went back to informing Mr. Boltwood of the true state of the markets.

"Talk to Claire too!" she demanded. She stopped, stared. From outside she heard a nervous pit-pit-pit, a blurred dialogue between Mr. James Barmberry and another man. Into the room rambled Milt Daggett, dusty of unpressed blue suit, tired of eyes, and not too well shaved of chin, grumbling, "Thought I'd never catch up with you, Claire—— Why——"

"Oh! Oh, Milt—Mr. Daggett—— Oh, Jeff, this is our good friend Milt Daggett, who has helped us along the road."

Jeff's lucid rimless spectacles stared at Milt's wind-reddened eyes; his jaunty patch-pocket outing clothes sniffed at Milt's sweater; his even voice followed

Milt's grunt of surprise with a curt "Ah. Mr. Daggett."

"Pleased meet you," faltered Milt.

Jeff nodded, turned his shoulder on Milt, and went on, "The fact is, Mr. Boltwood, the whole metal market——"

Milt was looking from one to another. Claire was now over her first shocked comparison of candied fruits with motor grease. She rose, moved toward Milt, murmuring, "Have you had dinner?"

The door opened again. A pink-haired, red-faced man in a preposterous green belted suit lunged in, swept his broad felt hat in greeting, and boomed like a cheap actor:

"Friends of my friend Milt, we about to dine salute you. Let me introduce myself as Westlake Parrott, better known to the vulgar as Pinky Parrott, gentleman adventurer, born in the conjunction of Mars and Venus, with Saturn ascendant."

Jeff had ignored Milt. But at this absurd second intrusion on his decidedly private dinner-party he flipped to the center of the room and said "I beg your pardon!" in such a head-office manner that the pink-locked Mystery halted in his bombast. Claire felt wabbly. She had no theories as to where Milt had acquired a private jester, nor as to what was about to happen to Milt—and possibly to her incautious self.

CHAPTER XVII

THE VAGABOND IN GREEN

AS Milt had headed westward from Butte, as he rattled peacefully along the road, conscious of golden haze over all the land, and the unexpectedness of prairie threshing-crews on the sloping fields of mountainsides, a man had stepped out from bushes beside the road, and pointed a .44 navy revolver.

The man was not a movie bandit. He wore a green imitation of a Norfolk jacket, he had a broad red smile, and as he flourished his hat in a bow, his hair was a bristly pompadour of gray-streaked red that was almost pink. He made oration:

"Pardon my eccentric greeting, brother of the open road, but I wanted you to give ear to my obsequious query as to how's chances on gettin' a lift? I have learned that obsequiousness is best appreciated when it is backed up by prayer and ca'tridges."

"What's the idea? I seem to gather you'd like a lift. Jump in."

"You do not advocate the Ciceronian style, I take it," chuckled the man as he climbed aboard.

Milt was not impressed. Claire might have been, but Milt had heard politics and religion argued about the stove in Rauskukle's store too often to be startled

by polysyllabomania. He knew it was often the sign
of a man who has read too loosely and too much by
himself. He snorted. "Huh! What are you—newspaper, politics, law, preacher, or gambler?"

"Well, a little of all those interesting occupations.
And ten-twent-thirt trouping, and county-fair spiel-
ing, and selling Dr. Thunder Rapids' Choctaw Herbal
Sensitizer. How far y' going?"

"Seattle."

"Honest? Say, kid, this is—— Muh boy, we
shall have the rare privilege of pooling adventures as
far as Blewett Pass, four to six days' run from here—
a day this side of Seattle. I'm going to my gold-mine
there. I'll split up on the grub—I note from your kit
that you camp nights. Quite all right, my boy. Pinky
Parrott is no man to fear night air."

He patted Milt's shoulder with patronizing inso-
lence. He filled a pipe and, though the car was
making twenty-five, he lighted the pipe with distinguished ease, then settled down to his steady stride:

"In the pride of youth, you feel that you have thoroughly categorized me, particularly since I am willing
to admit that, though I shall have abundance of the
clinking iron men to buy my share of our chow, I
chance just for the leaden-footed second to lack the
wherewithal to pay my railroad fare back to Blewett;
and the bumpers and side-door Pullman of the argo-
nauts like me not. Too damn dusty. But your analy-

sis is unsynthetic, though you will scarce grasp my paradoxical metaphor."

"The hell I won't. I've taken both chemistry and rhetoric," growled Milt, strictly attending to driving, and to the desire to get rid of his parasite.

"Oh! Oh, I see. Well, anyway: I am no mere nimble knight of wits, as you may take it. In fact, I am lord of fair acres in Arcady."

"Don't know the burg. Montana or Idaho?"

"Neither! In the valley of dream!"

"Oh! That one. Huh!"

"But I happen to back them up with a perfectly un-dreamlike gold-mine. Prospected for it in a canyon near Blewett Pass and found it, b' gum, and my lady wife, erstwhile fairest among the society favorites of North Yakima, now guards it against her consort's return. Straight goods. Got the stuff. Been to Butte to get a raise on it, but the fell khedives of commerce are jealous. They would hearken not. Gee, those birds certainly did pull the frigid mitt! So I wend my way back to the demure Dolores, the houri of my heart, and the next time I'll take a crack at the big guns in Seattle. And I'll sure reward you for your generosity in taking me to Blewett, all the long, long, languid, languorous way——"

"Too bad I got to stop couple of days at Spokane."

"Well, then you shall have the pleasure of taking me that far."

" And about a week in Kalispell! " "

" 'Twill discommode me, but 'pon honor, I like your honest simple face, and I won't desert you. Besides! I know a guy in Kalispell, and I .can panhandle the sordid necessary chuck while I wait for you. Little you know, my cockerel, how facile a brain your 'bus so lightly bears. When I've cashed in on the mine, I'll take my rightful place among the motored gentry. Not merely as actor and spieler, promoter and inventor and soldier and daring journalist, have I played my rôle, but also I am a mystic, an initiate, a clairaudient, a psychometrist, a Rosicrucian adept, and profoundly psychic—in fact, my guide is Hermes Trismegistus himself! I also hold a degree as doctor of mentopractic, and my studies in astro-biochemistry——"

" Gonna stop. All off. Make little coffee," said Milt.

He did not desire coffee, and he did not desire to stop, but he did desperately desire not to inflict Pinky Parrott upon the Boltwoods. It was in his creed as a lover of motors never to refuse a ride to any one, when he had room. He hoped to get around his creed by the hint implied in stopping. Pinky's reaction to the hint was not encouraging:

" Why, you have a touch of the psychic's flare! I could do with coffee myself. But don't trouble to make a fire. I'll do that. You drive—I do the camp work. Not but that I probably drive better than you,

if you will permit me to say so. I used to do a bit
of racing, before I took up aviation."

"Huh! Aviation! What machine d'you fly?"

"Why, why—a biplane!"

"Huh! What kind of motor?"

"Why, a foreign one. The—the—— It was a
French motor."

"Huh! What track you race on?"

"The—— Pardon me till I build a fire for our
al fresco collation, and I my driving history will un-
fold."

But he didn't do either.

After he had brought seven twigs, one piece of
sagebrush, and a six-inch board, Pinky let Milt finish
building the fire, while he told how much he knew
about the mysteries of ancient Egyptian priests.

Milt gave up hope that Pinky would become bored
by waiting and tramp on. After one hour of conversational deluge, he decided to let Pinky drive—to
make him admit that he couldn't. He was wrong.
Pinky could drive. He could not drive well, he wabbled in his steering, and he killed the engine on a grade,
but he showed something of the same dashing idiocy
that characterized his talk. It was Milt not Pinky,
who was afraid of their running off the road, and
suggested resuming the wheel.

Seven times that day Milt tried to lose him. Once
he stopped without excuse, and merely stared up at

rocks overhanging the hollowed road. Pinky was not embarrassed. He leaned back in the seat and sang two Spanish love songs. Once Milt deliberately took a wrong road, up a mountainside. They were lost, and took five hours getting back to the highway. Pinky loved the thrill and—in a brief address lasting fifteen minutes—he said so.

Milt tried to bore him by driving at seven miles an hour. Pinky affectionately accepted this opportunity to study the strata of the hills. When they camped, that night, Pinky loved him like a brother, and was considering not stopping at Blewett Pass, to see his gold-mine and Dolores the lady-wife, but going clear on to Seattle with his playmate.

The drafted host lay awake, and when Pinky awoke and delivered a few well-chosen words on the subject of bird-song at dawn, Milt burst out:

"Pinky, I don't like to do it, but—— I've never refused a fellow a lift, but I'm afraid you'll have to hike on by yourself, the rest of the way."

Pinky sat up in his blankets. "Afraid of me, eh? You better be! I'm a bad actor. I killed Dolores's husband, and took her along, see? I——"

"Are you trying to scare me, you poor four-flusher?" Milt's right hand expanded, fingers arching, with the joyous tension of a man stretching.

"No. I'm just reading your thoughts. I'm telling you you're scared of me! You think that if I went on, I might steal your car! You're afraid because I'm so suave. You aren't used to smooth ducks. You don't dare to let me stick with you, even for today! You're afraid I'd have your mis'able car by tonight! You don't dare!"

"The hell I don't!" howled Milt. "If you think I'm afraid—— Just to show you I'm not, I'll let you go on today!"

"That's sense, my boy. It would be a shame for two such born companions of the road to part!" Pinky had soared up from his blankets; was lovingly shaking Milt's hand.

Milt knew that he had been tricked, but he felt hopeless. Was it impossible to insult Pinky? He tried again:

"I'll be frank with you. You're the worst wind-jamming liar I ever met. Now don't reach for that gat. of yours. I've got a hefty rock right here handy."

"But, my dear, dear boy, I don't intend to reach for any crude lethal smoke-wagon. Besides, there isn't anything in it. I hocked the shells in Butte. I am not angry, merely grieved. We'll argue this out as we have breakfast and drive on. I can prove to you that, though occasionally I let my fancy color mere untutored fact with the pigments of a Robert J. Ingersoll—— By the way, do you know his spiel on whisky?"

"Stick to the subject. We'll finish our arguing

right now, and I'll give you breakfast, and we'll sadly
part."

"Merely because I am lighter of spirits than this
lugubrious old world? No! I decline to be dropped.
I'll forgive you and go on with you. Mind you, I am
sensitive. I will not intrude where I am not welcome.
Only you must give me a sounder reason than my
diverting conversational powers for shucking me. My
logic is even stronger than my hedonistic contempt for
hitting the pike."

"Well, hang it, if you must know—— Hate to say
it, but I'd do almost anything to get rid of you. Fact
is, I've been sort of touring with a lady and her father,
and you would be in the way!"

"Aaaaaaah! You see! Why, my boy, I will not
only stick, but for you, I shall do the nimble John
Alden and win the lady fair. I will so bedizen your
virile, though somewhat crassly practical gifts——
Why, women are my long suit. They fall for——"

"Tut, tut, tut! You're a fool. She's no beanery
mistress, like you're used to. She really is a lady."

"How blind you are, cruel friend. You do not
even see that whatever my vices may be, my social
standing——"

"Oh—shut—up! Can't you see I'm trying to be
kind to you? Have I simply got to beat you up before
you begin to suspect you aren't welcome? Your social
standing isn't even in the telephone book. And your

vocabulary—— You let too many 'kids' slip in among the juicy words. Have I got to lick——"

"Well. You're right. I'm a fliv. Shake hands, m' boy, and no hard feelings."

"Good. Then I can drive on nice and alone, without having to pound your ears off?"

"Certainly. That is—we'll compromise. You take me on just a few miles, into more settled country, and I'll leave you."

So it chanced that Milt was still inescapably accompanied by Mr. Pinky Parrott, that evening, when he saw Claire's Gomez standing in the yard at Barmberry's and pulled up.

Pinky had voluntarily promised not to use his eloquence on Claire, not to try to borrow money from Mr. Boltwood. Without ever having quite won permission to stay, he had stayed. He had also carried out his promise to buy his half of the provisions by adding a five-cent bag of lemon drops to Milt's bacon and bread.

When they had stopped, Milt warned, "There's their machine now. Seems to be kind of a hotel here. I'm going in and say howdy. Good-by, Pink. Glad to have met you, but I expect you to be gone when I come out here again. If you aren't—— Want granite or marble for the headstone? I mean it, now!"

"I quite understand, my lad. I admire your chivalric delicacy. Farewell, old *compagnon de voyage!*"

Milt inquired of Mr. Barmberry whether the Bolt-woods were within, and burst into the parlor-living-room-library. As he cried to Claire, by the fire, " Thought I'd never catch up with you," he was conscious that standing up, talking to Mr. Boltwood, was an old-young man, very suave, very unfriendly of eye. He had an Oxford-gray suit, unwrinkled cordovan shoes; a pert, insultingly well-tied blue bow tie, and a superior narrow pink bald spot. As he heard Jeff Saxton murmur, "Ah. Mr. Daggett!" Milt felt the luxury in the room—the fleecy robe over Claire's shoulders, the silver box of candy by her elbow, the smell of expensive cigars, and the portly complacence of Mr. Boltwood.

" Have you had any dinner?" Claire was asking, when a voice boomed, " Let me introduce myself as Westlake Parrott."

Jeff abruptly took charge. He faced Pinky and demanded, " I beg pardon!"

Claire's eyebrows asked questions of Milt.

" This is a fellow I gave a lift to. Miner—I mean actor—well, kind of spiritualistic medium——"

Mr. Boltwood, with the geniality of dinner and cigar, soothed, " Jeff, uh, Daggett here has saved our lives two distinct times, and given us a great deal of help. He is a motor expert. He has always refused to let us do anything in return but—— I noticed there was almost a whole fried chicken left. I wonder if he wouldn't share it with, uh, with his acquaintance here before—before they make camp for the night?"

In civil and vicious tones Jeff began, "Very glad to reward any one who has been of service to——"

He was drowned out by Pinky's effusive, "True hospitality is a virtue as delicate as it is rare. We accept your invitation. In fact I should be glad to have one of those cigarros elegantos that mine olfactory——"

Milt cut in abruptly, "Pink! Shut up! Thanks, folks, but we'll go on. Just wanted to see if you had got in safe. See you tomorrow, some place."

Claire was close to Milt, her fingers on his sleeve. "Please, Milt! Father! You didn't make your introduction very complete. You failed to tell Mr. Daggett that this is Mr. Saxton, a friend of ours in Brooklyn. Please, Milt, do stay and have dinner. I won't let you go on hungry. And I want you to know Jeff—Mr. Saxton. . . . Jeff, Mr. Daggett is an engineer, that is, in a way. He's going to take an engineering course in the University of Washington. Some day I shall make you bloated copper magnates become interested in him. . . . Mrs. Barmberry. Mrsssssss. Barrrrrrrmberrrrrry! Oh. Oh, Mrs. Barmberry, won't you please warm up that other chicken for——"

"Oh, now, that's too bad. Me and Jim have et it all up!" wept the landlady, at the door.

" I'll go on," stammered Milt.

Jeff looked at him expressionlessly.

" You will not go on!" Claire was insisting. " Mrs. Barmberry, won't you cook some eggs or steak or something for these boys?"

" Perhaps," Jeff suggested, " they'd rather make their own dinner by a campfire. Must be very jolly, and that sort of thing."

" Jeff, if you don't mind, this is my party, just for the moment!"

" Quite right. Sorry!"

" Milt, you sit here by the fire and get warm. I'm not going to be robbed of the egotistic pleasure of being hospitable. Everybody look happy now!"

She got them all seated—all but Pinky. He had long since seated himself, by the fire, in Claire's chair, and he was smoking a cigar from the box which Jeff had brought for Mr. Boltwood.

Milt sat farthest from the fire, by the dining-table. He was agonizing, " This Jeff person is the real thing. He's no Percy in riding-breeches. He's used to society and nastiness. If he looks at me once more— young garage man found froze stiff, near Flathead Lake, scared look in eyes, believed to have met a grizzly, no signs of vi'lence. And I thought I could learn to mingle with Claire's own crowd! I wish I was out in the bug. I wonder if I .can't escape?"

CHAPTER XVIII

THE FALLACY OF ROMANCE

DURING dinner Milt watched Jeff Saxton's manner and manners. The hot day had turned into
a cold night. Jeff tucked the knitted robe about
Claire's shoulders, when she returned to the fire. He
moved quietly and easily. He kept poking up the fire,
smiling at Claire as he did so. He seemed without
difficulty to maintain two conversations: one with Mr.
Boltwood about finances, one with Clare about mysterious persons called Fannie and Alden and Chub and
Bobbie and Dot, the mention of whom made Milt
realize how much a stranger he was. Once, as he
passed by Claire, Jeff said gently, " You *are* lovely! "
Only that, and he did not look at her. But Milt saw
that Claire flushed, and her eyes dimmed.

Pinky was silent till he had eaten about two-thirds
of the total amount of fried eggs, cold lamb and ice-
box curios. When Claire came over to see how they
fared, Pinky removed himself, with smirking humility,
and firmly joined himself to Jeff and Mr. Boltwood.
He caught the subject of finance and, while Claire
dropped down in the chair by Milt, Pinky was lectur-
ing the two men from New York:

" Ah, finance! Queen of the sociological pantheon!

I don't know how come I am so graced by Fortune as to have encountered in these wilds two gentlemen so obviously versed in the stratagems of the great golden game, but I will take the opportunity to give you gentlemen some statistics about the gold-deposits still existent in the Cascades and other ranges that may be of benefit and certainly will be a surprise to you. It happens that I have at the present time a mine——"

Claire was whispering to Milt, "If we can get rid of your dreadful passenger, I do want you to meet Mr. Saxton. He may be of use to you some day. He's terribly capable, and really quite nice. Think! He happened to be out here, and he traced me by telephone—oh, he treats long-distance 'phoning as I do a hair-pin. He brought down the duckiest presents— divertissements for dinner, and that knitted robe, and some real René Bleuzet perfume—I was all out of it—— And after the grime of the road——"

"Do you really care for things like that, all those awfully expensive luxuries?" begged Milt.

"Of course I do. Especially after small hotels."

"Then you don't really like adventuring?"

"Oh yes—in its place! For one thing, it makes a clever dinner seem so good by contrast!"

"Well—— Afraid I don't know much about clever dinners," Milt was sighing, when he was aware of Jeff Saxton looming down on him, demanding:

"Daggett, would you mind trying to inform your

friend that neither Mr. Boltwood nor I care to invest in his gold-mine? We can't seem to get that into his head. I don't mind being annoyed myself, but I really feel I must protect Mr. Boltwood."

"What can I do?"

"My dear sir, since you brought him here——"

It was the potassium cyanide and cracked ice and carpet tacks and TNT and castor oil in Jeff's "My dear sir" that did it. Milt discovered himself on his feet, bawling, "I am not your dear sir! Pinky is my guest, and—— Gee, sorry I lost my temper, Claire, terrible sorry. See you along the road. Good night. Pink! You take your hat! Git!"

Milt followed Pinky out of the door, snarling, "Git in the car, and do it quick. I'll take you clear to Blewett Pass. We drive all night."

Pinky was of great silence and tact. Milt lumped into the bug beside him. But he did not start the all-night drive. He wanted to crawl back, on his knees, to apologize to Claire—and to be slapped by Jeff Saxton. He compromised by slowly driving a quarter of a mile up the road, and camping there for the night.

Pinky tried to speak words of philosophy and cheer—just once he tried it.

For hours, by a small fire, Milt grieved that all his pride was gone in a weak longing to see Claire again. In the morning he did see her—putting off on the lake, in a motor-boat with Jeff and Mr. Barmberry.

He saw the boat return, saw Jeff get into the car
which had brought him from Kalispell, saw the farewell, the long handclasp, the stoop of Jeff's head, and
Claire's quick step backward before Jeff could kiss
her. But Claire waved to Jeff long after his car had
started.

When Claire and her father came along in the
Gomez, Milt was standing by the road. She stopped.
She smiled. " Night of sadness and regrets? You
were fairly rude, Milt. So was Mr. Saxton, but I've
lectured him, and he sends his apologies."

" I send him mine—'deed I do," said Milt gravely.

" Then everything's all right. I'm sure we were
all tired. We'll just forget it."

" Morning, Daggett," Mr. Boltwood put in. " Hope
you lose that dreadful red-headed person."

" No, I can't, Mr. Boltwood. When Mr. Saxton
turned on me, I swore I'd take Pinky clear through
to Blewett Pass . . . though not to Seattle, by
golly!"

" Foolish oaths should be broken," Claire platitudi-
nized.

" Claire—look—— You don't really care so terribly much about these little luxuries, food and fixin's
and six-dollar-a-day-hotel junk, do you?"

" Yes," stoutly, " I do."

" But not compared with mountains and——"

"Oh, it's all very well to talk, and be so superior about these dear old grandeurs of Nature, and the heroism of pioneers, and I do like a glimpse of them. But the niceties of life do mean something and even if it is weak and dependent, I shall always simply adore them!"

"All these things are kind of softening." And he meant that she was still soft.

"At least they're not rude!" And she meant that he was rude.

"They're absolutely trivial. They shut off——"

"They shut off rain and snow and dirt, and I still fail to see the picturesqueness of dirt! Good-by!"

She had driven off, without looking back. She was heading for Seattle and the Pacific Ocean at forty miles an hour—and they had no engagement to meet either in Seattle or in the Pacific.

Before Milt went on he completed a task on which he had decided the night before while he had meditated on the tailored impertinence of Jeff Saxton's gray suit. The task was to give away the Best Suit, that stolid, very black covering which at Schoenstrom had seemed suitable either to a dance or to the Y. P. S. C. E. The recipient was Mr. Pinky Parrott, who gave in return a history of charity and high souls.

Milt did not listen. He was wondering, now that they had started, where they had started for. Certainly not for Seattle! Why not stop and see Pinky's gold-mine? Maybe he did have one. Even Pinky had to tell the truth sometimes. With a good popular gold-mine in his possession, Milt could buy quantities of clothes like Jeff Saxton's, and——

"And," he reflected, " I can learn as good manners as his in one hour, with a dancing lesson thrown in. If I didn't, I'd sue the professor!"

CHAPTER XIX

THE NIGHT OF ENDLESS PINES

ON the edge of Kootenai Canyon, feeling more like an aviator than like an automobilist, Claire had driven, and now, nearing Idaho, she had entered a national forest. She was delayed for hours, while she tried to change a casing, after a blow-out when the spare tire was deflated. She wished for Milt. She would never see him again. She was sorry. He hadn't meant——

But hang it, she panted, if he admired her at all, he'd be here now and get on this per-fect-ly beast-ly casing, over which she had been laboring for a dozen years; and she was simply too ridiculously tired; and was there any respectful way of keeping Henry B. from beaming in that benevolent manner while she was killing herself; and look at those fingernails; and —oh, drrrrrrat that casing!

To make the next town, after this delay, she had to drive for hours by night through the hulking pines of the national forest. It was her first long night drive.

A few claims, with log cabins of recent settlers, once or twice the shack of a forest-ranger, a telephone in a box by the road or a rough R. F. D. box nailed to a pine trunk, these indicated that civilization still

existed, but they were only melancholy blurs. She
was in a cold enchantment. All of her was dead save
the ability to keep on driving, forever, with no hope
of the tedium ending. She was bewildered. She
passed six times what seemed to be precisely the same
forest clearing, always with the road on a tiny ridge
to the left of the clearing, always with a darkness-
stilled house at one end and always, in the pasture at
the other end, a horse which neighed. She was in a
panorama stage-scene; things moved steadily by her,
there was a sound of the engine, and a sensation of
steering, but she was forever in the same place, among
the same pines, with the same scowling blackness between their bare clean trunks. Only the road ahead
was clear: a one-way track, the foot-high earthy bank
and the pine-roots beside it, two distinct ruts, and a
roughening of strewn brown bark and pine-needles,
which, in the beating light of the car's lamps, made
the sandy road scabrous with little incessant shadows.

She had never known anything save this strained
driving on. Jeff and Milt were old tales, and untrue.
Was it ten hours before that she had cooked dinner
beside the road? No matter. She wasn't hungry any
longer. She would never reach the next town—and
she didn't care. It wasn't she, but a grim spirit which
had entered her dead body, that kept steering, feeding
gas, watching the road.

In the darkness outside the funnel of light from her

lamps were shadows that leaped, and gray hands hastily jerked back out of sight behind tree trunks as she came up; things that followed her, and hidden men waiting for her to stop.

As drivers will, she tried to exorcise the creeping fear by singing. She made up what she called her driving-song. It was intended to echo the hoofs of a fat old horse on a hard road:

> The old horse trots with a jog, jog, jog,
> And a jog, jog, jog; and a jog, jog, jog.
> And the old road makes a little jog, jog, jog,
> To the west, jog, jog; and the north, jog, jog.
> While the farmer drinks some cider from his jug,
>   jug, jug,
> From his coy jug, jug; from his joy jug, jug.
> Till he accumulates a little jag, jag, jag,
> And he jigs, jigs, jigs, with his jug, jug, jug——

The song was a comfort, at first—then a torment. She drove to it, and she steered to it, and when she tried to forget, it sang itself in her tired brain: " Jog, jog, jog—oh, *damn!* "

Her father had had a chill. Miserable, weak as a small boy, he had curled up on the bottom of the car, his head on the seat, and gone to sleep. She was alone. The mile-posts went by slowly. The posts said there was a town ahead called Pellago, but it never came——

And when it did come she was too tired to care. In a thick dream she drove through midnight streets of the town. In stupid paralysis she kicked at the door of the galvanized-iron-covered garage. No answer. She gave it up. She drove down the street and into the yard of a hotel marked by a swing sign out over the plank sidewalk. She got out the traveling bags, awakened her father, led him up on the porch.

The Pellago Tavern was a transformed dwelling house. The pillars of the porch were aslant, and the rain-warped boards snapped beneath her feet. She hesitatingly opened the door. The hallway was dark and musty. A sound like a moan filtered down the unlighted stairs.

There seemed to be light in the room on the right. Trying to assure herself that her father was a protection, she pushed open the door. She looked into an airless room, scattered with rubber boots, unsavory old corduroy caps, tattered magazines. By the stove nodded a wry-mouthed, squat old woman, and a tall, cheaply handsome man of forty. Tobacco juice stained the front of his stiff-bosomed, collarless shirt. His hands were white but huge.

The old woman started. " Well? "

" I want to get two rooms for the night, please."

The man smirked at her. The woman creaked, " Well, I don't know. Where d' you come from, heh ? "

198 FREE AIR

"We're motoring through."

"Heh? Who's that man?"

"He's my father, madam."

"Needn't to be so hoity-toity about it, 'he's my father, madam!' F' that matter, that thing there is my husband!"

The man had been dusting his shabby coat, stroking his mustache, smiling with sickly gallantry. He burbled, "Shut up, Teenie. This lady is all right. Give her a room. Number 2 is empty, and I guess Number 7 has been made up since Bill left—if 'tain't, the sheets ain't been slept on but one night."

"Where d' you come——"

"Now don't go shooting off a lot of questions at the lady, Teenie. I'll show her the rooms."

The woman turned on her husband. He was perhaps twenty-five years younger; a quarter-century less soaked in hideousness. Her yellow, concave-sided teeth were bared at him, her mouth drew up on one side above the gums. "Pete, if I hear one word more out of you, out you go. Lady! Huh! Where d' you come from, young woman?"

Claire was too weak to stagger away. She leaned against the door. Her father struggled to speak, but the woman hurled:

"Wherdjuhcomfromised!"

"From New York. Is there another hotel——"

"Nah, there ain't another hotel! Oh! So you come

from New York, do you? Snobs, that's what N'
Yorkers are. I'll show you some rooms. They'll be
two dollars apiece, and breakfast fifty cents extra."

The woman led them up-stairs. Claire wanted to
flee, but—— Oh, she couldn't drive any farther!
She couldn't!

The floor of her room was the more bare in contrast to a two-foot-square splash of gritty ingrain
carpet in front of the sway-backed bed. On the bed
was a red comforter that was filthy beyond disguise.
The yellow earthenware pitcher was cracked. The
wall mirror was milky. Claire had been spoiled. She
had found two excellent hotels since Yellowstone
Park. She had forgotten how badly human beings can
live. She protested:

"Seems to me two dollars is a good deal to charge
for this!"

"I didn't say two dollars. I said three! Three
each for you and your pa. If you don't like it you
can drive on to the next town. It's only sixteen
miles!"

"Why the extra dollar—or extra two dollars?"

"Don't you see that carpet? These is our best
rooms. And three dollars—— I know you New
Yorkers. I heard of a gent once, and they charged
him five dollars—five dol-lars!—for a room in New
York, and a boy grabbed his valise from him and
wanted a short-bit and——"

" Oh—all—right! Can we get something to eat?"

" Now!?"

" We haven't eaten since noon."

" That ain't my fault! Some folks can go gadding around in automobuls, and some folks has to stay at home. If you think I'm going to sit up all night cooking for people that come chassayin' in here God knows what all hours of the day and night——! There's an all-night lunch down the street."

When she was alone Claire cried a good deal.

Her father declined to go out to the lunch room. The chill of the late ride was still on him, he croaked through his door; he was shivering; he was going right to bed.

" Yes, do, dear. I'll bring you back a sandwich."

" Safe to go out alone?"

" Anything's safe after facing that horrible—— I do believe in witches, now. Listen, dear; I'll bring you a hot-water bag."

She took the bag down to the office. The landlady was winding the clock, while her husband yawned. She glared.

" I wonder if I may have some hot water for my father? He has a chill."

" Stove's out. No hot water in the house."

" Couldn't you heat some?"

" Now look here, miss. You come in here, asking for meals and rooms at midnight, and you want a cut rate on everything, and I do what I can, but enough's enough!"

The woman stalked out. Her husband popped up. "Mustn't mind the old girl, lady. Got a grouch. Well, you can't blame her, in a way; when Bill lit out, he done her out of four-bits! But I'll tell you!" he leered. "You leave me the hot-water biznai, and I'll heat you some water myself!"

"Thank you, but I won't trouble you. Good night."

Claire was surprised to find a warm, rather comfortable all-night lunch room, called the Alaska Café, with a bright-eyed man of twenty-five in charge. He nodded in a friendly way, and made haste with her order of two ham-and-egg sandwiches. She felt adventurous. She polished her knife and fork on a napkin, as she had seen people do in lunches along the way. A crowd of three rubbed their noses against the front window to stare at the strange girl in town, but she ignored them, and they drifted away.

The lunchman was cordial: "At a hotel, ma'am? Which one? Gee, not the Tavern?"

"Why yes. Is there another?"

"Sure. First-rate one, two blocks over, one up."

"The woman said the Tavern was the only hotel."

"Oh, she's an old sour-face. Don't mind her. Just bawl her out. What's she charging you for a room?"

"Three dollars."

"Per each? Gee! Well, she sticks tourists any-

wheres from one buck to three. Natives get by for
fifty cents. She's pretty fierce, but she ain't a patch on
her husband. He comes from Spokane—nobody
knows why—guess he was run out. He takes some
kind of dope, and he cheats at rummy."

"But why does the town stand either of them?
Why do you let them torture innocent people? Why
don't you put them in the insane hospital, where they
belong?"

"That's a good one!" her friend chuckled. But
he saw it only as a joke.

She thought of moving her father to the good hotel,
but she hadn't the strength.

Claire Boltwood, of Brooklyn Heights, went
through the shanty streets of Pellago, Montana, at
one A.M. carrying a sandwich in a paper bag which had
recently been used for salted peanuts, and a red rubber hot-water bag filled with water at the Alaska
Café. At the Tavern she hastened past the office door.
She made her father eat his sandwich; she teased him
and laughed at him till the hot-water bag had relieved
his chill-pinched back; she kissed him boisterously,
and started for her own room, at the far end of the
hall.

The lights were off. She had to feel her way, and
she hesitated at the door of her room before she entered. She imagined voices, creeping footsteps,
people watching her from a distance. She flung into

the room, and when the kindled lamp showed her familiar traveling bag, she felt safer. But once she was in bed, with the sheet down as far as possible over the loathly red comforter, the quiet rustled and snapped about her, and she could not relax. Sinking into sleep seemed slipping into danger, and a dozen times she started awake.

But only slowly did she admit to herself that she actually did hear a fumbling, hear the knob of her door turning.

" W-who's there? "

" It's me, lady. The landlord. Brought you the hot water."

" Thanks so much, but I don't need it now."

" Got something else for you. Come to the door. Don't want to holler and wake ev'body up."

At the door she said timorously, " Nothing else I want, thank you. D-don't bother me."

" Why, I've brought you up a sandwich, girlie, all nice and hot, and a nip of something to take the chill off."

" I don't want it, I tell you! "

" Be a sport now! You use Pete right, and he'll use you right. Shame to see a lady like you not gettin' no service here. Open the door. Dandy sandwich! " The knob rattled again. She said nothing. The heel of her palm pressed against the door till the molding ate into it. The man was snorting:

"I ain't going to all this trouble and then throw away a good sandwich. You asked me——"

"M-must I s-shout?"

"S-shout your fool head off!" He kicked the door. "Good friends of mine, 'long this end of the hall. Aw, listen. Just teasing. I'm not going to rob you, little honey bird. Laws, you could have a million dollars, and old Pete wouldn't take two-bits. I just get so darn lonely in this hick town. Like to chat to live ones from the big burg. I'm a city fella myself —Spokane and Cheyenne and everything."

In her bare feet, Claire had run across the room, looked desperately out of the window. Could she climb out, reach her friend of the Alaska Café? If she had to——

Then she grinned. The world was rose-colored and hung with tinkling bells. "I love even that Pinky person!" she said. In the yard of the hotel, beside her Gomez, was a Teal bug, and two men were sleeping in blankets on the ground.

She marched over to the door. She flung it open. The man started back. He was holding an electric torch. She could not see him, but to the hovering ball of light she remarked, "Two men, friends of mine, are below, by their car. You will go at once, or I'll call them. If you think I am bluffing, go down and look. Good night!"

CHAPTER XX

THE FREE WOMAN

BEFORE breakfast, Claire darted down to the hotel yard. She beamed at Milt, who was lacing a rawhide patch on a tire, before she remembered that they were not on speaking terms. They both looked extremely sheepish and young. It was Pinky Parrott who was the social lubricant. Pinky was always on speaking terms with everybody. "Ah, here she is! The little lady of the mutinous eyes! Our colonel of the flivver hussars!"

But he got no credit. Milt straightened up and lumbered, "Hel-lo!"

She peeped at him and whispered, "Hel-lo!"

"Say, oh please, Claire—— I didn't mean——"

"Oh, I know! Let's—let's go have breakfast."

"Was awfully afraid you'd think we were fresh, but when we came in last night, and saw your car—didn't like the looks of the hotel much, and thought we'd stick around."

"I'm so glad. Oh, Milt—yes, and you, Mr. Parrott—will you whip—lick—beat up—however you want to say it—somebody for me?"

With one glad communal smile Milt and Pinky

curved up their wrists and made motions as of pulling up their sleeves.

"But not unless I say so. I want to be a Citizeness Fixit. I've been good for so long. But now——"

"Show him to me!" and "Up, lads, and atum!" responded her squad.

"Not till after breakfast."

It was a sufficiently vile breakfast, at the Tavern. The feature was curious cakes whose interior was raw creepy dough. A dozen skilled workmen were at the same long table with Claire, Milt, Pinky, and Mr. Boltwood—the last two of whom were polite and scenically descriptive to each other, but portentously silent about gold-mines. The landlady and a slavey waited on table; the landlord could be seen loafing in the kitchen.

Toward the end of the meal Claire insultingly crooked her finger at the landlady and said, "Come here, woman."

The landlady stared, then ignored her.

"Very well. Then I'll say it publicly!" Claire swept the workmen with an affectionate smile. "Gentlemen of Pellago, I want you to know from one of the poor tourists who have been cheated at this nasty place that we depend on you to do something. This woman and her husband are criminals, in the way they overcharge for hideous food and——"

The landlady had been petrified. Now she charged

down. Behind her came her husband. Milt arose.
The husband stopped. But it was Pinky who faced
the landlady, tapped her shoulder, and launched into,
" And what's more, you hag, if our new friends here
have any sense, they'll run you out of town."

That was only the beginning of Pinky's paper on
corrections and charities. He enjoyed himself. Before he finished, the landlady was crying . . . she
voluntarily promised to give her boarders waffles, some
morning, jus' soon as she could find the waffle-iron.

With her guard about her, at the office desk, Claire
paid one dollar apiece for the rooms, and discussion
was not.

Before they started, Milt had the chance to say to
her, " I'm getting so I can handle Pinky now. Have
to. Thinking of getting hold of his gold-mine. I
just give him the eye, as your friend Mr. Saxton
would, and he gets so meek——"

" But don't! Please understand me, Milt; I do admire Mr. Saxton; he is fine and capable, and really
generous; only—— He may be just a bit snippish at
times, while you—you're a playmate—father's and
mine—and—— I did face that landlady, didn't I!
I'm not soft and trivial, am I! Praise!"

She had driven through the panhandle of Idaho
into Washington, through Spokane, through the writhing lava deposits of Moses Coulee where fruit trees

grow on volcanic ash. Beyond Wenatchee, with its
rows of apple trees striping the climbing fields like
corduroy in folds, she had come to the famous climb
of Blewett Pass. Once over that pass, and Snoqualmie, she would romp into Seattle.

She was sorry that she hadn't come to know Milt
better, but perhaps she would see him in Seattle.

Not adventure alone was she finding, but high intellectual benefit in studying the names of towns in the
state of Washington. Not Kankakee nor Kalamazoo
nor Oshkosh can rival the picturesque fancy of Washington, and Claire combined the town-names in a lyric
so emotion-stirring that it ought, perhaps, to be the
national anthem. It ran:

> Humptulips, Tum Tum, Moclips, Yelm,
> Satsop, Bucoda, Omak, Enumclaw,
> Tillicum, Bossburg, Chettlo, Chattaroy,
> Zillah, Selah, Cowiche, Keechelus,
> Bluestem, Bluelight, Onion Creek, Sockeye,
> Antwine, Chopaka, Startup, Kapowsin,
> 　　Skamokawa, Sixprong, Pysht!
>
> Klickitat, Kittitas, Spangle, Cedonia,
> Pe Ell, Cle Elum, Sallal, Chimacum,
> Index, Taholah, Synarep, Puyallup,
> Wallula, Wawawai, Wauconda, Washougal,
> Walla Walla, Washtucna, Wahluke,
> Solkulk, Newaukum, Wahkiakus,
> 　　Penawawa, Ohop, Ladd!

Harrah, Olalla, Umtanum, Chuckanut,
Soap Lake, Loon Lake, Addy, Ace, Usk,
Chillowist, Moxee City, Yellepit, Cashup,
Moonax, Mabton, Tolt, Mukilteo,
Poulsbo, Toppenish, Whetstone, Inchelium,
Fishtrap, Carnation, Shine, Monte Cristo,
 Conconully, Roza, Maud!

China Bend, Zumwalt, Sapolil, Riffle,
Touchet, Chesaw, Chew, Klum, Bly,
Humorist, Hammer, Nooksack, Oso,
Samamish, Dusty, Tiger, Turk, Dot,
Scenic, Tekoa, Nellita, Attalia,
Steilacoom, Tweedle, Ruff, Lisabeula,
Latah, Peola, Towal, Eltopia,
 Steptoe, Pluvius, Sol Duc, Twisp!

"And then," complained Claire, "they talk about Amy Lowell! I leave it to you, Henry B., if any union poet has ever written as gay a refrain as 'Ohop Ladd'!"

She was not merely playing mental whist. She was trying to keep from worry. All the way she had heard of Blewett Pass; its fourteen miles of climbing, and the last half mile of stern pitch. On this eastern side of the pass, the new road was not open; there was a tortuous, flint-scattered trail, too narrow, in most places, for the passing of other cars. Claire was glad that Milt and Pinky were near her.

If so many of the race of kind advisers of tourists

had not warned her about it, doubtless she would have
gone over the pass without difficulty. But their vol-
untary croaking sapped her nerve, and her father's.
He kept worrying, " Do you think we better try it? "
When they stopped at a ranch house at the foot of the
climb, for the night, he seemed unusually tired. He
complained of chill. He did not eat breakfast. They
started out silent, depressed.

He crouched in the corner of the seat. She looked
at him and was anxious. She stopped on the first
level space on the pass, crying, " You are perfectly
miserable. I'm afraid of—— I think we ought to
see a doctor."

" Oh, I'll be all right."

But she waited till Milt came pit-pattering up the
slope. " Father feels rather sick. What shall I do?
Turn round and drive to the nearest doctor—at Cash-
mere, I suppose? "

" There's a magnolious medico ahead here on the
pass," Pinky Parrott interrupted. " A young thing,
but they say he's a graduate of Harvard. He's out
here because he has some timber-claims. Look, Milt
o' the Daggett, why don't you drive Miss Boltwood's
'bus—make better time, and hustle the old gent. up to
the doc, and I'll come on behind with your machine."

" Why," Claire fretted, " I hate——"

A new Milt, the boss, abrupt, almost bullying,
snapped out of his bug. " Good idee. Jump in, Claire.

I'll take your father up. Heh, whasat, Pink? Yes, I get it; second turn beyond grocery. Right. On we go. Huh? Oh, we'll think about the gold-mine later, Pink."

With the three of them wedged into the seat of the Gomez, and Pinky recklessly skittering after them in the bug, they climbed again—and lo! there was no climb! Unconsciously Claire had hesitated before dashing at each sharp upsloping bend; had lost headway while she was wondering, " Suppose the car went off this curve?" Milt never sped up, but he never slackened. His driving was as rhythmical as music.

They were so packed in that he could scarcely reach gear lever and hand-brake. He halted on a level, and curtly asked, "That trap-door in the back of the car —convertible extra seat?"

" Yes, but we almost never use it, and it's stuck. Can't get it open."

" I'll open it all right! Got a big screwdriver? Want you sit back there. Need elbow room."

" Perhaps I'd better drive with Mr. Pinky."

" Nope. Don't think better."

With one yank he opened the trap-door, revealing a folding seat, which she meekly took. Back there, she reflected, " How strong his back looks. Funny how the little silvery hairs grow at the back of his neck."

They came to a settlement and the red cedar bungalow of Dr. Hooker Beach. The moment Claire saw the doctor's thin demanding face, she trusted him. He spoke to Mr. Boltwood with assurance: " All you need is some rest, and your digestion is a little shaky. Been eating some pork? Might stay here a day or two. We're glad to have a glimpse of Easterners."

Mr. Boltwood went to bed in the Beaches' guest-room. Mrs. Beach gave Claire and Milt lunch, with thin toast and thin china, on a porch from which an arroyo dropped down for a hundred feet. Fir trees scented the air, and a talking machine played the same Russian music that was popular that same moment in New York. And the Beaches knew people who knew Claire.

Claire was thinking. These people were genuine aristocrats, while Jeff Saxton, for all his family and his assumptions about life, was the eternal climber. Milt, who had been uncomfortable with Jeff, was serene and un-self-conscious with the Beaches, and the doctor gratefully took his advice about his stationary gas engine. " He's rather like the Beaches in his simplicity—yes, and his ability to do anything if he considers it worth while," she decided.

After lunch, when the doctor and his wife had to trot off to a patient, Claire proposed, " Let's walk up to that ledge of rock and see the view, shall we, Milt? "

" Yes! And keep an eye on the road for Pinky. The poor nut, he hasn't showed up. So reckless; hope he hasn't driven the Teal off the road."

She crouched at the edge of a rock, where she would have been frightened, a month before, and looked across the main road to a creek in a pine-laced gully. He sat beside her, elbows on knees.

"Those Beaches—their kin are judges and senators and college Presidents, all over New England," she said. "This doctor must be the grandson of the ambassador, I fancy."

"Honest? I thought they were just regular folks. Was I nice?"

"Of course you were."

"Did I—did I wash my paws and sit up and beg?"

"No, you aren't a little dog. I'm that. You're the big mastiff that guards the house, while I run and yip." She was turned toward him, smiling. Her hand was beside him. He touched the back of it with his forefinger, as though he was afraid he might soil it.

There seemed to be no reason, but he was trembling as he stammered, "I—I—I'm d-darn glad I didn't know they were anybody, or 'd have been as bad as a flivver driver the first time he tries a t-twelve-cylinder machine. G-gee your hand is little!"

She took it back and inspected it. "I suppose it is. And pretty useless."

"N-no, it isn't, but your shoes are. Why don't you wear boots when you're out like this?" A flicker of his earlier peremptoriness came into his voice. She resented it:

"My shoes are perfectly sensible! I will not wear those horrible vegetarian uplift sacks on my feet!"

"Your shoes may be all right for New York, but you're not going to New York for a while. You've simply got to see some of this country while you're out here—British Columbia and Alaska."

"Would be nice, but I've had enough rough-ing——"

"Chance to see the grandest mountains in the world, almost, and then you want to go back to tea and all that junk!"

"Stop trying to bully me! You have been dicta-torial ever since we started up——"

"Have I? Didn't mean to be. Though I suppose I usually am bullying. At least I run things. There's two kinds of people; those that give orders, and those that naturally take them; and I belong to the first one, and——"

"But my dear Milt, so do I, and really——"

"And mostly I'd take them from you. But hang it, Seattle is just a day away, and you'll forget me. Wish I could kidnap you. Have half a mind to. Take you way up into the mountains, and when you got used to roughing it in sure-enough wilderness—say you'd helped me haul timber for a flume—then we'd be real pals. You have the stuff in you, but you still need toughening before——"

"Listen to me, Milton. You have been reading fiction, about this man—sometimes he's a lumberjack, and sometimes a trapper or a miner, but always he's frightfully hairy—and he sees a charming woman in the city, and kidnaps her, and shuts her up in some unspeakable shanty, and makes her eat nice cold boiled potatoes, and so naturally, she simply adores him! A hundred men have written that story, and it's an example of their insane masculine conceit, which I, as a woman, resent. Shakespeare may have started it, with his silly *Taming of the Shrew*. Shakespeare's men may have been real, but his women were dolls, designed to please some majesty. You may not know it, but there are women today who don't live just to please majesties' fancies. If a woman like me were kidnapped, she would go on hating the brute, or if she did give in, then the man would lose anyway, because she would have degenerated; she'd have turned into a slave, and lost exactly the things he'd liked in her. Oh, you cavemen! With your belief that you can force women to like you! I have more courage than any of you!"

"I admit you have courage, but you'd have still more, if you bucked the wilds."

"Nonsense! In New York I face every day a hundred complicated problems you don't know I ever heard of!"

"Let me remind you that Brer Julius Cæsar said he'd rather be mayor in a little Spanish town than

police commissioner in Rome. I'm king in Schoenstrom, while you're just one of a couple hundred
thousand bright people in New York——"

" Really? Oh, at least a million. Thanks! "

" Oh—gee—Claire, I didn't mean to be personal,
and get in a row and all, but—can't you see—kind of
desperate—Seattle so soon——"

Her face was turned from him; its thin profile was
firm as silver wire. He blundered off into silence and
—they were at it again!

" I didn't mean to make you angry," he gulped.

" Well, you did! Bullying—— You and your men
of granite, in mackinaws and a much-needed shave,
trying to make a well-bred woman satisfied with a
view consisting of rocks and stumps and socks on the
line! Let me tell you that compared with a street
canyon, a mountain canyon is simply dead, and yet
these unlettered wild men——"

" See here! I don't know if you're firing these adjectives at me, but I don't know that I'm so much
more unlettered—— You talked about taking French
in your finishing-school. Well, they taught American
in mine! "

" They would! "

Then he was angry. " Yes, and chemistry and
physics and Greek and Latin and history and mathematics and economics, and I took more or less of a
whirl at all of them, while you were fiddling with

ribbons, and then I had to buck mechanics and business methods."

"I also 'fiddled' with manners—an unfortunate omission in your curriculum, I take it! You have been reasonably rude——"

"So have you!"

"I had to be! But I trust you begin to see that even your strong hand couldn't control a woman's taste. Kidnapping! As intelligent a boy as you wanting to imitate these boorish movie——"

"Not a darn bit more boorish than your smart set, with its champagne and these orgies at country clubs——"

"You know so much about country clubs, don't you! The worst orgy I ever saw at one was the golf champion reading the beauty department in *Boudoir*. Would you mind backing up your statements about the vices of myself and my friends——"

"Oh, you. Oh, I didn't mean——"

"Then why did you——"

"Now you're bullying me, and you know that if the smart set isn't vicious, at least it's so snobbish that it can't see any——"

"Then it's wise to be snobbish, because if it did condescend——"

"I won't stand people talking about condescending——"

"Would you mind not shouting so?"

"Very well! I'll keep still!"

Silence again, while both of them looked unhappy, and tried to remember just what they had been fighting about. They did not at first notice a small red car larruping gaily over the road beneath the ledge, though the driver was a pink-haired man in a green coat. He was almost gone before Milt choked, "It's Pinky!"

"Pink! Pinky!" he bellowed.

Pinky looked back but, instead of stopping, he sped up, and kept going.

CHAPTER XXI

THE MINE OF LOST SOULS

THAT couldn't have been Pinky! Why! Why, the car he had was red," cried Claire.

" Sure. The idiot's got hold of some barn paint somewhere, and tried to daub it over. He's trying to make a getaway with it!"

" We'll chase him. In my car."

" Don't you mind?"

" Of course not. I do not give up my objections to the roughing philosophy, but—— You were right about these shoes—— Oh, don't leave me behind! Want to go along!"

These sentences she broke, scattered, and totally lost as she scrambled after him, down the rocks. He halted. His lips trembled. He picked her up, carried her down, hesitated a second while his face—curiously foreshortened as she looked up at it from his big arms—twisted with emotion. He set her down gently, and she climbed into the Gomez.

It seemed to her that he drove rather too carefully, too slowly. He took curves and corners evenly. His face was as empty of expression, as unmelodramatic, as that of a jitney driver. Then she looked at the speedometer. He was making forty-eight miles an hour down hill and forty to thirty on upgrades.

They were in sight of the fleeing Pinky in two miles. Pinky looked back; instantly was to be seen pulling his hat low, stooping over—the demon driver. Milt merely sat more erect, looked more bland and white-browed and steady.

The bug fled before them on a winding shelf road. It popped up a curve, then slowed down. " He took it too fast. Poor Pink! " said Milt.

They gained on that upslope, but as the road dropped, the bug started forward desperately. Another car was headed toward them; was drawn to the side of the road, in one of the occasional widenings. Pinky passed it so carelessly that, with crawling spine, Claire saw the outer wheels of the bug on the very edge of the road—the edge of a fifty-foot drop. Milt went easily past the halted car—even waved his hand to the waiting driver.

This did not seem to Claire at all like the chase of a thief. She looked casually ahead at Pinky, as he whirled round an S-shaped curve on the downslope, then—— It was too quick to see what happened. The bug headed directly toward the edge of the road, shot out, went down the embankment, over and over. It lay absurdly upside-down, its muffler and brake-rods showing in place of the seat and hood.

Milt quite carefully stopped the Gomez. The day

was still—just a breathing of running water in the deep gully. The topsy-turvy car below them was equally still; no sight of Pinky, no sound.

The gauche boy gone from him, Milt took her hand, pressed it to his cheek. "Claire! You're here! You might have gone with him, to make room—— Oh, I was bullying you because I was bullying myself! Trying to make myself tell you—but oh, you know, you know! Can you stand going down there? I hate to have you, but you may be needed."

"Yes. I'll come," she whispered.

Their crawl down the rock-rolling embankment seemed desperately slow.

"Wait here," bade Milt, at the bottom.

She looked away from the grotesque car. She had seen that one side of it was crumpled like paper in an impatient hand.

Milt was stooping, looking under; seemed to be saying something. When he came back, he did not speak. He wiped his forehead. "Come. We'll climb back up. Nothing to do, now. Guess you better not try to help, anyway. You might not sleep well."

He gave her his hand up the embankment, drove to the nearest house, telephoned to Dr. Beach. Later she waited while Milt and the doctor, with two other men, were raising the car. As she waited she thought of the Teal bug as a human thing—as her old friend, to which she had often turned in need.

Milt returned to her. "There is one thing for you to do. Before he died, Pinky asked me to go get his wife—Dolores, I think it is. She's up in a side canyon, few miles away. She may want a woman around. Beach will take care of—of him. Can you come?"

"Of course. Oh, Milt, I didn't——"

"I didn't——"

"—mean you were a caveman! You're my big brother!"

"—mean you were a snob!"

They drove five miles along the highway, then up a trail where the Gomez brushed the undergrowth on each side as it desperately dug into moss, rain-gutted ruts, loose rocks, all on a vicious slant which seemed to push the car down again. Beside them, the mountain woods were sacredly quiet, with fern and lily and green-lit spaces. They came out in a clearing, before dusk. Beside the clearing was a brook, with a crude cradle—sign of a not very successful gold miner. Before a log cabin, in a sway-sided rocker, creaked a tall, white, flabby woman, once nearly beautiful, now rubbed at the edges. She rose, huddling her wrapper about her bosom, as they drove into the clearing and picked their way through stumps and briars.

"Where you folks think you're going?" she whimpered.

"Why, why just——"

"I cer'nly am glad to see somebody! I been 'most scared to death. Been here alone two weeks now. Got a shotgun, but if anybody come, I guess they'd take it away from me. I was brought up nice, no rough-house or—— Say, did you folks come to see the gold-mine?"

"M-mine?" babbled Milt.

"Course not. Pinky said I was to show it, but I'm so sore on that low-life hound now, I swear I won't even take the trouble and lie about it. No more gold in that crick than there is in my eye. Or than there's flour or pork in the house!"

The woman's voice was rising. Her gestures were furious. Claire and Milt stood close, their hands slipping together.

"What d' you think of a man that'd go off and leave a lady without half enough to eat, while he gallivanted around, trying to raise money by gambling, when he was offered a good job up here? He's a gambler—told me he was a rich mine-owner, but never touched a mine in his life. Lying hound—worst talker in ten counties! Got a gambler's hand on him, too—I ought to seen it! Oh, wait till I get hold of him; just wait!"

Claire thought of the still hand—so still—that she had seen under the edge of the upturned car. She tried to speak, while the woman raved on, wrath feeding wrath:

"Thank God, I ain't really his wife! My husband

is a fine man—Mr. Kloh—Dlorus Kloh, my name is. Mr. Kloh's got a fine job with the mill, at North Yakima. Oh, I was a fool! This gambler Pinky Parrott, he comes along with his elegant ways, and he hands me out a swell line of gab, and I ups and leaves poor Kloh, and the kid, and the nicest kid—— Say, please, could you folks take me wherever you're going? Maybe I could get a job again—used to was a good waitress, and I ain't going to wait here any longer for that lying, cheating, mean-talking——"

" Oh, Mrs. Kloh, please don't! He's dead!" wailed Claire.

" Dead? Pinky? Oh—my—God! And I won't ever see him, and he was so funny and——"

She threw herself on the ground; she kicked her heels; she tore at her loosely caught, tarnished blonde hair.

Claire knelt by her. " You mustn't—you mustn't —we'll——"

" Damn you, with your smug-faced husband there, and your fine auto and all, butting into poor folks' troubles!" shrieked Dlorus.

Claire stumbled to her feet, stood with her clenched right hand to her trembling lips, cupping it with her nervous left hand. Her shoulders were dejected. Milt pleaded, " Let's hike out. I don't mind decent honest grease, but this place—look in at table! Dirty dishes—— And gin bottles on the floor!"

" Desert her? When she needs me so?" Claire started forward, but Milt caught her sleeve, and admired, " You were right! You've got more nerve than I have!"

" No. I wouldn't dare if—— I'm glad you're here with me!"

Claire calmed the woman; bound up her hair; washed her face—which needed it; and sat on the log doorstep, holding Dlorus's head in her lap, while Dlorus sobbed, " Pinky—dead! Him that was so lively! And he was so sweet a lover, oh, so sweet. He was a swell fellow; my, he could just make you laugh and cry, the way he talked; and he was so educated, and he played the vi'lin—he could do anything—and athaletic—he would have made me rich. Oh, let me alone. I just want to be alone and think of him. I was so bored with Kloh, and no nice dresses or nothin', and—I did love the kid, but he squalled so, just all the time, and Pinky come, and he was so funny—— Oh, let me alone!"

Claire shivered, then, and the strength seemed to go from the steady arms that had supported Dlorus's head. Dusk had sneaked up on them; the clearing was full of swimming grayness, and between the woman's screams, the woods crackled. Each time Dlorus spoke, her screech was like that of an animal in the woods, and round about them crept such sinister echoes that Milt kept wanting to look back over his shoulder.

" Yes," sighed Claire at last, " perhaps we'd better go."

" If you go, I'll kill myself! Take me to Mr. Kloh! Oh, he was—— My husband, Mr. Kloh. Oh, so good. Only he didn't understand a lady has to have her good times, and Pink danced so well——"

Dlorus sprang up, flung into the cabin, stood in the dimness of the doorway, holding a butcher knife and clamoring, " I will! I'll kill myself if you leave me! Take me down to Mr. Kloh, at North Yakima, to-night! "

Milt sauntered toward her.

" Don't you get flip, young man! I mean it! And I'll kill you——"

Most unchivalrously, quite out of the picture of gray grief, Milt snapped, " That'll be about enough of you! Here! Gimme that knife! "

She dropped the knife, sniveling, " Oh Gawd, some-body's always bullying me! And all I wanted was a good time! "

Claire herded her into the cabin. " We'll take you to your husband—tonight. Come, let's wash up, and I'll help you put on your prettiest dress."

" Honest, will you? " cried the woman, in high spirits, all grief put aside. " I got a dandy China silk dress, and some new white kid shoes! My, Mr. Kloh, he won't hardly know me. He'll take me back. I know how to handle him. That'll be swell, going back in an automobile. And I got a new hair-comb, with genuine Peruvian diamonds. Say, you aren't kidding me along?"

In the light of the lantern Milt had kindled, Claire looked questioningly at him. Both of them shrugged. Claire promised, "Yes. Tonight. If we can make it."

"And will you jolly Mr. Kloh for me? Gee, I'll be awfully scared of him. I swear, I'll wash his dishes and everything. He's a good man. He—— Say, he ain't seen my new parasol, neither!"

CHAPTER XXII

ACROSS THE ROOF OF THE WORLD

CLAIRE dressed Dlorus, cooked a dinner of beet greens, potatoes, and trout; and by bullying and great sweetness kept Dlorus from too many trips to the gin bottle. Milt caught the trout, cut wood, locked in a log shed Pinky's forlorn mining-tools. They started for North Yakima at eight of the evening, with Dlorus, back in the spare seat, alternately sobbing and to inattentive ears announcing what she'd say to the Old Hens.

Milt was devoted to persuading the huge cat of a car to tiptoe down the slippery gouged ruts of the road, and Claire's mind was driving with him. Every time he touched the foot-brake, she could feel the strain in the tendons of her own ankle.

A mile down the main road they stopped at a store-postoffice to telephone back to Mr. Boltwood and Dr. Beach. On the porch was a man in overalls and laced boots. He was lean and quick-moving. As he raised his head, and his spectacles flashed, Claire caught Milt's arm and gasped, "Oh, my dear, I'm in a beautiful state of nerves. For a moment I thought that was Jeff Saxton. I bet it is his astral body!"

"And you thought he was going to forbid your

running away on this fool expedition, and you were scared," chuckled Milt, as they sat in the car.

"Of course I was! And I still am! I know what he'll say afterward! He *is* here, reasoning with me. Oughtn't I to be sensible? Oughtn't I to have you leave me at the Beaches' before you start—jolly jaunt to take a strange woman to her presumably homicidal husband! Why am I totally lacking in sense? Just listen to what Jeff is saying!"

"Of course you ought to go back, and let me drive alone. Absolutely insane, your——"

"But you would like me to go along, wouldn't you!"

"Like you to? It's our last ride together, and that bloomin' old Browning never thought of a ride together by midnight over the roof of the world! No, it's really our first ride together, and tomorrow—you're gone."

"No, I sha'n't be gone, but——" Addressing herself to the astounded overalled man on the porch, she declared, "You're quite right, Jeff. And Milt is wrong. Insane adventure. Only, it's wonderful to be young enough to do insane adventures. Falling down abyssy places is so much more interesting than bridge. I'm going—going—going! . . . Milt, you telephone."

"Don't you think you better?"

"No, siree! Father would forbid me. Try not

to get him—just tell Dr. Beach where we're going, and hang up, and scoot!"

All night they drove; down the Pacific side of Blewett Pass; down the sweeping spirals to a valley. Dlorus drowsed in the extra seat. Claire's sleepy head was fantastically swaying. She was awakened by an approaching roar and, as though she sat at a play, she watched a big racing machine coming toward them, passing them with two wheels in the ditch. She had only a thunderous glimpse of the stolid driver; a dark, hooded, romantic figure, like a sailor at the helm in a storm.

Milt cried, "Golly! May be a transcontinental racer! Be in New York in five days—going night and day—take mud at fifty an hour—crack mechanic right from the factory—change tires in three minutes —people waiting up all night to give him gasoline and a sandwich! That's my idea of fun!"

Studying Milt's shadowed face, Claire considered, "He could do it, too. Sitting there at the wheel, taking danger and good road with the same steadiness. Oh, he's—well, anyway, he's a dear boy."

But what she said was:

"Less dramatic things for you, now, Milt. Trigonometry is going to be your idea of fun; blueprints and engineering books."

"Yes. I know. I'm going to do it. Do four years' work in three—or two. I'll tack pages of

formulas on the wall, in my bum hallroom, and study
'em while I'm shaving. Oh, I'll be the grind! But
learn to dance the fox-trot, though! If America gets
into the war, I'll get into the engineering corps, and
come back to school afterward."

" Will the finances——"

" I'll sell my garage, by mail. Rauskukle will take
it. He won't rob me of more than a thousand dollars
on price—not much more."

" You're going to love Seattle. And we'll have some
good tramps while I'm there, you and I."

" Honestly? Will you want to?"

" Do you suppose for one second I'd give up my
feeling of free air? If you don't come and get me,
I'll call on you and make you come!"

"Warn you I'll probably be living over some
beanery."

" Probably. With dirty steps leading up to it. I'll
sweep the steps. I'll cook supper for you. I can do
things, can't I! I did manage Dlorus, didn't I!"

He was murmuring, " Claire, dear!" when she
changed her tone to the echo of Brooklyn Heights,
and hurried on, " You do understand, don't you!
We'll be, uh, good friends."

" Yes." He drove with much speed and silence.

Though they were devouring the dark road, though
roadside rocks, caught by the headlights, seemed to
fly up at them, though they went on forever, chased

by a nightmare, Claire snuggled down in security.
Her head drooped against his shoulder. He put his
arm about her, his hand about her waist. She sleepily
wondered if she ought to let him. She heard herself
muttering, "Sorry I was so rude when you were so
rude," and her chilly cheek discovered that the smooth-
worn shoulder of his old blue coat was warm, and she
wondered some more about the questions of waists
and hands and—— She was asleep.

She awoke, bewildered to find that dawn was slipping into the air. While she had slept Milt had taken
his arm from about her and fished out a lap-robe for
her. Behind them, Dlorus was slumbering, with her
soft mouth wide open. Claire felt the luxury of the
pocket of warmth under the lap-robe; she comfortably
stretched her legs while she pictured Milt driving on
all the night, rigid, tireless, impersonal as the engineer of a night express.

They came into North Yakima at breakfast time,
and found the house of Mr. Kloh, a neat, bare, drab
frame box, with tight small front and back yards.
Dlorus was awake, and when she wasn't yawning, she
was enjoying being hysterical.

"Miss Boltwood," she whined, "you go in and
jolly him up."

Milt begged, "Better let me do it, Claire."

They looked squarely at each other. "No, I think
I'd better," she decided.

" Right, Claire, but—I wish I could do more things for you."

" I know!"

He lifted her stiff, cold little body from the car. His hands under her arms, he held her on the running-board an instant, her eyes level with his. "Little sister—plucky little sister!" he sighed. He lowered her to the ground.

Claire knocked at the back door. To it came a bald, tired man, in an apron wet at the knees. The kitchen floor was soaped, and a scrubbing-brush rode amid the seas. A rather dirty child clung to his hand. "Trying to clean up, ma'am. Not very good at it. I hope you ain't the Cruelty to Children lady. Willy looks mussed, but fact is, I just can't get time to wash the clothes, but he means a terrible lot to me. What was it? Will you step in?"

Claire buttoned the child's rompers before she spoke. Then:

" Mr. Kloh, I want to be perfectly honest with you. I've had word from your wife. She's unhappy, and she loves and admires you more than any other man in the world, and I think she would come back—misses the child so."

The man wiped his reddened hands. "I don't know—— I don't wish her no harm. Trouble was, I'm kind of pokey. I guess I couldn't give her any good times. I used to try to go to dances with her,

but when I'd worked late, I'd get sleepy and——
She's a beautiful woman, smart 's a whip, and I guess
I was too slow for her. No, she wouldn't never come
back to me."

"She's out in front of the house now—waiting!"

"Great Cæsar's ghost, and the floor not scrubbed!"
With a squawk of anxiety he leaped on the scrubbing-
brush, and when Milt and Dlorus appeared at the door,
Mr. Kloh and Miss Claire Boltwood were wiping up
the kitchen floor.

Dlorus looked at them, arms akimbo, and sighed,
"Hello, Johnny, my, ain't it nice to be back, oh, you
had the sink painted, oh, forgive me, Johnny, I was
a bad ungrateful woman, I don't care if you don't
never take me to no more dances, hardly any, Willy
come here, dear, oh, he is such a sweet child, my, his
mouth is so dirty, will you forgive me, Johnny, is my
overcoat in the moth-balls?"

When Mr. Kloh had gone off to the mill—thrice
returning from the gate to kiss Dlorus and to thank
her rescuers—Claire sat down and yawningly lashed
off every inch of Dlorus's fair white skin:

"You're at it already; taking advantage of that
good man's forgiveness, and getting lofty with him,
and rather admiring yourself as a spectacular sinner.
You are a lazy, ignorant, not very clean woman, and
if you succeed in making Mr. Kloh and Willy happy,
it will be almost too big a job for you. Now if I

come back from Seattle and find you misbehaving
again——"

Dlorus broke down. "You won't, miss! And I
will raise chickens, like he wanted, honest I will!"

"Then you may let me have a room to take a
nap in, and perhaps Mr. Daggett could sleep in there
on the sofa, and we'll get rested before we start
back."

Both Milt and Dlorus meekly followed the boss.

It was noon before Milt and Claire woke, and discovered that Dlorus had prepared for them scrambled
eggs and store celery, served on an almost clean table-
cloth. Mr. Kloh came home for lunch, and while
Dlorus sat on his lap in the living-room, and repeated
that she had been a "bad, naughty, 'ittle dirl—what
did the fellows say at the mill?" Milt and Claire
sat dumpily on the back porch, regarding scenery
which featured of seven tin cans, a broken patent
washing-machine, and a rheumatic pear tree.

"I suppose we ought to start," groaned Claire.

"I have about as much nerve as a rabbit, and as
much punch as a bale of hay," Milt admitted.

"We're like two children that have been playing
too long."

"But don't want to go home!"

"Quite! Though I don't think much of your idea
of a playhouse—those tin cans. But it's better than
having to be grown-up."

In the midst of which chatter they realized that Mr. Henry B. Boltwood and Dr. Hooker Beach had come round the corner of the house, and were gaping at them.

CHAPTER XXIII

THE GRAEL IN A BACK YARD IN YAKIMA

"I MUST say that you two have chosen a fine pastoral scene!" observed Mr. Boltwood.

"Hhhhhhhhow did you get here?" gasped Claire.

"Auto 'bus over Blewett Pass, train here from Ellensburg. That woman—everything all right?"

"Yes, everything's fine. We were just starting back, sir," implored Milt.

"Huh!"

"Awfully sorry, sir, to take Claire on such a hike——"

"I don't blame you particularly. When that young woman gets an idea into her head, the rest of us are pawns. Why, even me—she's dragged me all over the Rocky Mountains. And I will admit, Claire, that it's been good for me. But I begin to feel human again, and I think it's about time I took charge. We'll catch the afternoon train for Seattle, Claire. The trip has been extremely interesting, but I think perhaps we'll call it enough. Daggett, want to get you to drive the Gomez on to Seattle. Beach tells me your car is completely wrecked. Lose any money in it?"

"No, sir. Had my roll in the bug. I'll have to go back to it and get some clothes out of it, though."

"Well, then, will you drive my car in? Charge me anywhere up to fifty dollars, if you want to——"

"I'd rather not——"

"It's a perfectly honest job—I'd do it, too quick! Or if your confounded pride won't let you charge anything, bring the car on anyway. Come, dolly, I have a jitney here, please observe my graceful use of 'jitney,' and I have the bags. We'll hustle to the station now. No! No arguments, chick!"

On the station platform, Claire and Milt were under the surveillance of Mr. Boltwood, who was extremely irritable as every two minutes the train was reported to be two minutes later. They tramped up and down, speaking in lowered voices, very meek but in their joint naughtiness very intimate.

"That was a nice place to end a transcontinental drive—in the back yard of Mr. Johnny Kloh, with an unrestricted view of tin cans!" lamented Claire.

"Still, your drive didn't end at Kloh's; it ended way up in the mountains."

Mr. Boltwood bumbled down on them: "Another minute late! Like to know what the matter is!"

"Yes, father!"

When Mr. Boltwood's impatiently waiting back was turned, Claire gripped Milt's hand, and whispered to him, "You see, I'm captured! I thought I was father's lord and chauffeur, but he sniffs the smoke of the ticker. In his mind, he's already back in the office, running things. He'll probably turn me over to Jeff, for disciplining! You won't let them change me back into a pink-face, will you? Come to tea, at the Gilsons', just as soon as you reach Seattle."

"Tea—— Now we're so near your Gilsons, I begin to get scared. Wouldn't know what to do. Gee, I've heard you have to balance a tea-cup and a sandwich and a hunk o' cake and a lot of conversation all at once! I'd spill the tea, and drop crumbs, and probably have the butler set on me."

"You will not! And if you did—can't you see?—it wouldn't matter! It just wouldn't matter!"

"Honestly? Claire dear, do you know why I came on this trip? In Schoenstrom, I heard you say you were going to Seattle. That moment, I decided I would, too, and get acquainted with you, if murder would do it. But, oh, I'm clumsy."

"You've seen me clumsy, in driving. You taught me to get over it. Perhaps I can teach you some things. And we'll study—together—evenings! I'm a thoroughly ignorant parasite woman. Make me become real! A real woman!"

"Dear—dear——"

Mr. Boltwood loomed on them. "The train 's coming, at last. We'll have a decent sleep for once, at the Gilsons'. I've wired them to meet us." He departed.

"Terribly glad your father keeps coming down on

us, because it scares me so I get desperate," said Milt. " Golly, I think I can hear the train. I, uh, Claire, Claire dear——"

" Milt, are you proposing to me? Please hurry, because that is the train. Isn't it absurd—some day you'll have to propose all over again formally, for the benefit of people like father, when you and I already know we're partners! We've done things together, not just danced together! When you're an engineer, you'll call me, and I'll come a-running up to Alaska. And sometimes you'll come with me to Brooklyn— we'll be a couple of bombs—— There's the train. Oh, playmate, hurry with your engineering course! Hurry, hurry, hurry! Because when it's done, then—— Whither thou goest, there I go also! And you did bully me, you did, you did, and I like it, and—— Yes, father, the bags are right here. Telephone me, minute you reach Seattle, dear, and we'll have a private lesson in balancing tea-cups—— Yes, father, I have the tickets. So glad, dear, the trip smashed up like this—shocked me into reality—made me realize I've been with you every hour since I dismissed you, back in Dakota, and you looked at me, big hurt eyes, like a child, and—— Yes, father, Pullman's at the back. Yes, I'm coming! "

" W-wait! D-did you know I was going to propose? "

" Yes. Ever since the Yellowstone. Been trying to

think of a nice way to refuse you. But there isn't
any. You're like Pinky—can't get rid of you—
have t' adopt you. Besides, I've found out——"

"You love me?"

"I don't know! How can I tell? But I do like
to drive with my head on your shoulder and——
Yesssss, father, coming!"

CHAPTER XXIV

HER OWN PEOPLE

M R. HENRY B. BOLTWOOD was decorously asleep in a chair in the observation car, and Claire, on the wide back platform, sat unmoving, apparently devoted to agriculture and mountain scenery. But it might have been noted that her hand clenched one of the wooden supports of her camp-stool, and that her hunched back did not move.

When she had turned to follow her father into the train, Milt had caught her shoulders and kissed her.

For half an hour that kiss had remained, a perceptible warm pressure on her lips. And for half an hour she had felt the relief of gliding through the mountains without the strain of piloting, the comfort of having the unseen, mysterious engineer up ahead automatically drive for her. She had caroled to her father about nearing the Pacific. Her nervousness had expressed itself in jerky gaiety.

But when he had sneaked away for a nap, and Claire could no longer hide from herself by a veil of chatter the big decision she had made on the station platform, then she was lonely and frightened—and very anxious to undecide the decision. She could not think clearly. She could see Milt Daggett only as a

solemn young man in an inferior sweater, standing by
the track in a melancholy autumnal light, waving to
her as the train pulled out, disappearing in a dun
obscurity, less significant than the station, the reced-
ing ties, or the porter who was, in places known only
to his secretive self, concealing her baggage.

She could only mutter in growing panic, " I'm crazy.
In-sane! Pledging myself to this boy before I know
how he will turn out. Will he learn anything besides
engineering? I know it—I do want to stroke his
cheek and—his kiss frightened me, but—— Will I
hate him when I see him with nice people? Can I
introduce him to the Gilsons? Oh, I was mad; so
wrought up by that idiotic chase with Dlorus, and so
sure I was a romantic heroine and—— And I'm
simply an indecisive girl in a realistic muddle!"

Threatened by darkness and the sinister evening
chill of the mountains, with the train no longer cheerfully climbing the rocky ridge but rumbling and snorting in the defiles, and startling her with agitating forward leaps as though the brakes had let go, she could
not endure the bleak platform, and even less could she
endure sitting in the chair car, eyed by the smug
tourists—people as empty of her romance as they
were incapable of her sharp tragedy. She balanced
forward to the vestibule. She stood in that cold,
swaying, darkling place that was filled with the smell
of rubber and metal and grease and the thunderous

clash of steel on steel; she tried to look out into the
fleeing darkness; she tried to imagine that the train
was carrying her away from the pursuing enemy—
from her own weak self.

Her father came puffing and lip-pursing and jolly,
to take her to dinner. Mr. Boltwood had no tearing
meditations; he had a healthy interest in soup. But
he glanced at her, across the bright, sleek dining-table;
he seemed to study her; and suddenly Claire saw that
he was a very wise man. His look hinted, "You're
worried, my dear," but his voice ventured nothing
beyond comfortable drawling stories to which she had
only, from the depth of her gloomy brooding, to nod
mechanically.

She got a great deal of satisfaction and
horror out of watching two traveling-men after
dinner. Milt had praised the race, and one of
the two traveling-men, a slender, clear-faced
youngster, was rather like Milt, despite plastered hair,
a watch-chain slung diagonally across his waistcoat,
maroon silk socks, and shoes of pearl buttons, gray
tops, and patent-leather bottoms. The other man was
a butter-ball. Both of them had harshly pompous
voices—the proudly unlettered voices of the smoking
compartment. The slender man was roaring:

" Yes, sir, he's got a great proposition there—believe me, he's got a great proposition—he's got one
great little factory there, take it from me. He can

turn out toothpicks to compete with Michigan. He's simply piling up the shekels—why say, he's got a house with eighteen rooms—every room done different."

Claire wondered whether Milt, when the sting and faith of romance were blunted, would engage in Great Propositions, and fight for the recognition of his— toothpicks. Would his creations be favorites in the best lunch rooms? Would he pile up shekels?

Then her fretting was lost in the excitement of approaching Seattle and their host—Claire's cousin, Eugene Gilson, an outrageously prosperous owner of shingle-mills. He came from an old Brooklyn Heights family. He had married Eva Gontz of Englewood. He liked music and wrote jokey little letters and knew the addresses of all the best New York shops. He was of Her Own People, and she was near now to the security of his friendship, the long journey done.

Lights thicker and thicker—a factory illuminated by arc-lamps,—the baggage—the porter—the eager trail of people in the aisle—climbing down to the platform—red caps—passing the puffing engine which had brought them in—the procession to the gate—faces behind a grill—Eugene Gilson and Eva waving— kisses, cries of "How was the trip?" and "Oh! Had won-der-ful drive!"—the huge station, and curious waiting passengers, Jap coolies in a gang, lumbermen in corks—the Gilsons' quiet car, and baggage stowed away by the chauffeur instead of by their own tired hands—streets strangely silent after the tumult of the train—Seattle and the sunset coast at last attained.

Claire had forgotten how many charming, most desirable things there were in the world. The Gilsons drove up Queen Anne Hill to a bay-fronting house on a breezy knob—a Georgian house of holly hedge, French windows, a terrace that suggested tea, and a great hall of mahogany and white enamel with the hint of roses somewhere, and a fire kindled in the paneled drawing-room to be seen beyond the hall. Warmth and softness and the Gilsons' confident affection wrapped her around; and in contented weariness she mounted to a bedroom of Bakst sketches, a four-poster, and a bedside table with a black and orange electric lamp and a collection of Arthur Symons' essays.

She sank by the bed, pitifully rubbed her cheek against the silk comforter that was primly awaiting her commands at the foot of the bed, and cried, " Oh, four-posters *are* necessary ! I can't give them up! I won't! They—— No one has a right to ask me." She mentally stamped her foot. " I simply won't live in a shack and take in washing. It isn't worth it."

A bath, faintly scented, in a built-in tub in her own marble bathroom. A preposterously and delightfully enormous Turkish towel. One of Eva Gilson's foamy negligées. Slow exquisite dressing—not the scratchy hopping over ingrown dirt, among ingrown smells, of a filthy small-hotel bedroom, but luxurious wandering over rugs velvety to her bare feet. A languid inspection of the frivolous colors and curves in the drawings by Bakst and George Plank and Helen Dryden. A glance at the richness of the toilet-table, at the velvet curtains that shut out the common world.

Expanding to the comfort as an orchid to cloying tropic airs, she drew on her sheerest chemise, her most frivolous silk stockings. In a dreaming enervated joy she saw how smooth were her arms and legs; she sleepily resented the redness of her wrists and the callouses of the texture of corduroy that scored her palms from holding the steering wheel.

Yes, she was glad that she had made the experiment—but gladder that she was safely in from the long dust-whitened way, back in her own world of beauty; and she couldn't imagine ever trying it again. To think of clumping out into that world of deliberate and brawling crudeness——

Of one Milt Daggett she didn't think at all.

Georgeously sleepy—and gorgeously certain that by and by she would go, not to a stingy hotel bed, with hound-dog ribs to cut into her tired back, but to a feathery softness of slumber—she wavered down to the drawing-room, and on the davenport, by the fire, with Victoria chocolates by her elbow, and pillows behind her shoulders, she gossiped of her adventure, and asked for news of friends and kin back East.

Eugene and Eva Gilson asked with pyrotechnic mer-
riness about the " funny people she must have met
along the road." With a subdued, hidden unhappiness, Claire found that she could not mention Milt—
that she was afraid her father would mention Milt—
to these people who took it for granted that all persons
who did not live in large houses and play good games
of bridge were either " queer " or " common "; who
believed that their West was desirable in proportion
as it became like the East; and that they, though
Westerners, were as superior to workmen with hard
hands as was Brooklyn Heights itself.

Claire tried to wriggle out from under the thought
of Milt while, with the Gilsons as the perfect audience,
she improvised on the theme of wandering. With
certain unintended exaggerations, and certain not
quite accurate groupings of events, she described the
farmers and cowpunchers, the incredible hotels and
garages. Indeed they had become incredible to her
own self. Obviously this silken girl couldn't possibly
take seriously a Dlorus Kloh—or a young garage man
who said " ain't."

Eva Gilson had been in Brooklyn within the month,
and in a passion of remembrance of home, Claire cried,
" Oh, do tell me about everybody."

" I had such a good time with Amy Dorrance," said
Mrs. Gilson. " Of course Amy is a little dull, but she's
such an awfully good sort and—— We did have the

jolliest party one afternoon. We went to lunch at the Ritz, and a matinée, and we saw such an interesting man—Gene is frightfully jealous when I rave about him—I'm sure he was a violinist—simply an exquisite thing he was—I wanted to kiss him. Gene will now say, ' Why didn't you ? ' "

And Gene said, "Well, why *didn't* you?" and Claire laughed, and her toes felt warm and pink and good, and she was perfectly happy, and she murmured, " It would be good to hear a decent violinist again. Oh! What had George Worlicht been doing, when you were home? "

" Don't you think Georgie is wonderful?" fluttered Mrs. Gilson. " He makes me rue my thirty-six sad years. I think I'll adopt him. You know, he almost won the tennis cup at Long Branch."

Georgie had a little mustache and an income, just enough income to support the little mustache, and he sang inoffensively, and was always winning tennis cups —almost—and he always said, at least once at every party, " The basis of *savoir faire* is knowing how to be rude to the right people." Fire-enamored and gliding into a perfumed haze of exquisite drowsiness, Claire saw Georgie as heroic and wise. But the firelight got into her eyes, and her lids wouldn't stay open, and in her ears was a soft humming as of a million bees in a distant meadow golden-spangled—and Gene was helping her upstairs; sleepiness submerged her like bathing in sweet waters; she fumbled at buttons and hooks and stays, let things lie where they fell—and of all that luxury nothing was more pleasant than the knowledge that she did not have to take precautions against the rats, mice, cockroaches, and all their obscene little brothers which—on some far-off fantastic voyaging when she had been young and foolish—she seemed to remember having found in her own room. Then she was sinking into a bed like a tide of rainbow-colored foam, sinking deep, deep, deep——

And it was morning, and she perceived that the purpose of morning light was to pick out surfaces of mahogany and orange velvet and glass, and that only an idiot would ever leave this place and go about begging dirty garage men to fill her car with stinking gasoline and oil.

The children were at breakfast—children surely not of the same species as the smeary-cheeked brats she had seen tumbling by roadsides along the way—sturdy Mason, with his cap of curls, and Virginia, with bobbed ash-blond hair prim about her delicate face. They curtsied, and in voices that actually had intonations they besought her, "Oh, Cousin Claire, would you pleasssssse tell us about drive-to-the-coast?"

After breakfast, she went out on the terrace for the View.

In Seattle, even millionaires, and the I. W. W., and

men with red garters on their exposed shirt-sleeves
who want to give you real estate, all talk about the
View. The View is to Seattle what the car-service,
the auditorium, the flivver-factory, or the price of coal
is to other cities. At parties in Seattle, you discuss the
question of whether the View of Lake Union or the
View of the Olympics is the better, and polite office-
managers say to their stenographers as they enter,
" How's your View this morning? " All real-estate
deeds include a patent on the View, and every native
son has it as his soundest belief that no one in Tacoma
gets a View of Mount Rainier.

Mrs. Gilson informed Claire that they had the finest
View in Seattle.

Below Claire was the harbor, with docks thrust far
out into the water, and steamers alive with smoke.
Mrs. Gilson said they were Blue Funnel Liners, loading for Vladivostok and Japan. The names, just the
names, shot into Claire's heart a wistful unexpressed
desire that was somehow vaguely connected with a
Milt Dagget who, back in the Middlewestern mud and
rain, had longed for purple mountains and cherry blos-
soms and the sea. But she cast out the wish, and lifted
her eyes to mountains across the sound—not purple
mountains, but sheer silver streaked with black, like
frozen surf on a desolate northern shore—the
Olympics, two-score miles away.

Up there, one could camp, with a boy in a deteriorated sweater singing as he watched the coffee——

Hastily she looked to the left, across the city, with
its bright new skyscrapers, its shining cornices and
masses of ranked windows, and the exclamation-point
of the " tallest building outside of New York "—far
livelier than her own rusty Brooklyn. Beyond the
city was a dun cloud, but as she stared, far up in the
cloud something crept out of the vapor, and hung there
like a dull full moon, aloof, majestic, overwhelming,
and she realized that she was beholding the peak of
Mount Rainier, with the city at its foot like white
quartz pebbles at the base of a tower.

A landing-stage for angels, she reflected.

It did seem larger than dressing-tables and velvet
hangings and scented baths.

But she dragged herself from the enticing path
of that thought, and sighed wretchedly, " Oh, yes, he
would appreciate Rainier, but how—how would he
manage a grape-fruit?   I mustn't be a fool!   I
mustn't!"   She saw that Mrs. Gilson was peeping at
her, and she made herself say adequate things about
the View before she fled inside—fled from her sput-
tering inquiring self.

In the afternoon they drove to Capitol Hill; they
dropped in at various pretty houses and met the sort
of people Claire knew back home.   Between people
they had Views; and the sensible Miss Boltwood,
making a philosophic discovery, announced to herself,

" After all, I've seen just as much from this limousine as I would from a bone-breaking Teal bug. Silly to make yourself miserable to see things. Oh yes, I will go wandering some more, but not like a hobo. But—— What can I say to him? Good heavens, he may be here any time now, with our car. Oh, why —why—why was I insane on that station platform?"

CHAPTER XXV

THE ABYSSINIAN PRINCE

SNOQUALMIE PASS lies among mountains prickly with rocks and burnt stumps, but the road is velvet, with broad saucer curves; and to Milt it was pure beauty, it was release from life, to soar up coaxing inclines and slip down easy grades in the powerful car. " No more Teals for me," he cried, in the ecstasy of handling an engine that slowed to a demure whisper, then, at a touch of the accelerator, floated up a rise, effortless, joyous, humming the booming song of the joy in speed. He suddenly hated the bucking tediousness of the Teal. The Gomez-Dep symbolized his own new life.

So he came to Lake Washington, and just across it was the city of his long dreams, the city of the Pacific —and of Claire. There was no ferry in sight, and he rounded the lake, struck a brick pavement, rolled through rough woods, suburban villas, and petty business streets, to a region of factories and mills, with the funnels of ships beyond.

And every minute he drove more slowly and became more uneasy.

The pavement—the miles of it; the ruthless lumbermills, with their thousands of workmen quite like himself; the agitation of realizing that every three minutes he was passing a settlement larger than Schoenstrom; the strangeness of ships and all the cynical ways of the sea—the whole scene depressed him as he perceived how little of the world he knew, and how big and contemptuous of Milt Daggetts that world must be.

"Huh!" he growled. "Quite some folks living here. Don't suppose they spend such a whale of a lot of time thinking about Milt Daggett and Bill McGolwey and Prof Jones. I guess most of these people wouldn't think Heinie Rauskukle's store was so gosh-awful big. I wasn't scared of Minneapolis—much —but there they didn't ring in mountains and an ocean on you. And I didn't have to go up on the hill and meet folks like Claire's relations, and figure out whether you shake hands catch-as-catch-can or Corinthian. Look at that sawmill chimney—isn't it nice of 'em to put the fly-screen over it so the flies won't get down into the flames. No, they haven't got much more than a million feet of lumber in that one pile. And here's a bum little furniture store—it wouldn't cost more 'n about ten times all I've got to buy one of those Morris chairs. Oh Gooooooosh, won't these houses ever stop? Say, that must be a jitney. The driver snickered at me. Will the whole town be onto me? Milt, you're a kind young fellow, and you know what's the matter with Heinie's differential, but they don't need you here. Quite a few folks to carry on the business. Gosh, look at that building ahead—nine stories!"

He had planned to stop at a hotel, to wash up, and to gallop to Claire. But—well—wouldn't it maybe be better to leave the car at a public garage, so the Boltwoods could get it when they wanted to? He'd better "just kind of look around before he tackled the watch-dog."

It was the public garage which finally crushed him. It was a garage of enameled brick and colored tiles, with a plate-glass-enclosed office in which worked young men clad as the angels. One of them wore a carnation, Milt noted.

"Huh! I'll write back and tell Ben Sittka that hereafter he's to wear his best Sunday-go-to-meeting clothes and a milk-weed blossom when he comes down to work at the Red Trail Garage!"

Milt drove up the brick incline into a room thousands of miles long, with millions of new and recently polished cars standing in lines as straight as a running-board. He begged of a high-nosed colored functionary—not in khaki overalls but in maroon livery—"Where'll I put this boat?"

The Abyssinian prince gave him a check, and in a tone of extreme lack of personal interest snapped, "Take it down the aisle to the elevator."

Milt had followed the natural lines of traffic into

the city; he had spoken to no one; the prince's snort was his welcome to Seattle.

Meekly he drove past the cars so ebon and silvery, so smug and strong, that they would have regarded a Teal bug as an insult. Another attendant waved him into the elevator, and Milt tried not to look surprised when the car started, not forward, but upward, as though it had turned into an aeroplane.

When these adventures were over, when he had had a shave and a shine, and washed his hands, and looked into a department-store window that contained ten billion yards of silk draped against polished satinwood, when he had felt unhappy over a movie theater large enough to contain ten times the population of Schoenstrom, and been cursed by a policeman for jaywalking, and had passed a hotel entirely full of diplomats and marble and caviare—then he could no longer put off telephoning to Claire, and humbly, in a booth meant for an umbrella-stand, he got the Eugene Gilson house, and to a female who said "Yes?" in a tone which made it mean "No!" he ventured, "May I speak to Miss Boltwood?"

Miss Boltwood, it seemed, was out.

He was not sorry. He was relieved. He ducked out of the telephone-booth with a sensation of escape.

Milt was in love with Claire; she was to him the purpose of life; he thought of her deeply and tenderly and longingly. All the way into Seattle he had brooded about her; remembered her every word and gesture; recalled the curve of her chin, and the fresh feeling of her hands. But Claire had suddenly become too big. In her were all these stores, these office buildings for clever lawyers and surgeons, these contemptuous trolley cars, these careless people in beautiful clothes. They were too much for him. Desperately he was pushing them back—back—fighting for breath. And she belonged with them.

He mailed the check for the stored car to her, with a note—written standing before a hacked wall-desk in a branch post-office—which said only, " Here's check for the boat. Did not know whether you would have room for it at house. Tried to get you on phone, phone again just as soon as rent room etc. hope having happy time, M.D."

He went out to the university. On the trolley he relaxed. But he did not exultantly feel that he had won to the Pacific; he could not regard Seattle now as a magic city, the Bagdad of modern caravans, with Alaska and the Orient on one hand, the forests to the north, and westward the spacious Inland Empire of the wheat. He saw it as a place where you had to work hard just to live; where busy policemen despised you because you didn't know which trolley to take; where it was incredibly hard to remember even the names of the unceasing streets; where the conductors said " Step lively! " and there was no room to whistle, no time to swap stories with a Bill McGolwey at an Old Home lunch-counter.

He found the university; he talked with the authorities about entering the engineering school; the Y. M. C. A. gave him a list of rooms; and, because it was cheap, he chose a cubbyhole in a flat over a candy store—a low room, which would probably keep out the rain, but had no other virtues. It had one bed, one table, one dissipated bureau, two straight bare chairs, and one venerable lithograph depicting a girl with ringlets shaking her irritating forefinger at a high-church kitten.

The landlady consented to his importing an oil-stove for cooking his meals. He bought the stove, with a box of oatmeal, a jar of bacon, and half a dozen eggs. He bought a plane and solid geometry, and an algebra. At dinner time he laid the algebra beside his plate of anemic bacon and leaking eggs. The eggs grew cold. He did not stir. He was reviewing his high-school algebra. He went down the pages, word by word, steadily, quickly, absolutely concentrated—as concentrated as he would recently have been in a new problem of disordered transmission. Not once did he stop to consider how glorious it would be to marry Claire—or how terrifying it would be to marry Miss Boltwood.

Three hours went by before he started up, bewildered, rubbed his eyes, picked at the chill bacon

and altogether disgusting eggs, and rambled out into
the street.

Again he risked the scorn of conductors and jitney
drivers.　He found Queen Anne Hill, found the resi-
dence of Mr. Eugene Gilson.　He sneaked about it,
slipped into the gate, prowled toward the house.
Flabby from the intensity of study, he longed for the
stimulus of Claire's smile.　But as he stared up at the
great squares of the clear windows, at the flare of
white columns in the porch-lights, that smile seemed
unreachable.　He felt like a rustic at court.　From the
shelter of the prickly holly hedge he watched the
house.　It was "some kind of a party?—or what
would folks like these call a party?"　Limousines
were arriving; he had a glimpse of silken ankles,
frothy underskirts; heard easy laughter; saw people
moving through a big blue and silver room; caught
a drifting tremor of music.

At last he saw Claire.　She was dancing with a
young man as decorative as "that confounded Saxton
fellow" he had met at Flathead Lake, but younger
than Saxton, a laughing young man, with curly black
hair.　For the first time in his life Milt wanted to kill.
He muttered, "Damn—damn—DAMN!" as he saw
the young man carelessly embracing Claire.

His fingers tingling, his whole body yearning till
every cell seemed a beating hammer, Milt longed just
once to slip his hand about Claire's waist like that.

He could feel the satin of her bodice and its warmth.

Then it seemed to him, as Claire again passed the window, that he did not know her at all. He had once talked to a girl who resembled her, but that was long ago. He could understand a Gomez-Dep and appreciate a brisk sports-suit, but this girl was of a world unintelligible to him. Her hair, in its dips and convolutions, was altogether a puzzle. "How did she ever fix it like that?" Her low evening dress— "what was it made of—some white stuff, but was it silk or muslin or what?" Her shoulders were startling in their bare powdery smoothness—"how dare that young pup dance with her?" And her face, that had seemed so jolly and friendly, floated past the window as pale and illusive as a wisp of fog. His longing for her passed into clumsy awe. He remembered, without resentment, that once on a hilltop in Dakota she had coldly forbidden him to follow her.

With all the pleasure of martyrdom—to make quite sure that he should realize how complete a fool he had been to intrude on Miss Boltwood—he studied the other guests. He gave them, perhaps, a glory they did not have. There were girls sleek as ivory. There was a lean stooped man, very distinguished. There was a bulky man in a dinner coat, with a semi-circle of mustache, and eyes that even at a distance seemed to give impatient orders. He would be a big banker, or a lumberman.

It was the easy friendliness of all of them that most made Milt feel like an outsider. If a servant had come out and ordered him away, he would have gone meekly . . . he fancied.

He straggled off, too solidly unhappy to think how unhappy he was. In his clammy room he picked up the algebra. For a quarter-hour he could not gather enough vigor to open it. In his lassitude, his elbows felt feeble, his fingers were ready to drop off. He slowly scratched the book open——

At one o'clock he was reading algebra, his face still and grim. But already it seemed less heartily brick-red.

He listlessly telephoned to Claire, in the morning.

"Hello? Oh! Miss Boltwood? This is Milt Daggett."

"Oh! Oh, how are you?"

"Why, why I'm—I've got settled. I can get into the engineering school all right."

"I'm glad."

"Uh, enjoying Seattle?"

"Oh! Oh yes. The mountains—— Do you like it?"

"Oh! Oh yes. Sea and all—— Great town."

"Uh, w-when are we going to see you? Daddy had to go East, left you his regards. W-when——?"

"Why—why I suppose you're awful—awfully busy, meeting people and all——"

"Yes, I am, rather, but——" Her hedging uncomfortable tone changed to a cry of distress. "Milt! I must see you. Come up at four this afternoon."

"Yes!"

He rushed to a small, hot tailor-shop. He panted "Press m' suit while I wait?" They gave him a pair of temporary trousers, an undesirable pair of trousers belonging to a short fat man with no taste in fabrics, and with these flapping about his lean legs, he sat behind a calico curtain, reading *The War Cry* and looking at a "fashion-plate" depicting nine gentlemen yachtsmen each nine feet tall, while the Jugoslav in charge unfeelingly sprinkled and ironed and patted his suit.

He spent ten minutes in blacking his shoes, in his room—and twenty minutes in getting the blacking off his fingers.

He was walking through the gate in the Gilson hedge at one minute to four.

But he had reached Queen Anne Hill at three. For an hour he had walked the crest road, staring at the steamers below, alternately gripping his hands with desire of Claire, and timorously finally deciding that he wouldn't go to her house—wouldn't ever see her again.

He came into the hall tremblingly expecting some great thing, some rending scene, and she met him with a cool, " Oh, this is nice. Eva had some little white cakes made for us." He felt like a man who has asked for a drink of cold charged water and found it warm and flat.

" How—— Dandy house," he muttered, limply shaking her limp hand.

" Yes, isn't it a darling. They do themselves awfully well here. I'm afraid your bluff, plain, democratic Westerners are a fraud. I hear a lot more about ' society' here than I ever did in the East. The sets seem frightfully complicated." She was drifting into the drawing-room, to a tapestry stool, and Milt was awkwardly stalking a large wing chair, while she fidgeted:

" Everybody tells me about how one poor dear soul, a charming lady who used to take in washing or salt gold-mines or something, and she came here a little while ago with billions and billions of dollars, and tried to buy her way in by shopping for all the charities in town, and apparently she's just as out of it here as she would be in London. You and I aren't exclusive like that, are we ! "

Somehow——

Her " you and I " was too kindly, as though she was trying to put him at ease, as though she knew he couldn't possibly be at ease. With a horribly elaborate politeness, with a smile that felt hot on his twitching

cheeks, he murmured, "Oh no. No, we—— No, I
guess——"

If he knew what it was he guessed, he couldn't get
it out. While he was trying to find out what had become of all the things there were to say in the world,
a maid came in with an astonishing object—a small,
red, shelved table on wheels, laden with silver vessels,
and cake, and sandwiches that were amazingly small
and thin.

The maid was so starched that she creaked. She
glanced at Milt—— Claire didn't make him so
nervous that he thought of his clothes, but the maid
did. He was certain that she knew that he had blacked
his own shoes, knew how old were his clothes. He
was urging himself, "Must get new suit tomorrow—
ready-made—mustn't forget, now—be sure—get suit
tomorrow." He wanted to apologize to the maid for
existing. . . . He wouldn't dare to fall in love with
the maid. . . . And he'd kill the man who said he
could be fool enough to fall in love with Miss Boltwood.

He sipped his tea, and dropped sandwich crumbs,
and ached, and panted, and peeped at the crushing
quantities of pictures and sconces and tables and
chairs in the room, and wondered what they did with
all of them, while Claire chattered:

"Yes, we weren't exclusive out on the road. Didn't
we meet funny people though! Oh, somehow that

'funny people' sounds familiar. But—— What fun
that morning was at—Pellago, was it? Heavens, I'm
forgetting those beastly little towns already—that
place where we hazed the poor landlady who over-
charged me."

"Yes." He was thinking of how much Claire
would forget, now. "Yes. We certainly fixed her,
all right. Uh—did you get the storage check for your
car?"

"Oh yes, thank you. So nice of you to bother
with it."

"Oh, nothing at all, nothing—— Nothing at all.
Uh—— Do you like Seattle?"

"Oh yes. Such views—the mountains—— Do you
like it?"

"Oh yes. Always wanted to see the sea."

"Yes, and—— Such a well-built town."

"Yes, and—— They must do a lot of business
here."

"Yes, they—— Oh yes, I do like Seat——"

He had darted from his chair, brushed by the tea-
wagon, ignoring its rattle and the perilous tipping of
cups. He put his hand on her shoulder, snorted,
"Look here. We're both sparring for time. Stop
it. It's—it's all right, Claire. I want you to like
me, but I'm not—I'm not like that woman you were
telling about that's trying to butt in. I know, Lord I
know so well what you're thinking! You're thinking

I'm not up to the people you've been seeing last couple of days—not up to 'em yet, anyway. Well—— We'll be good friends."

Fearless, now, his awe gone in tenderness, he lifted her chin, looked straight into her eyes, smiled. But his courage was slipping. He wanted to run and hide.

He turned abruptly, grumbling, " Well, better get back to work now, I guess."

Her cry was hungry: " Oh, please don't go." She was beside him, shyly picking at his sleeve. " I know what you mean. I like you for being so understanding. But—— I do like you. You were the perfect companion. Let's—— Oh, let's have a walk—and try to laugh again."

He definitely did not want to stay. At this moment he did not love her. He regarded her as an estimable young woman who, for a person so idiotically reared, had really shown a good deal of pluck out on the road —where he wanted to be. He stood in the hall disliking his old cap while she ran up to put on a top coat.

Mute, casual, they tramped out of the house together, and down the hill to a region of shabby old brown houses like blisters on the hillside. They had little to say, and that little was a polite reminiscence of incidents in which neither was interested.

When they came back to the Gilson hedge, he

stopped at the gate, with terrific respectableness removed his cap.

"Good night," she said cheerily. "Call me up soon again."

He did not answer "Good night." He said "Goodby"; and he meant it to be his last farewell. He caught her hand, hastily dropped it, fled down the hill.

He was, he told himself, going to leave Seattle that evening.

That, doubtless, is the reason why he ran to a trolley, to get to a department-store before it closed; and why, precipitating himself upon a startled clerk, he purchased a new suit of chaste blue serge, a new pair of tan boots (curiously like some he had seen on the university campus that morning) and a new hat so gray and conservative and felty that it might have been worn by Woodrow Wilson.

He spent the evening in reading algebra and geometry, and in telling himself that he was beautifully not thinking about Claire.

In the midst of it, he caught himself at it, and laughed.

"What you're doing, my friend, is pretending you don't like Claire, so that you can hide from your fool self the fact that you're going to sneak back to see her the first chance you get—first time the watch-dog is out. Seriously now, son, Claire is impossible for you. No can do. Now that you've been chump enough to leave home—— Oh Lord, I wish I hadn't promised to take this room for all winter. Wish I hadn't matriculated at the U. But I'm here now, and I'll stick it out. I'll stay here one year anyway, and go back home. Oh! And to—— By Golly! She liked me!"

He was thinking of the wild-rose teacher to whom he had given a lift back in Dakota. He was remembering her daintiness, her admiration.

"Now there's somebody who'd make me keep climbing, but wouldn't think I was a poor hick. If I were to drive back next spring, I could find her——"

CHAPTER XXVI

A CLASS IN ENGINEERING AND OMELETS

THE one thing of which Milt Daggett was certain was that now he had managed to crawl into the engineering school, he must get his degree in mechanical engineering. He was older than most of his classmates. He must hurry. He must do four years' work in two.

There has never been a Freshman, not the most goggle-eyed and earnest of them, who has seen less of classmates, thought less about "outside activities," more grimly centered the universe about his work.

Milt had sold his garage, by mail, to Ben Sittka and Heinie Rauskukle. He had enough money to get through two years, with economy. His life was as simple and dull as it had been in Schoenstrom. He studied while he cooked his scrappy meals; he pinned mathematical formulæ and mechanical diagrams on the wall, and pored over them while he was dressing —or while he was trying to break in the new shoes, which were beautiful, squeaky, and confoundedly tight.

He was taking French and English and "composition-writing" in addition to engineering, and he made out a schedule of life as humorlessly as a girl grind who intends to be a Latin teacher. When he was not at work, or furiously running and yanking chest-weights in the gymnasium, he was attending concerts, lectures.

Studying the life about him, he had discovered that the best way to save time was to avoid the lazy friend-ships of college; the pipe-smoking, yawning, com-fortable, rather heavy, altogether pleasant wondering about " what'll we do next? " which occupies at least four hours a day for the average man in college. He would have liked it, as he had liked long talks about nothing with Bill McGolwey at the Old Home Lunch. But he couldn't afford it. He had to be ready to——

That was the point at which his reflections always came up with a jolt. He was quite clear about the method of getting ready, but he hadn't the slightest idea of what he was getting ready for. The moment he had redecided to marry Claire, he saw that his only possible future would be celibate machinery-installing in Alaska; and the moment he was content with the prospect of an engineer's camp in Alaskan wilds, his thoughts went crazily fluttering after Claire.

Despite his aloofness, Milt was not unpopular in his class. The engineers had few of them the interest in dances, athletics, college journalism, which dis-tinguished the men in the academic course. They were older, and more conscious of a living to earn. And Milt's cheerful, " How's the boy? " his manner of waving his hand—as though to a good customer leaving the Red Trail Garage with the generator at last tamed—indicated that he was a "good fellow."

One group of collegians Milt did seek. It is true that he had been genuine in scorning social climbers. But it is also true that the men whom he sought to know were the university smart set. Their satisfaction in his allegiance would have been lessened, however, had they known how little he cared for what they thought of him, and with what cruel directness he was using them as models for the one purpose of pleasing Miss Claire Boltwood.

The American state universities admit, in a pleased way, that though Yale and Harvard and Princeton may be snobbish, the state universities are the refuge of a myth called "college democracy." But there is no university near a considerable city into which the inheritors of the wealth of that city do not carry all the local social distinctions. Their family rank, their place in the unwritten peerage, determines to which fraternity they shall be elected, and the fraternity determines with whom—men and girls—they shall be intimate. The sons and daughters of Seattle and Tacoma, the scions of old families running in an unbroken line clear back to 1880, were amiable to poor outsiders from the Yakima valley and the new claims of Idaho, but they did not often invite them to their homes on the two hills and the Boulevard.

Yet it was these plutocrats whom Milt followed; they whose boots and table manners, cigarettes and lack of interest in theology, he studied. He met them in his English class. He remarked " Hello, Smith," and " Mornin', Jones," as though he liked them but didn't care a hang whether they liked him. And by and by he drifted into their fraternity dwelling-house, with a question about the next day's assignment, and met their friends. He sat pipe-smoking, silent, cheerful, and they seemed to accept him. Whenever one of them felt that Milt was intruding, and asked impertinent questions in the manner of a Pullman porter at a Darktown ball, Milt had a peculiar level look which had been known to generate courtesy even in the offspring of a million dollars. They found that he knew more about motor-cars than any of them, and as motor-cars were among their greater gods, they considered him wise. He was incomparably simple and unpretentious; they found his presence comfortable.

But there is a question as to what they would have thought had they known that, lying awake in the morning, Milt unsmilingly repeated:

" Hair always straight down at the back. Never rounded. Nix on clippers over the ears.

" Matisse is a popular nut artist. Fashionable for the swells to laugh at him, and the fellows on the college papers to rave about him.

"Blinx and Severan the swellest—the smartest haberdashery in the city.

"The one way to get in Dutch is to mention labor leaders.

"Never say 'Pleased to meet you.' Just look about halfway between bored and tol'able and say, 'How do you do?'"

All these first three weeks of his life in Seattle, he had seen Claire only on his first call. Twice he had telephoned to her. On one of these high occasions she had invited him to accompany the family to the theater—which meant to the movies—and he had wretchedly refused; the other time she had said that she might stay in Seattle all winter, and she might go any day, and they "must be sure to have that good long walk"; and he had said "oh yes," ten or twelve unhappy times, and had felt very empty as he hung up the receiver.

Then she wrote to invite him to late Sunday breakfast at the Gilsons'—they made a function of it, and called it bruncheon. The hour was given as ten-thirty; most people came at noon; but Milt arrived at ten-thirty-one, and found only a sleepy butler in sight.

He waited in the drawing-room for five minutes, feeling like a bill-collector. Into the room vaulted a medium-sized, medium-looking, amiable man, Eugene

Gilson, babbling, "Oh, I say, so sorry to keep you waiting, Mr. Daggett. Rotten shame, do come have a bun or something, frightfully informal these bruncheons, play auction?"

"Zallright—no," said Milt.

The host profusely led him to a dining-room where —in English fashion, or something like English fashion, or anyway a close approximation to the fictional pictures of English fashion—kidneys and sausages and omelets waited in dishes on the sideboard. Mr. Gilson poured coffee, and chanted:

"Do try the kidneys. They're usually very fair. Miss Boltwood tells me that you were very good to her on the trip. Must have been jolly trip. You going to be in town some time, oh yes, Claire said you were in the university, engineering, wasn't it? have you ever seen our lumber mills, do drop around some—— Try the omelet before the beastly thing gets cold, do you mind kicking that button, we'll have some more omelet in—any time at the mill and I'll be glad to have some one show you through, how did you find the roads along the Red Trail?"

"Why, pretty fair," said Milt.

Into the room precipitated Mrs. Gilson, in a smile, a super-sweater, and a sports skirt that would have been soiled by any variety of sport more violent than pinochle, and she was wailing as she came:

"We're disgraced, Gene, is this Mr. Daggett? how do you do, so good of you to come, do try the kidneys, they're usually quite decent, are the omelets warm, you might ring for some more, Gene, for heaven's sake give me some coffee, Miss Boltwood will be right down, Mr. Daggett, she told us how fortunate they were that they met you on the road, did you like the trip, how were the roads?"

"Why, they were pretty good," said Milt.

Claire arrived, fresh and serene in white taffeta, and she cried prettily, "I ought to have known that you'd be prompt even if no one else in the world is, so glad you came, have you tried the kidneys, and do have an—oh, I see you have tried the omelets, how goes the work at the university?"

"Why, fine," said Milt.

He ate stolidly, and looked pleased, and sneaked in a glance at his new (and still tight and still squeaky) tan boots to make sure that they were as well polished as they had seemed at home.

From nowhere appeared a bustling weighty woman, purring, "Hello, hello, hello, is it possible that you're all up—— Mr. Daggett. Yes, do lead me to the kidneys."

And a man with the gray hair of a grandfather and the giggle of a cash-girl bounced in clamoring, "Mornin'—expected to have bruncheon alone—do we have some bridge? Oh, good morning, Mr. Daggett, how do you like Seattle? Oh, thanks so much, yes, just two."

Then Milt ceased to keep track of the conversation, which bubbled over the omelets, and stewed over the kidneys, and foamed about the coffee, and clashed above a hastily erected bridge table, and altogether sounded curiously like four cars with four quite different things the matter with them all being tried out at once in a small garage. People flocked in, and nodded as though they knew one another too well to worry about it. They bowed to him charmingly, and instantly forgot him for the kidneys and sausages. He sat looking respectable and feeling lonely, by a cup of coffee, till Claire—dropping the highly unreal smile with which she had been listening to the elderly beau's account of a fishing-trip he hadn't quite got around to taking—slipped into a chair beside him and begged, " Are they looking out for you, Milt? "

" Oh yes, thank you."

" You haven't been to see me."

" Oh no, but—— Working so darn hard."

" What a strikingly original reason! But have you really? "

" Honest."

Suddenly he wanted—eternal man, forever playing confidential small boy to the beloved—to tell her about his classes and acquaintances; to get pity for his bare room and his home-cooking. But round them blared the brazen interest in kidneys, and as Claire glanced up with much brightness at another arrival, Milt lost momentum, and found that there was absolutely nothing in the world he could say to her.

He made a grateful farewell to the omelets and kidneys, and escaped.

He walked many miles that day, trying to remember how Claire looked.

CHAPTER XXVII

THE VICIOUSNESS OF NICE THINGS

"WHAT did you think of my nice Daggett boy?" Claire demanded of Eva Gilson, the moment bruncheon was over.

"Which one was—— Oh, the boy you met on the road? Why, really, I didn't notice him particularly. I'd rather fancied from the way you referred to him that he was awfully jolly and forceful, but rather crude. But I didn't notice him at all. He seemed perfectly well-bred, but slightly heavy."

"No, he isn't that—— He—— Why did you lead spades?" reflected Claire.

They were in the drawing-room, resting after the tact and tumult of the bruncheon. Claire had been here long enough now for the Gilsons to forget her comfortably, and be affectionate and quarrelsome and natural, and to admit by their worrying that even in their exalted social position there were things to fuss about.

"I do think we ought to have invited Belle Torrens," fretted Mrs. Gilson. "We've simply got to have her here soon."

Mr. Gilson speculated intensely, "But she's the dullest soul on earth, and her husband spends all his spare time in trying to think up ways of doing me dirt in business. Oh, by the way, did you get the water tap in the blue room fixed? It's dripping all the time."

"No, I forgot it."

"Well, I *do* wish you'd have it attended to. It simply drips all the time."

"I know. I intended to 'phone the plumber—— Can't you 'phone him tomorrow, from the office?"

"No, I haven't time to bother with it. But I do wish you would. It keeps on dripping——"

"I know, it doesn't seem to stop. Well, you remind me of it in the morning."

"I'm afraid I'll forget. You better make a note of it. If it keeps on dripping that way, it's likely to injure something. And I do wish you'd tell the Jap not to put so much parsley in the omelet. And I say, how would an omelet be with a butter sauce over it?"

"Oh, no, I don't think so. An omelet ought to be nice and dry. Butter makes it so greasy—besides, with the price of butter——"

"But there's a richness to butter—— You'd better make a note about the tap dripping in the blue room right now, before you forget it. Oh! Why in heaven's name did we have Johnny Martin here? He's dull as ditchwater——"

"I know, but—— It is nice to go out to his place on the Point. Oh, Gene, I do wish you'd try and

remember not to talk about your business so much.
You and Mr. Martin were talking about the price
of lumber for at least half an hour——"

"Nothing of the kind. We scarcely mentioned it.
Oh! What car are you going to use this afternoon?
If we get out to the Barnetts', I thought we might use
the limousine—— Or no, you'll probably go out before I do, I have to read over some specifications, and
I promised to give Will a lift, couldn't you take the
Loco, maybe you might drive yourself, no, I forgot,
the clutch is slipping a little, well, you might drive
out and send the car back for me—still, there wouldn't
hardly be time——"

Listening to them as to a play, Claire suddenly de-
sired to scream, "Oh, for heaven's sake quit fussing!
I'm going up and drown myself in the blue-room tap!
What does it matter! Walk! Take a surface car!
Don't fuss so!"

Her wrath came from her feeling of guilt. Yes,
Milt had been commonplace. Had she done this to
him? Had she turned his cheerful ignorances into a
careful stupor? And she felt stuffy and choking and
overpacked with food. She wanted to be out on the
road, clear-headed, forcing her way through, an independent human being—with Milt not too far behind.

Mrs. Gilson was droning, "I do think Mattie Vin-
cent is so nice."

"Rather dull I'd call her," yawned Mr. Gilson.

Mattie was the seventh of their recent guests whom he had called dull by now.

"Not at all—oh, of course she doesn't dance on tables and quote Maeterlinck, but she does have an instinct for the niceties and the proprieties—her little house is so sweet—everything just exactly right—it may be only a single rose, but always chosen so carefully to melt into the background; and such adorable china—I simply die of envy every time I see her Lowestoft plates. And such a quiet way of reproving any bad taste—the time that crank university professor was out there, and spoke of the radical labor movement, and Mattie just smiled at him and said, 'If you don't mind, let's not drag filthy lumberjacks into the drawing-room—they'd hate it just as much as we would, don't you think, perhaps?'"

"Oh, *damn* nice china! Oh, let's hang all spinsters who are brightly reproving," Claire was silently raging. "And particularly and earnestly confound all nicety and discretion of living."

She tried to break the spell of the Gilsons' fussing. She false-heartedly fawned upon Mr. Gilson, and inquired:

"Is there anything very exciting going on at the mills, Gene?"

"Exciting?" asked Mr. Gilson incredulously. "Why, how do you mean?"

"Don't you find business exciting? Why do you do it then?"

"Oh, welllllll—— Of course—— Oh, yes, exciting in a way. Well—— Well, we've had a jolly interesting time making staves for candy pails—promises to be wonderfully profitable. We have a new way of cutting them. But you wouldn't be interested in the machinery."

"Of course not. You don't bore Eva with your horrid, headachy business-problems, do you?" Claire cooed, with low cunning.

"Indeed no. Don't think a chap ought to inflict his business on his wife. The home should be a place of peace."

"Yes," said Claire.

But she wasn't thinking "Yes." She was thinking, "Milt, what worries me now isn't how I can risk letting the 'nice people' meet you. It's how I can ever waste you on the 'nice people.' Oh, I'm spoiled for cut-glass-and-velvet afternoons. Eternal spiritual agony over blue-room taps is too high a price even for four-poster beds. I want to be driving! hiking! living!"

That afternoon, after having agreed that Mr. Johnny Martin was a bore, Mr. and Mrs. Gilson decided to run out to the house of Mr. Johnny Martin. They bore along the lifeless Claire.

Mr. Martin was an unentertaining bachelor who

entertained. There were a dozen supercilious young married people at his bayside cottage when the Gilsons arrived. Among them were two eyebrow-arching young matrons whom Claire had not met—Mrs. Corey and Mrs. Betz.

"We've all heard of you, Miss Boltwood," said Mrs. Betz. "You come from the East, don't you?"

"Yes," fluttered Claire, trying to be cordial.

Mrs. Corey and Mrs. Betz looked at each other in a motionless wink, and Mrs. Corey prodded:

"From New York?"

"No. Brooklyn." Claire tried not to make it too short.

"Oh." The tacit wink was repeated. Mrs. Corey said brightly—much too brightly—"I was born in New York. I wonder if you know the Dudenants?"

Now Claire knew the Dudenants. She had danced with that young ass Don Dudenant a dozen times. But the devil did enter into her and possess her, and, to Eva Gilson's horror, Claire said stupidly, "No-o, but I think I've heard of them."

The condemning wink was repeated.

"I hear you've been doing such interesting things—motoring and adventuring—you must have met some terrible people along the way," fished Mrs. Betz.

"Yes, everybody does seem to feel that way. But I'm afraid I found them terribly nice," flared Claire.

"I always say that common people can be most

agreeable," Mrs. Corey patronized. Before Claire could kill her—there wasn't any homicidal weapon in sight except a silver tea-strainer—Mrs. Corey had pirouetted on, " Though I do think that we're much too kind to workmen and all—the labor situation is getting to be abominable here in the West, and upon my word, to keep a maid nowadays, you have to treat her as though she were a countess."

" Why shouldn't maids be like countesses? They're much more important," said Claire sweetly.

It cannot be stated that Claire had spent any large part of her time in reading Karl Marx, leading syndicalist demonstrations, or hemming red internationalist flags, but at this instant she was a complete revolutionist. She could have executed Mrs. Corey and pretty Mrs. Betz with zeal; she disliked the entire bourgeoisie; she looked around for a Jap boy to call " comrade " and she again thought about the possibilities of the tea-strainer for use in assassination. She stolidly wore through the combined and exclamatory explanations of Mrs. Corey, Mrs. Betz, Mrs. Gilson, and Mr. Johnny Martin about the inherent viciousness of all maids, and when the storm was over, she said in a manner of honey and syrup:

" You were speaking of the Dudenants, weren't you, Mrs. Corey? I do remember them now. Poor Don Dudenant, isn't it a pity he's such a fool? His father is really a very decent old bore."

"I," observed Mrs. Corey, in prim horror, "regard the Dudenants as extremely delightful people. I fancy we must be thinking of different families. I mean the Manhattan Dudenants, not the Brooklyn family."

"Oh, yes, I meant the Manhattan family, too—the one that made its fortune selling shoddy woolens in the Civil War," caressed Claire.

Right there, her welcome by Mrs. Corey and Mrs. Betz ceased; and without any of the unhappiness which the thought would have caused her three months before, Claire reflected, "How they hate me!"

The Gilsons had a number of thoughts upon the subject of tact to express to Claire on the way home. But she, who had always smiled, who had been the obedient guest, shrugged and snapped, "They're idiots, those young women. They're impertinent shopgirls in good frocks. I like your Seattle. It's a glorious city. And I love so many of the fine, simple, real people I've met here. I admire your progress. I do know how miraculously you've changed it from a mining camp. But for heaven's sake don't forget the good common hardiness of the miners. Somehow, London social distinctions seem ludicrous in American cities that twenty years ago didn't have much but board sidewalks and saloons. I don't care whether it's Seattle or Minneapolis or Omaha or Denver, I refuse to worry about the Duchess of Corey and the Baroness Betz and all the other wonderful imitations of gilt. When a pair of finishing-school flappers like Betz and Corey try to impress me with their superiority to workmen, and their extreme aristocracy and Easternness, they make me tired. I *am* the East!"

She had made peace with the Gilsons by night; she had been reasonably repentant about not playing the game of her hosts; but inside her eager heart she snuggled a warm thought. She remembered how gaily she had once promised, out on the road, to come to Milt's room and cook for him. She thought of it with homesick desire. His room probably wasn't particularly decorative, and she doubted his having an electric range, but it would be fun to fry eggs again, to see him fumbling with the dish-washing, to chatter and plan golden futures, and not worry about the opinions of Mrs. Corey and Mrs. Betz.

The next afternoon the limousine was not busy and she borrowed it, with the handsome Greek chauffeur.

She gave him an address not far from the university.

He complained, " Pardon me, miss, but I think you have the wrong number. That block is a low quarter."

" Probably! But that's the right number!"

He raised his Athenian eyebrows, and she realized what a mistake she had made in not bringing the lethal tea-strainer along. When they had stopped in front of a cheap candy-store, he opened the door of the car with such frigid reserve that she thought seriously about slapping him.

She climbed the stingy, flapping stairs, and knocked at the first door in the upper hall. It was opened by a large apron, to which a sleepy woman was an unimportant attachment, and out of the mass of apron and woman came a yawning, " Mr. Daggett's room is down the hall on the right."

Claire knocked at a door which had at various epochs been blue, yellow, and pink, and now was all three. No answer. She tried the knob, went in.

She could not tell whether it was the barrenness of the room, or Milt's carefulness, that caught her. The uncarpeted boards of the floor were well swept. He had only one plate, one spoon, but they were scoured, and put away on newspaper-covered shelves in a cupboard made of a soap-box. Behind a calico curtain was his new suit, dismayingly neat on its hanger. On the edge of the iron sink primly washed and spread out to dry, was a tattered old rag. At the sight of it, at the thought of Milt solemnly washing dishes, the tears began to creep to her eyes.

There was but one picture in the room—a half-tone of a girl, clipped from a magazine devoted to actresses. The name was cut off. As she wondered at it, Claire saw that the actress was very much like herself.

The only other ornament was a papier-mâché figure of a cat, a cat reminiscent of the Lady Vere de Vere.

Claire picked it up. On the bottom was the price-mark—three cents.

It was the price-mark that pierced her. She flung across the room, dropped on his creaky cot-bed, howled, "Oh, I've been a beast—a beast—a beast! All the pretty things—limousines and marble baths—thinking so much of them, and not wanting them for *him!* And he with so little, with just nothing—he that would appreciate jolly things so much—here in this den, and making it as tolerable as he can—and me half ashamed of him instead of fighting for him—— I belong with Corey and Betz. Oh, I'm so ashamed, so bitterly ashamed."

She patted his bed smooth with nervous eager fingers.

She scraped a pin-point of egg-yolk off a platter.

Before she had been home five minutes she had written a note asking him to tea for next day.

CHAPTER XXVIII

THE MORNING COAT OF MR. HUDSON B. RIGGS

MR. HUDSON B. RIGGS now enters the tale —somewhat tardily, and making a quick exit, all in a morning coat too tight about the shoulders, and a smile of festivity too tight about the lips. He looked as improbable as an undertaker's rubber-plant. Yet in his brief course he had a mighty effect upon the progress of civilization as exemplified in the social career of Mr. Milton Daggett.

Mr. Riggs had arrived at a golden position in Alaskan mining engineering by way of the farm, the section gang, the surveyor's chain, and prospecting; and his thick hands showed his evolution. His purpose in life was to please Mrs. Riggs, and he wasn't ever going to achieve his purpose in life. She wore spangles, and her corsets creaked, and she smiled nervously, and could tell in a glance quicker than the 1/100 kodak shutter whether or not a new acquaintance was "worth cultivating." She had made Mr. Riggs thoroughly safe and thoroughly unhappy in the pursuit of society. He stood about keeping from doing anything he might want to, and he was profusely polite to young cubs whom he longed to have in his office—so that he could get even with them.

What Mr. Riggs wanted to do, at the third large tea given by Mrs. Gilson for Miss Claire Boltwood, was to sneak out on the sun-porch and play over the new records on the phonograph; but the things he had heard from Mrs. Riggs the last time he'd done that had convinced him that it was not a wise method of escape. So he stood by the fireplace—safe on one side at least—and ate lettuce sandwiches, which he privately called " cow feed," and listened to a shining, largely feminine crowd rapidly uttering unintelligible epigrams from which he caught only the words, " Ripping hand—trained nurse—whipcord—really worth seeing—lost the ball near the second hole—most absurd person—new maid—thanks so much." He was hoping that some one would come around and let him be agreeable. He knew that he stood the ride home with Mrs. Riggs much better after he had been agreeable to people he didn't like.

What Mr. Riggs did not know was that a young man in uninteresting blue, who looked like a good tennis-player, was watching him. It wasn't because he detected a fellow soul in purgatory but because he always was obsequious outside of his office that Mr. Riggs bowed so profusely that he almost lost his teacup, when the young man in blue drifted to him and suggested, " I hear you're in the Alaskan mining-game, Mr. Riggs."

" Oh yes."

"Do you get up there much now?"

"No, not much."

"I hope to hit Alaska some day—I'm taking engineering at the U."

"Do you? Straight?" Mr. Riggs violently set his cup down on a table—Mrs. Riggs would later tell him that he'd put it down in the wrong place, but never mind. He leaned over Milt and snarled, "Offer me a cigarette. I don't know if they smoke here, and I dassn't be the first to try. Say, boy, Alaska—— I wish I was there now! Say, it beats all hell how good tea can taste in a tin cup, and how wishy-washy it is in china. Boy, I don't know anything about you, but you look all right, and when you get ready to go to Alaska, you come to me, and I'll see if I can't give you a chance to go up there. But don't ever come back!"

When the crowd began bubblingly to move toward the door, Milt prepared to move—and bubble—with them. Though Claire's note had sounded as though she was really a little lonely, at the tea she had said nothing to him except, "So glad you came. Do you know Dolly Ransome? Dolly, this is my nice Mr. Daggett. Take him and make him happy."

Dolly hadn't made him in the least happy. She had talked about tennis; she had with some detail described her remarkable luck in beating one Sally Saunders three sets. Now Milt was learning tennis.

He was at the present period giving two hours a week to tennis, two to dancing, two to bridge. But he preferred cleaning oil-wells to any of these toilsome accomplishments, and it must sadly be admitted that all the while he was making his face bright at Dolly, he was wondering what would happen if he interrupted Dolly's gurgling, galloping, giggling multitudinousness by shouting, "Oh, shut up!"

When it seemed safe to go, and he tried to look as though he too were oozing out to a Crane-Simplex, Claire slipped beside him, soft as a shadow, and whispered, "Please don't go. I want to talk to you. *Please!*" There was fluttering wistfulness in her voice, though instantly it was gone as she hastened to the door and was to be heard asserting that she did indeed love Seattle.

Milt looked out into the hall. He studied a console with a curious black and white vase containing a single peacock feather, and a gold mirror shimmering against a gray wall.

"Lovely stuff. I like that mirror. Like a slew in the evening. But it isn't worth being a slave for. I'm not going to be a Mr. Riggs. Poor devil, he's more of a servant than any of these maids. Certainly am sorry for that poor fish. He'll have a chance to take his coat off and sit down and smoke—when he's dead!"

The guests were gone; the Gilsons up-stairs. Claire

came running, seized Milt's sleeve, coaxed him to the davenport in the drawing-room—then sighed, and rubbed her forehead, and looked so tired that he could say nothing but, "Hope you haven't been overdoing."

"No, just—just talking too much."

He got himself to say, "Miss Ransome—the one that's nuts about tennis—she's darn nice."

"Is she?"

"Yes, she's—she's——   What do you hear from your father?"

"Oh, he's back at work."

"Trip do him good?"

"Oh, a lot."

"Did he——"

"Milt! Tell me about you. What are you doing? What are you studying? How do you live? Do you really cook your own meals? Do you begin to get your teeth into the engineering? Oh, do tell me everything. I want to know, so much!"

"There isn't a whole lot to tell. Mostly I'm getting back into math. Been out of touch with it. I find that I know more about motors than most of the fellows. That helps. And about living—oh, I keep conservative. Did you know I'd sold my garage?"

"Oh, I didn't, I didn't!"

He wondered why she said it with such stooping shame, but he went on mildly, "Well, I got a pretty good price, but of course I don't want to take any chances on running short of coin, so I'm not splurging much. And——" He looked at his nails, and whistled a bar or two, and turned his head away, and looked back with a shy, " And I'm learning to play bridge and tennis and stuff!"

"Oh, my dear!" It was a cry of pain. She beat her hands for a moment before she murmured, " When are we going to have our lessons in dancing—and in making an impression on sun-specks like Dolly Ransome?"

"I don't know," he parried. Then, looking at her honestly, he confessed, " I don't believe we're ever going to. Claire, I can't do it. I'm no good for this tea game. You know how clumsy I was. I spilled some tea, and I darn near tripped over some woman's dress and—— Oh, I'm not afraid of them. Now that I get a good close look at this bunch, they seem pretty much like other folks, except maybe that one old dame says ' cawn't.' But I can't do the manners stunt. I can't get myself to give enough thought to how you ought to hold a tea-cup."

"Oh, those things don't matter—they don't *matter!* Besides, everybody likes you—only you're so terribly cautious that you never let them see the force and courage and all that wonderful sweet dear goodness that's in you. And as for your manners—heaven knows I'm no P. G. Wodehouse valet. But I'll teach you all I know."

"Claire, I appreciate it a lot but—— I'm not so darn sure I want to learn. I'm getting scared. I watched that bird named Riggs here today. He's a regular fellow, or he was, but now he's simply lost in the shuffle. I don't want to be one of the million ghosts in a city. Seattle is bad enough—it's so big that I feel like a no-see-um in a Norway pine reserve. But New York would be a lot worse. I don't want to be a Mr. Riggs."

"Yes, but—I'm not a Mrs. Riggs!"

"What do you——"

He did not finish asking her what she meant. She was in his arms; she was whispering, "My heart is so lonely;" and the room was still. The low sun flooded the windows, swam in the mirror in the hall, but they did not heed, did not see its gliding glory.

Not till there was a sound of footsteps did she burst from his arms, spring to her reflection in the glass of a picture, and shamefacedly murmur to him over her shoulder, "My hair—it's a terrible giveaway!"

He had followed her; he stood with his arm circling her shoulder.

She begged, "No. Please no. I'm frightened. Let's—oh, let's have a walk or something before you scamper home."

"Look! My dear! Let's run away, and explore the town, and not come back till late evening."

"Yes. Let's."

They walked from Queen Anne Hill through the city to the docks. There was nothing in their excited, childish, " Oh, see that! " and " There's a dandy car! " and " Ohhhhh, that's a Minnesota license—wonder who it is?" to confess that they had been so closely, so hungrily together.

They swung along a high walk overlooking the city wharf. They saw a steamer loading rails and food for the government railroad in Alaska. They exclaimed over a nest of little, tarry fishing-boats. They watched men working late to unload Alaska salmon.

They crossed the city to Jap Town and its writhing streets, its dark alleys and stairways lost up the hillsides. They smiled at black-eyed children, and found a Japanese restaurant, and tried to dine on raw fish and huge shrimps and roots soaked in a very fair grade of light-medium motor oil.

With Milt for guide, Claire discovered a Christianity that was not of candles and shifting lights and insinuating music, nor of carpets and large pews and sound oratory, but of hoboes blinking in rows, and girls in gospel bonnets, and little silver and crimson placards of Bible texts. They stopped on a corner to listen to a Pentecostal brother, to an I. W. W. speaker, to a magnificent negro who boomed in an operatic baritone that the Day of Judgment was coming on April 11, 1923, at three in the morning.

In the streets of Jap Town, in cheap motion-picture
theaters, in hotels for transient workmen, she found
life, running swift and eager and many-colored; and
it seemed to her that back in the house of four-posters
and walls of subdued gray, life was smothered in the
very best pink cotton-batting. Milt's delight in every
picturesque dark corner, and the colloquial eloquence
of the street-orators, stirred her. And when she saw
a shopgirl caress the hand of a slouching beau in
threadbare brown, her own hand slipped into Milt's
and clung there.

But they came shyly up to the Gilson hedge, and
when Milt chuckled, " Bully walk; let's do it again,"
she said only, "Oh, yes, I did like it. Very much."

He had abruptly dropped his beautiful new felt hat.
He was clutching her arms, demanding, " Can you
like me? Oh my God, Claire, I can't play at love.
I'm mad—I just live in you. You're my blood and
soul. Can I become—the kind of man you like?"

"My dear!" She was fiercely addressing not him
alone but the Betzes and Coreys and Gilsons and Jeff
Saxtons, " don't you forget for one moment that all
these people—here or Brooklyn either—that seem so
aloof and amused, are secretly just plain people with
enamel on, and you're to have the very best enamel,
if it's worth while. I'm not sure that it is——"

" You're going to kiss me! "

" No! Please no! I don't—I don't understand us,

even now. Can't we be just playmates a while yet?
But—I do like you!"

She fled. When she reached the hall she found her
eyelids wet.

It was the next afternoon——

Claire was curled on the embroidered linen counter-
pane of her bed, thinking about chocolates and Brooklyn and driving through Yellowstone Park and corn
fritters and satin petticoats versus *crêpe de chine* and
Mount Rainier and Milt and spiritualism and manicur-
ing, when Mrs. Gilson prowled into her room and demanded "Busy?" so casually that Claire was suspicious.

"No. Not very. Something up?"

"A nice party. Come down and meet an amusing
man from Alaska."

Claire took her time powdering her nose, and ambled down-stairs and into the drawing-room, to
find——

Jeff Saxton, Mr. Geoffrey Saxton, who is the height
of Brooklyn Heights, standing by the fireplace, smiling
at her.

CHAPTER XXIX

THE ENEMY LOVE

BUT at second glance—was it Jeff? This man was tanned to a thick even brown in which his eyes were startlingly white. His hands were burned red; there was a scar across one of them; and he was standing with them cockily at his hips, all unlike the sleekly, noisily quiet Jeff of Brooklyn. He was in corduroy trousers and belted corduroy jacket, with a khaki-colored flannel shirt.

But his tranquilly commanding smile was Jeff's, and his lean grace; and Jeff's familiar amused voice greeted her paralyzed amazement with:

"Hello, pard! Ain't I met you some place in Montana?"

"Well—where—in—the——"

"Just landed from Alaska. Had to run up there from California. How are you, little princess?"

His hand was out to her, then both hands, beseechingly, but she did not run to him, as she had at Flathead Lake. She stalked him cautiously, and shook hands—much too heartily. She sought cover in the wing-chair and—much too cordially—she invited:

"Tell me all about it."

He was watching her. Already his old pursuing

determination, his steady dignity, were beginning to frighten her. But he calmly dropped into a straight chair, and obliged:

"It's really been quite a lively journey. Didn't know I could like roughing-it so well. And it was real roughing-it, pretty much. Oh, not dangerous at all, but rather vigorous. I had to canoe up three hundred miles of a shallow river, with one Indian guide, making a portage every ten miles or so, and we got tipped over in the rapids now and then—the Big Chief almost got drowned once—and we camped at night in the original place where they invented mosquitoes—and one morning I shot a black bear just in time to keep him from eating my boots."

"Oh!" she sighed in admiration, and "Oh!" again, uneasily.

Nothing had been said about it; Jeff was the last person in the world to spoil his triumph by commenting on it; but both of them knew that they had violently changed places; that now it was she who was the limp indoor-dweller, and he who was the ruddy ranger; that as he had admired her at Flathead Lake, so now it was hers to admire, and his to be serenely heroic.

She was not far from the worshiping sub-deb in her sighing, "How *did* you get the scar?"

"That? Oh, nothing."

"Please tell me."

" Really and truly. Nothing at all. Just a drunken fellow with a knife, playing the fool. I didn't have to touch him—quite sure he could have given me a frightful beating and all that sort of thing. It was the Big Chief who got rid of him."

" He—cut you? With a kniiiiiiife? Ohhhhhhh!"

She ran to him, pityingly stroked the scar, looked down at him with filmy eyes. Then she tried to retreat, but he retained her hand, glanced up at her as though he knew her every thought. She felt weak. How could she escape him? " Please! " she begged flutteringly.

If he held her hand another moment, she trembled, she'd be on his lap, in his arms—lost. And he was holding it. He was——

Oh, he was too old for her. Yes, and too paternal. But still—— Life with Jeff would be protected, kindly, honorable.

Yet all the time she wanted, and stormily knew she wanted, to be fleeing to the boy Milt, her mate; to run away with him, hand in hand, discovering all the colored world, laughing at life, not afraid of losing dignity. In fear of Jeff's very kindliness and honor, she jerked her hand free. Then she tried to smile like a clever fencer.

As she retreated to her chair she stammered, " Did you—— Was Alaska interesting? "

He did not let her go, this time. Easy, cat-like for

all his dry gravity, he sauntered after her, and with a fine high seriousness pleaded his case:

"Claire dear, those few weeks of fighting nature were a revelation to me. I'm going to have lots more of it. As it happens, they need me there. There's plenty of copper, but there's big transportation and employment problems that I seem better able to solve than the other chaps—though of course I'm an absolute muff when it comes to engineering problems. But I've had certain training and—I'm going to arrange things so that I get up there at least once a year. Next summer I'll make a much longer trip—see the mountains—oh, glorious mountains—and funny half-Russian towns, and have some fishing—— Wandering. The really big thing. Even finer than your superb plucky trip through——"

"Wasn't plucky! I'm a cry baby," she said, like a bad, contradictory little girl.

He didn't argue it. He smiled and said "Tut!" and placidly catalogued her with, "You're the pluckiest girl I've ever seen, and it's all the more amazing because you're not a motion-picture Tomboy, but essentially exquisite——"

"I'm a grub."

"Very well, then. You're a grub. So am I. And I like it. And when I make the big Alaskan trip next year I want you to go along! Claire! Haven't you any idea how terribly close to me the thought of you has been these weeks? You've guided me through the wilderness——"

"It's—— I'm glad." She sprang up, beseeching, "Jeff dear, you're going to stay for tea? I must run up and powder my nose."

"Not until you say you're glad to see me. Child dear, we've been ambling along and—— No. You aren't a child any more. You're a woman. And if I've never been quite a man, but just a dusty office-machine, that's gone now. I've got the wind of the wilderness in my lungs. Man and woman! My woman! That's all I'm going to say now, but—— Oh my God, Claire, I do need you so!"

He drew her head to his shoulder, and for an instant she rested there. But as she looked up, she saw coming age in the granulated skin of his throat.

"He needs me—but he'd boss me. I'd be the cunning child-wife, even at fifty," she worried, and "Hang him, it's like his superiority to beat poor Milt even at adventuring—and to be such a confounded Modest Christian Gentleman about it!"

"You'd—you're so dreadfully managing," she sighed aloud.

For the first time in all their acquaintanceship, Jeff's pride broke, and he held her away from him, while his lips were pathetic, and he mourned, "Why do you always try to hurt me?"

"Oh, my dear, I don't."

"Is it because you resent the decent things I have managed to do?"

"I don't understand."

"If I have an idea for a party, you think I'm 'managing.' If I think things out deeply, you say I'm dull."

"Oh, you aren't. I didn't mean——"

"What are you? A real woman, or one of these flirts, that love to tease a man because he's foolish enough to be honestly in love?"

"I'm not—hon-estly I'm not, Jeff. It's—— You don't quite make me—— It's just that I'm not in love with you. I like you, and respect you terribly, but——"

"I'm going to make you love me." His clutching fingers hurt her arm, and somehow she was not angry, but stirred. "But I'm not going to try now. Forget the Alaskan caveman. Remember, I haven't even used the word 'love.' I've just chatted about fjords, or whatever they are, but one of these days—— No. I won't do it. I want to stay here in Seattle a few days, and take you on jolly picnics, but—— Would you rather I didn't even do that? I'm——" He dropped her arm, kneaded his forehead with the heel of his palm. "I can't stand being regarded as a bothersome puppy. I can't stand it! I can't!"

"Please stay, Jeff! We'll have some darling drives and things. We'll go up Rainier as far as we can."

He stayed.   He was anecdotal and amusing at tea, that afternoon.   Claire saw how the Gilsons, and two girls who dropped in, admired him.   That made her uneasy.   And when Mrs. Gilson begged him to leave his hotel and stay with them, he refused with a quick look at Claire that hurt her.

"He wants me to be free.   He's really so much more considerate than Milt.   And I hurt him.   Even his pride broke down.   And I've spoiled Milt's life by meddling.   And I've hurt the Gilsons' feelings.   And I'm not much of a comfort to father.   Oh, I'm absolutely no good," she agonized.

CHAPTER XXX

THE VIRTUOUS PLOTTERS

MR. GEOFFREY SAXTON, in Alaskan tan and New York evening clothes and Piccadilly poise, was talking to the Eugene Gilsons while Claire finished dressing for the theater.

Mrs. Gilson observed, " She's the dearest thing. We've become awfully fond of her. But I don't think she knows what she wants to do with life. She's rather at loose ends. Who is this Daggett boy —some university student—whom she seems to like? "

" Well, since you speak of him—— I hadn't meant to, unless you did. I want to be fair to him. What did she tell you about him? " Jeff asked confidentially.

" Nothing, except that he's a young engineer, and frightfully brave and all those uncomfortable virtues, and she met him in Yellowstone Park or somewhere, and he saved her from a bear—or was it a tramp? —from something unnecessary, at any rate."

" Eva, I don't want to be supercilious, but the truth is that this young Daggett is a rather dreadful person. He's been here at the house, hasn't he? How did he strike you? "

" Not at all. He's silent, and as dull as lukewarm tea, but perfectly inoffensive."

" Then he's cleverer than I thought! Daggett is anything but dull and inoffensive, and if he can play that estimable rôle——! It seems that he is the son of some common workman in the Middlewest; he isn't an engineer at all; he's really a chauffeur or a taxi-driver or something; and he ran into Claire and Henry B. on the road, and somehow insinuated himself into their graces—far from being silent and commonplace, he appears to have some strange kind of charm which," Jeff sighed, " I don't understand at all. I simply don't understand it!

" I met him in Montana with the most gorgeously atrocious person I've ever encountered—one Pinky Westlake, or some such a name—positively, a crook! He tried to get Boltwood and myself interested in the commonest kind of a mining swindle—hinted that we were to join him in cheating the public. And this Daggett was his partner—they actually traveled together. But I do want to be just. I'm not *sure* that Daggett was aware of his partner's dishonesty. That isn't what worries me about the lad. It's his utter impossibility. He's as crude as iron-ore. When he's being careful, he may manage to be inconspicuous, but give him the chance——

" Really, I'm not exaggerating when I say that at thirty-five he'll be dining in his shirt-sleeves, and sitting down to read the paper with his shoes off and feet up on the table. But Claire—you know what a dear Quixotic soul she is—she fancies that because this fellow repaired a puncture or something of the sort for her on the road, she's indebted to him, and the worse he is, the more she feels that she must help him. And affairs of that kind—— Oh, it's quite too horrible, but there have been cases, you know, where girls as splendid and fine and well-bred as Claire herself have been trapped into low marriages by their loyalty to cadging adventurers!"

"Oh!" groaned Mrs. Gilson; and "Good Lord!" lamented Mr. Gilson, delighted by the possibility of tragedy; and "Really, I'm not exaggerating," said Jeff enthusiastically.

"What are we going to do?" demanded Mrs. Gilson; while Mr. Gilson, being of a ready and inventive mind, exclaimed, "By Jove, you ought to kidnap her and marry her yourself, Jeff!"

"I'd like to. But I'm too old."

They beautifully assured him that he was a blithe young thing with milk teeth; and with a certain satisfaction Jeff suggested, "I tell you what we might do. Of course it's an ancient stunt, but it's good. I judge that Daggett hasn't been here at the house much. Why not have him here so often that Claire will awaken to his crudity, and get sick of him?"

"We'll do it," thrilled Mrs. Gilson. "We'll have him for everything from nine-course dinners with Grandmother Eaton's napkins on view, to milk and cold ham out of the ice-box. When Claire doesn't invite him, I will!"

CHAPTER XXXI

THE KITCHEN INTIMATE

MILT had become used to the Gilson drawing-room. He was no longer uncomfortable in the presence of its sleek fatness, though at first (not knowing that there were such resources as interior decorators), he had been convinced that, to have created the room, the Gilsons must have known everything in the world. Now he glanced familiarly at its white paneling, its sconces like silver candlesticks, the inevitable davenport inevitably backed by an amethyst-shaded piano lamp and a table crowded with silver boxes and picture-frames. He liked the winsomeness of light upon velvet and polished wood.

It was not the drawing-room but the kitchen that dismayed him.

In Schoenstrom he had known that there must somewhere be beautiful "parlors," but he had trusted in his experience of kitchens. Kitchens, according to his philosophy, were small smelly rooms of bare floors, and provided with one oilcloth-covered table, one stove (the front draft always broken and propped up with the lid-lifter), one cupboard with panes of tin pierced in rosettes, and one stack of dirty dishes.

But the Gilson kitchen had the efficiency of a

laboratory and the superciliousness of a hair-dresser's booth. With awe Milt beheld walls of white tiles, a cork floor, a gas-range large as a hotel-stove, a ceiling-high refrigerator of enamel and nickel, zinc-topped tables, and a case of utensils like a surgeon's knives. It frightened him; it made more hopelessly unapproachable than ever the Alexandrian luxury of the great Gilsons. . . . The Vanderbilts' kitchen must be like this. And maybe King George's.

He was viewing the kitchen upon the occasion of an intimate Sunday evening supper to which he had been yearningly invited by Mrs. Gilson. The maids were all out. The Gilsons and Claire, Milt and Jeff Saxton, shoutingly prepared their own supper. While Mrs. Gilson scrambled eggs and made coffee, the others set the table, and brought cold ham and a bowl of salad from the ice-box.

Milt had intended to be a silent but deft servitor. When he had heard that he was to come to supper with the returned Mr. Geoffrey Saxton, he had first been panic-shaken, then resolved. He'd "let old iron-face Saxton do the high and mighty. Let him stand around and show off his clothes and adjectives, way he did at Flathead Lake." But he, Milt, would be "on the job." He'd help get supper, and calmly ignore Jeff's rudeness.

Only—Jeff wasn't rude. He greeted Milt with, "Ah, Daggett! This is *so* nice!" And Milt had no chance to help. It was Jeff who anticipated him and with a pleasant, " Let me get that—I'm kitchen-broke," snatched up the cold ham and salad. It was Jeff who found the supper plates, while Milt was blunderingly wondering how any one family could use a " whole furniture-store-full of different kinds of china." It was Jeff who sprang to help Claire wheel in the tea-wagon, and so captured the chance to speak to her for which Milt had been maneuvering these five minutes.

When they were settled, Jeff glowed at him, and respectfully offered, " I thought of you so often, Daggett, on a recent little jaunt of mine. You'd have been helpful."

" Where was that? " asked Milt suspiciously (wondering, and waiting to see, whether you could take cold ham in your fingers).

" Oh, in Alaska."

" In—Alaska? " Milt was dismayed.

" Yes, just a business trip there. There's something I wish you'd advise me about."

He was humble. And Milt was uneasy. He grumbled, " What's that? "

" I've been wondering whether it would be possible to use wireless telephony in Alaska. But I'm such a dub at electricity. Do you know—— What would be the cost of installing a wireless telephone plant with a hundred-mile radius? "

"Gee, I don't know!"

"Oh, so sorry. Well, I wonder if you can tell me about wireless telegraphy, then?"

"No, I don't know anything about that either."

Milt had desperately tried to make his answer gracious but somehow—— He hated this devil's obsequiousness more than he had his chilliness at Flathead Lake. He had a feeling that the Gilsons had delightedly kicked each other under the table; that, for all her unchanging smile, Claire was unhappy. . . . And she was so far off, a white wraith floating beyond his frantic grasp.

"It doesn't matter, really. But I didn't know—— So you've started in the engineering school at the University of Washington," Saxton was purring. "Have you met Gid Childers there—son of old Senator Childers—charming people."

"I've seen him. He has a Stutz—no, his is the Mercer," sighed Milt.

He hated himself for it, but he couldn't quite keep the awe out of his voice. People with Mercers——

Claire seemed to be trying to speak. She made a delicate, feminine, clairesque approximation to clearing her throat. But Jeff ignored her and with almost osculatory affection continued to Milt:

"Do let me know if there's anything I can do to help you. We're acquainted with two or three of your engineering faculty at the Office. They write in about various things. Do you happen to know Dr. Philgren?"

"Oh yes. Say! He's a wonder!" Milt was betrayed into exclaiming.

"Yes. Good chap, I believe. He's been trying to get a job with us. We may give him one. Just tell him you're a friend of mine, and that he's to give you any help he can."

Milt choked on a "Thanks."

"And—now that we're just the family here together—how goes the financial side? Can I be of any assistance in introducing you to some engineering firm where you could do a little work on the side? You could make quite a little money——"

So confoundedly affectionate and paternal——

Milt said irritably, "Thanks, but I don't need to do any work. I've got plenty of money."

"How pleasant!" Saxton's voice was smooth as marshmallow. "You're fortunate. I had quite a struggle to get through Princeton."

Wasn't Mr. Gilson contrasting Saxton's silk shirt with Milt's darned cotton covering, and in light of that contrast chuckling at Milt's boast and Saxton's modesty? Milt became overheated. His scalp prickled and his shoulder-blades were damp. As Saxton turned from him, and crooned to Claire, "More ham, honey?" Milt hated himself. He was in much of the dramatic but undesirable position of a man in pajamas, not very good pajamas, who has been locked out in the hotel corridor by the slamming of his door. He was in the frame of mind of a mongrel, of a real Boys'-Dog, at a Madison Square dog-show. He had a faint shrewd suspicion of Saxton's game. But what could he do about it?

He felt even more out of place when the family forgot him and talked about people of whom he had never heard.

He sat alone on an extremely distant desert isle and ate cold ham and wished he were in Schoenstrom.

Claire had recovered her power of speech. She seemed to be trying to bring him into the conversation, so that the family might appreciate him.

She hesitated, and thought with creased brows, and brought out, "Uh, uh, oh—— Oh Milt: How much is gas selling at now?" . . .

Milt left that charming and intimate supper-party at nine. He said, "Got to work on—on my analytical geometry," as though it was a lie; and he threw "Good night" at Saxton as though he hated his kind, good benefactor; and when he tried to be gracious to Mrs. Gilson the best he could get out was, "Thanks f' inviting me." They expansively saw him to the door. Just as he thought that he had escaped, Saxton begged, "Oh, Daggett, I was arguing with a chap—— What color are Holstein-Friesian cattle? Red?"

" Black and white," Milt said eagerly.

He heard Mrs. Gilson giggle.

He stood on the terrace wiping his forehead and, without the least struggle, finally and irretrievably admitting that he would never see Claire Boltwood or any of her friends again. Not—never!

He had received from Mrs. Gilson a note inviting him to share their box at the first night of a three-night Opera Season. He had spent half a day in trying to think of a courteously rude way of declining.

A straggly little girl came up from the candy-shop below his room, demanding, " Say, are you Mr. Daggett? Say, there's some woman wants to talk to you on our telephone. Say, tell them we ain't supposed to be no messenger-office. You ain't supposed to call no up-stairs people on our telephone. We ain't supposed to leave the store and go trotting all over town to—— Gee, a nickel, gee, thank you, don't mind what ma says, she's always kicking."

On the telephone, he heard Claire's voice in an agitated, " Milt! Meet me down-town, at the Imperial Motion Picture Theater, right away. Something I've got to tell you. I'll be in the lobby. Hurry!"

When he bolted in she was already in the lobby, agitatedly looking over a frame of " stills." She ran to him, hooked her fingers in his lapel, poured out, " They've invited you to the opera? I want you to

come and put it all over them. I'm almost sure there's
a plot. They want to show me that you aren't used
to tiaras and saxophones and creaking dowagers and
tulle. Beat 'em! Beat 'em! Come to the opera and be
awf'ly aloof and supercilious. You can! Yes, you can!
And be sure—wear evening clothes. Now I've got to
hurry."

"B-but——"

"Don't disappoint me. I depend on you. Oh, say
you will!"

"I will!"

She was gone, whisking into the Gilson limousine.
He was in a glow at her loyalty, in a tremor of anger
at the meddlers.

But he had never worn evening clothes.

He called it "a dress-suit," and before the complications of that exotic garb, he was flabby with
anxiety. To Milt and to Schoenstrom—to Bill Mc-
Golwey, even to Prof Jones and the greasily prosperous Heinie Rauskukle—the dress-suit was the symbol
and proof, the indication and manner, of sophisticated
wealth. In Schoenstrom even waiters do not wear
dress-suits. For one thing there aren't any waiters.
There is one waitress at the Leipzig House, Miss
Annie Schweigenblat, but you wouldn't expect Miss
Schweigenblat to deal them off the arm in black
trousers with braid down the side.

No; a dress-suit was what the hero wore in the

movies; and the hero in the movies, when he wasn't a cowpuncher, was an ex-captain of the Yale football team, and had chambers and a valet. You could tell him from the valet because he wasn't so bald. It is true that Milt had heard that in St. Cloud there were people who wore dress-suits at parties, but then St. Cloud was a city, fifteen or sixteen thousand.

"How could he get away with a dress-suit? How could he keep from feeling foolish in a low-cut vest, and what the deuce would he do with the tails? Did you part 'em or roll 'em up, when you sat down? And wouldn't everybody be able to tell from his foolish look that he didn't belong in one?" He could hear A.D.T. boys and loafers in front of pool rooms whispering, "Look at the piker in the rented soup and fish!"

For of course he'd rent one. Nobody bought them —except plutes like Henry B. Boltwood.

He agitatedly walked up and down for an hour, peering into haberdashery windows, looking for a kind-faced young man. He found him, in Ye Pall Mall Toggery Shoppe & Shoes; an open-faced young man who was gazing through the window as sparklingly as though he was thinking of going as a missionary to India—and liked curry. Milt ironed out his worried face, clumped in, demanded fraternally, "Say, old man, don't some of these gents' furnishings stores have kind of little charts that tell just what you

wear with dress-suits and Prince Alberts and everything? "

" You bet," said the kind-faced young man.

West of Chicago, " You bet " means " Rather," and
" Yes indeed," and " On the whole I should be inclined
to fancy that there may be some vestiges of accuracy
in your curious opinion," and " You're a liar but I
can't afford to say so."

The kind-faced young man brought from behind the
counter a beautiful brochure illustrated with photo-
graphs of Phoebus Apollo in what were described as
" American Beauty Garments—neat, natty, nobby,
new." The center pages faithfully catalogued the
ties, shirts, cuff-links, spats, boots, hats, to wear with
evening clothes, morning clothes, riding clothes, tennis
costumes, polite mourning.

As he looked it over Milt felt that his wardrobe already contained all these gentlemanly possessions.

With the aid of the clerk and the chart he purchased
a tradition-haunted garment with a plate-armor bosom
and an opening as crooked as the Missouri River; a
white tie which in his strong red hands looked as silly
as a dead fish; waistcoat, pearl links, and studs. For
the first time, except for seizures of madness during
two or three visits to Minneapolis motor accessory
stores, he caught the shopping-fever. The long shining counter, the trim red-stained shelves, the glittering cases, the racks of flaunting ties, were beautiful

to him and beckoning. He revolved a pleasantly clicking rack of ties, then turned and fought his way out.

He bought pumps—which cost exactly twice as much as the largest sum which he had allowed himself. He bought a newspaper, and in the want-columns found the advertisement:

Silberfarb the Society Tailor
DRESS SUITS TO RENT
Snappiest in the City

Despite the superlative snappiness of Mr. Silberfarb's dress-suits his establishment was a loft over a delicatessen, approached by a splintery stairway along which hung shabby signs announcing the upstairs offices of " J. L. & T. J. O'Regan, Private Detectives," " The Zenith Spiritualist Church, Messages by Rev. Lulu Paughouse," " The International Order of Live Ones, Seattle Wigwam," and "Mme. Lavourie, Sulphur Baths." The dead air of the hallway suggested petty crookedness. Milt felt that he ought to fight somebody but, there being no one to fight, he banged along the flapping boards of the second-floor hallway to the ground-glass door of Silberfarb the Society Tailor, who was also, as an afterthought on a straggly placard, " Pressng & Cleang While U Wait."

He belligerently shouldered into a low room. The

light from the one window was almost obscured by racks of musty-smelling black clothes which stretched away from him in two dismal aisles that resembled a morgue of unhappy dead men indecently hung up on hooks. On a long, clumsily carpentered table, a small Jew, collarless, sweaty, unshaven, was darning trousers under an evil mantle gaslight. The Jew wrung out his hands and tried to look benevolent.

"Want to rent a dress-suit," said Milt.

"I got just the t'ing for you!"

The little man unfolded himself, galloped down the aisle, seized the first garment that came to hand, and came back to lay it against Milt's uncomfortable frame, bumbling, "Fine, mister, fy-en!"

Milt studied the shiny-seamed, worn-buttonholed, limp object with dislike. Its personality was disintegrated. The only thing he liked about it was the good garage stink of gasoline.

"That's almost worn out," he growled.

At this sacrilege Mr. Silberfarb threw up his hands, with the dingy suit flapping in them like a bed-quilt shaken from a tenement window. He looked Milt all over, coldly. His red but shining eyes hinted that Milt was a clodhopper and no honest wearer of evening clothes. Milt felt humble, but he snapped, "No good. Want something with class."

"Vell, that was good enough for a university professor at the big dance, but if you say so——"

In the manner of one who is being put to an unfair amount of trouble, Mr. Silberfarb returned the paranoiac dress-suit to the rack, sighing patiently as he laboriously draped it on a hanger. He peered and pawed. He crowed with throaty triumph and brought back a rich ripe thing of velvet collar and cuffs. He fixed Milt with eyes that had become as sulky as the eyes of a dog in August dust.

" Now that—you can't beat that, if you vant class, and it'll fit you like a glove. Oh, that's an elllegant garment! "

Shaking himself out of the spell of those contemptuous eyes Milt opened his brochure, studied the chart, and in a footnote found, " Never wear velvet collars or cuffs with evening coat."

"Nope. Nix on the velvet," he remarked.

Then the little man went mad and ran around in circles. He flung the elllegant garment on the table. He flapped his arms, and wailed, " What do you vant? What do you vannnnt? That's a hundred-and-fifty-dollar dress-suit! That belonged to one of the richest men in the city. He sold it to me because he was going to Japan."

" Well, you can send it to Japan after him. I want something decent. Have you got it—or shall I go some place else? "

The tailor instantly became affectionate. " How about a nice Tuxedo? " he coaxed.

" Nope. It says here—let me see—oh yes, here it is—it says here in the book that for the theater-with-ladies, should not wear ' dinner-coat or so-called Tuxedo, but——' "

"Oh, dem fellows what writes books they don't know nothing. Absolute! They make it up."

" Huh! Well, I guess I'll take my chance on them. The factory knows the ignition better 'n any repairman."

"Vell say, you're a hard fellow to please. I'll give you one of my reserve stock, but you got to leave me ten dollars deposit instead of five."

Mr. Silberfarb quite cheerfully unlocked a glass case behind the racked and ghostly dead; he brought out a suit that seemed to Milt almost decent. And it almost fitted when, after changing clothes in a broiling, boiling, reeking, gasoline-pulsing hole behind the racks, he examined it before a pier-glass. But he caught the tailor assisting the fit by bunching up a roll of cloth at the shoulder. Again Milt snapped, and again the tailor suffered and died, and to a doubting heathen world maintained the true gospel of " What do you vannnnt? It ain't stylish to have the dress-suit too tight! All the gents is wearing 'em loose and graceful." But in the end, after Milt had gone as far as the door, Mr. Silberfarb admitted that one dress-coat wouldn't always fit all persons without some alterations.

The coat did bag a little, and it was too long in the sleeves, but as Milt studied himself in his room—by placing his small melancholy mirror on the bureau, then on a chair, then on the floor, finally, to get a complete view, clear out in the hall—he admitted with stirring delight that he looked "pretty fair in the bloomin' outfit." His clear face, his shining hair, his straight shoulders, seemed to go with the costume.

He wriggled into his top-coat and marched out of his room, theater-bound, with the well-fed satisfaction of a man who is certain that no one is giggling, "Look at the hand-me-downs." His pumps did alternately pinch his toes and rub his heels; the trousers cramped his waist; and he suspected that his tie had gone wandering. But he swaggered to the trolley, and sat as one rich and famous and very kind to the Common People, till——

Another man in evening clothes got on the car, and Milt saw that he wore a silk hat, and a white knitted scarf; that he took out and examined a pair of white kid gloves.

He'd forgotten the hat! He was wearing his gray felt. He could risk the gloves, but the hat—the "stovepipe"—and the chart had said to wear one —he was ruined——

He turned up the collar of his top-coat to conceal his white tie, tried to hide each of his feet behind the other to cover up his pumps; sought to change his

expression from that of a superior person in evening
clothes to that of a decent fellow in honest Regular
Clothes. Had the conductor or any of the passengers
realized that he was a dub in a dress-suit without the
hat?

Once he thought that the real person in real evening clothes was looking at him. He turned his head
and bore the probable insult in weak misery.

Too feeble for anything but thick suffering he was
dragged on toward the theater, the opera, people in
silk hats—toward Jeff Saxton and exposure.

But his success in bullying the tailor had taught him
that dressing wasn't really a hidden lore to be known
only by initiates; that some day he too might understand the black and white magic of clothes. His
bruised self-consciousness healed. " I'll do—something," he determined. He waited, vacuously.

The Gilson party was not in the lobby when he
arrived. He tore off his top-coat. He draped it over
his felt hat, so that no one could be sure what sort
of hat it shamefully concealed. That unveiling did
expose him to the stare of everybody waiting in the
lobby. He was convinced that the entire ticket-buying
cue was glumly resenting him. Peeping down at the
unusual white glare of his shirt-front, he felt naked
and indecent. . . . " Nice kind o' vest. Must make
'em out of old piqué collars."

He endured his martyrdom till his party arrived

—the Gilsons, Claire, Jeff Saxton, and a glittering young woman whose name, Milt thought, was Mrs. Corey.

And Saxton wasn't wearing a high hat! He wore a soft one, and he didn't seem to care!

Milt straightened up, followed them through the manifold dangers of the lobby, down a perilous aisle of uptilted scornful faces, to a red narrow corridor, winding stairs, a secret passage, a mysterious dark closet—and he walked out into a room with one side missing, and, on that side, ten trillion people in a well, and nine trillion of them staring at him and noticing that he'd rented his dress-suit. Hot about the neck, he stumbled over one or two chairs, and was permitted to rest in a foolish little gilt chair in the farthest corner.

Once safe, he felt much better. Except that Jeff did put on white kid gloves, Milt couldn't see that they two looked so different. And neither of the two men in the next box wore gloves. Milt made sure of that comfort; he reveled in it; he looked at Claire, and in her loyal smile found ease.

He snarled, "She trusts you. Forget you're a dub. Try to be human. Hang it, I'm no greener at the opera than old horsehair sofa there would be at a garage."

There was something—— What was it he was trying to remember? Oh yes. When he'd worked in the Schoenstrom flour-mill, as engineer, at eighteen, the owner had tried to torment him (to " get his goat," Milt put it), and Milt had found that the one thing that would save him was to smile as though he knew more than he was telling. It did not, he remembered, make any difference whether or not the smile was real. If he merely looked the miller up and down, and smiled cynically, he was let alone.

Why not——

Saxton was bending toward him, asking in honeyed respectfulness:

" Don't you think that the new school in music—audible pointillage, one might call it—mistakes cacophony for power? "

Milt smiled, paternally.

Saxton waited for something more. He dug the nail of his right middle finger into his thumb, looked thoughtful, and attacked again:

"Which do you like better: the new Italian music, or the orthodox German? "

Milt smiled like two uncles watching a clever baby, and patronized Saxton with, " They both have their points."

He saw that Claire was angry; but that the Gilsons and Mrs. Corey, flap-eared, gape-mouthed, forward-bending, were very proud of their little Jeff. He saw that, except for their clothes and self-conscious coiffúres, they were exactly like a gang of cracker-box loafers at Heinie Rauskukle's badgering a new boy in town.

Saxton looked bad-tempered. Then Mrs. Corey bustled with her face and yearned at Milt, " Do tell me: what is the theme of the opera tonight. I've rather forgotten."

Milt ceased to smile. While all of them regarded him with interest he said clearly, " I haven't got the slightest idea. I don't know anything about music. Some day I hope I can get a clever woman like you to help me, Mrs. Corey. It must be great to know all about all these arts, the way you do. I wish you'd explain that—overture they call it, don't they?"

For some reason, Mr. Gilson was snickering, Mrs. Corey flushing, Claire looking well pleased. Milt had tried to be insulting, but had got lost in the intricacies of the insult. He felt that he'd better leave it in its apparently safe state, and he leaned back, and smiled again, as though he was waiting. Mrs. Corey did not explain the overture. She hastily explained her second maid, to Mrs. Gilson.

The opera was *Il Amore dei Tre Re*. Milt was bewildered. To him, who had never seen an opera, the convention that a girl cannot hear a man who is bellowing ten feet away from her, was absurd; and he wished that the singers would do something besides making their arms swim.

He discovered that by moving his chair forward, he

could get within a foot of Claire. His hand slipped across, touched hers. She darted a startled backward glance. Her fingers closed tight about his, then restlessly snuggled inside his palm—and Milt was lost in enchantment.

Stately kings of blood-red cloaks and chrysoberyls malevolent in crowns of ancient and massy gold—the quick dismaying roll of drums and the shadow of passing banners below a tower—a woman tall and misty-veiled and pale with dreams—a world of spirit where the soul had power over unseen dominions— this he saw and heard and tasted in the music. What the actual plot was, or the technique of the singing, he did not know, but it bore him beyond all reality save the sweet, sure happiness of Claire's nestling hand.

He held her fingers so firmly that he could feel the pulse beat in them.

In the clamminess of his room, when the enchantment was gone, he said gravely:

" How much longer can I keep this up? Sooner or later I bust loose and smash little Jeff one in the snoot, and he takes the count, and I'm never allowed to see Claire again. Turn the roughneck out on his ear. I s'pose I'm vulgar. I s'pose that fellow Michael in *Youth's Encounter* wouldn't talk about snoots. I don't care, I'll—— If I poke Saxton one—— I'm not afraid of the kid-glove precinct any more. My brain's as good as theirs, give it a chance. But oh, they're all against me. And they bust the Athletic Union's wrestling rule that 'striking, kicking, gouging, hair-pulling, butting, and strangling will not be allowed.' How long can I go on being good-natured? When I do break loose——"

Slowly, beneath the moral cuff of his dress-shirt, Milt's fist closed in a brown, broad-knuckled lump, and came up in the gesture of a right to the jaw. But it came up only a foot. The hand opened, climbed to Milt's face, rubbed his temples, while he sighed:

"Nope. Can't even do that. Bigger game now. Used to could—used to be able to settle things with a punch. But I've got to be more—oh, more diplomatic now. Oh Lord, how lonely I get for Bill McGolwey. No. That isn't true. I couldn't stand Bill now. Claire took all that out of me. Where am I, where am I? Why did I ever get a car that takes a 36 x 6?"

CHAPTER XXXII

THE CORNFIELD ARISTOCRAT

IT was an innocent little note from Jeff Saxton; a polite, humble little note; it said that Jeff had a card to the Astoria Club, and wouldn't Milt please have lunch with him? But Milt dropped it on the table, and he walked round it as though it were a dictagraph which he'd discovered in the table drawer after happy, happy, hidden hours at counterfeiting.

It seemed more dangerous to refuse than to go. He browned the celebrated new shoes; he pressed the distinguished new trousers, with a light and quite unsatisfactory flatiron; he re-re-retied his best spotted blue bow—it persisted in having the top flaps too short, but the retying gave him spiritual strength—and he modestly clumped into the aloof brick portal of the Astoria Club on time.

He had never been in a club before.

He looked at the red tiled floor of the entrance hall; he stared through the hall into an immense lounge with the largest and softest chairs in the world, with oil portraits of distinguished old bucks, and ninety per cent. of the wealth and power of Seattle pulling its several mustaches, reading the P.I., and ignoring the lone intruder out in the hall.

A small Zulu in blue tights and brass buttons glared at Milt; and a large, soft, suave, insulting young man demanded, " Yes, sir? "

" Mr. G-g-geoffrey Saxton? " ventured Milt.

" Not in, sir." The " sir " sounded like " And you know it." The flaming guardian retired behind a narrow section of a bookkeeper's desk and ignored him.

" I'm to meet him for lunch," Milt forlornly persisted.

The young man looked up, hurt and annoyed at finding that the person was still to be dealt with.

" If you will wait in there? " he groaned.

Milt sat in there, which was a small blue tapestry room with hard chairs intended to discourage bill-collectors. He turned his hat round and round and round, till he saw Jeff Saxton, slim and straight and hard as the stick hooked over his arm, sailing into the hall. He plunged out after him, took refuge with him from the still unconvinced inspection of the hall-man. For twenty seconds, he loved Jeff Saxton.

And Jeff seemed to adore him in turn. He solicitously led Milt to the hat-checking counter. He showed Milt the lounge and the billiard room, through which Milt crept with erect shoulders and easy eyes and a heart simply paralyzed with fear that one of these grizzled clubmen with clipped mustaches would look at him. He coaxed Milt into a grill that was a cross between the Chinese throne-room and a Viennese

Weinstube, and he implored his friend Milt to do him the favor of trying the "very fair" English mutton chops and potatoes *au gratin.*

"I did want to see you again before we go East, Daggett," he said pleasantly.

"Th-thanks. When do you go?"

"I'm trying to get Miss Boltwood to start soon now. The season is opening in the East. She does like your fine sturdy West, as I do, but still, when we think of the exciting new shows opening, and the dances, and the touch with the great world—— Oh, it does make one eager to get back."

"That's so," risked Milt.

"We, uh—— Daggett—— In fact, I'm going to call you Milt, as Claire does. You don't know what a pleasure it has been to have encountered you. There's a fine keen courage about you Western chaps that makes a cautious old fogy like me envious. I shall remember meeting you with a great deal of pleasure."

"Th-thanks. Been pleasure meet you."

"And I know Claire will, too."

Milt felt that he was being dealt with foully. He wanted to object to Saxton's acting as agent for Claire as incompetent, irrelevant, immaterial, and no foundation laid. But he could not see just where he was being led, and with Saxton glowing at him as warmly and greasily as the mutton chops, Milt could only smile wanly, and reflectively feel the table leg to see if it was loose enough to jerk out in case of need.

Saxton was being optimistic:

" In fact, Claire and I both hope that some day when you've finished your engineering course, we'll see you in the East. I wonder—— As I say, my dear fellow, I've taken the greatest fancy to you, and I do hope you won't think I'm too intimate if I say that I imagine that even in your charming friendship with Miss Boltwood, you've probably never learned what important people the Boltwoods are. I thought I'd tell you so that you could realize the privilege both you and I have in knowing them. Henry B. is—while not a man of any enormous wealth—regarded as one of the keenest intellects in New York wholesale circles. But beyond that, he is a scholar, and a man of the broadest interests. Of course the Boltwoods are too modest to speak of it, but he was chiefly instrumental in the establishment of the famous Brooklyn Symphony Orchestra. And his ancestors clear through —his father was a federal judge, and his mother's brother was a general in the Civil War, and afterwards an ambassador. So you can guess something of the position Claire holds in that fine, quiet, solid old Brooklyn set. Henry Ward Beecher himself was complimented at being asked to dine with the Boltwoods of his day, and——"

No, the table leg wouldn't come loose, so it was

only verbally that the suddenly recovered Milt attacked:

"Certainly is nice to have one of those old families. It's something like—— As you say, you and I have gotten pretty well acquainted along the line, so I guess I can say it to you—— My father and his folks came from that same kind of family. Father's dad was a judge, back in Maine, and in the war, grand-dad was quite friendly with Grant."

This tribute of Milt to his grandsire was loyal but inaccurate. Judge Daggett, who wasn't a judge at all, but a J. P., had seen General Grant only once, and at the time the judge had been in company with all the other privates in the Fourteenth Maine.

"Dad was a pioneer. He was a doctor. He had to give up all this easy-going stuff in order to help open up the West to civilization, but I guess it was worth it. He used to do the hardest kind of operations, on kitchen tables, with his driver giving the chloroform. I'm mighty proud of him. As you say, it's kind of what you might call inspiring to belong to the old Pilgrim aristocracy."

Never before had Milt claimed relation to a group regarding which his only knowledge was the information derived from the red school-history to the effect that they all carried blunderbusses, put people in the stocks for whistling, and frequently said, "Why don't you speak for yourself, John?" But he had made his boast with a clear eye and a pleasant, superior, calm smile.

"Oh! Very interesting," grunted Saxton.

"Would you like to see grandfather's daguerreotype?"

"Oh, yes, yes, uh, thanks, that would be very interesting—— Do let me see it, when—— Uh, as I was saying, Claire doubtless has a tremendous social career before her. So many people expecting her to marry well. Of course she has a rather unusual combination of charm and intelligence and—— In fact I think we may both be glad that——"

"Yes. That's right. And the best thing about her is the way she can shake off all the social stuff and go camping and be a regular human being," Milt caressed.

"Um, uh, no doubt, no doubt, though—— Of course, though, that isn't an inherent part of her. I fancy she's been rather tired by this long trip, poor child. Of course she isn't very strong."

"That's right. Real pluck. And of course she'll get stronger by hiking. You've never seen her bucking a dangerous hill—I kind of feel that a person who hasn't seen her in the wilds doesn't know her."

"I don't want to be contradictory, old man, but I feel on the other hand that no one who has failed to see her at the Junior League Dances, in a Poiret

frock, can know her! Come, come! Don't know how
we drifted into this chorus of praise of Claire! What
I wanted to ask was your opinion of the Pierce-
Arrow. I'm thinking of buying one. Do you think
that——"

All the way home Milt exulted, "I put it all over
him. I wasn't scared by the 'Don't butt into the
aristocracy, my young friend' stuff. I lied handsome.
But—— Darn it, now I'll have to live up to my
New England aristocracy. . . . Wonder if my grand-
dad's dad was a hired man or a wood-sawyer? . . .
Ne' mine; I'm Daggett of Daggett from now on." He
bounded up to his room vaingloriously remarking,
" I'm there with the ancestors. I was brought up in
the handsome city of Schoenstrom, which was founded
by a colony of Vermont Yankees, headed by Herman
Skumautz. I was never allowed to play with the
Dutch kids, and——" He opened the door. "—the
Schoenstrom minister taught me Greek and was my
bosom frien'——"

He stopped with his heart in his ankles. Lolling
on the bed, grinning, waving a cigarette, was Bill
McGolwey, proprietor of the Old Home Lunch, of
Schoenstrom, Minnesota.

" Wwwwwwwwwwwwwwwwwwwwwwwwwhy
where the heck did you come from?" stammered the
deposed aristocrat to his bosom friend Bill.

" You old lemon-pie-faced, lollygagging, flap-footed,

crab-nosed son of misery, gee, but it's good to see you,
Milt!"

Bill was off the bed, wringing Milt's hand with
simple joy, with perfect faith that in finding his friend
all the troubles of life were over. And Milt was
gloomily discovering the art of diplomacy. Bill was
his friend, yes, but——

It was hard enough to carry his own self.

He pictured Jeff Saxton leering at the door, and
while he pounded Bill's shoulder, and called him the
name which, west of Chicago, is the token of hatred
and of extreme gladness at meeting, he discovered that
some one had stolen his stomach and left a piece of
ice in its place.

They settled down on bed and chair, Bill's ears red
with joy, while Milt demanded:

"How the deuce did you get here?"

"Well, tell you, old hoss. Schoenstrom got so darn
lonely after you left, and when Ben and Heinie got
your address and bought the garage, think's I, lez go
off on a little bum."

Milt was realizing—and hating himself for realizing—that Bill's face was dirty, his hair linty, the bottoms of his trousers frayed masses of mud, while Bill
chuckled:

"I figured out maybe I could get a job here in a
restaurant, and you and me could room together. I
sold out my good will in the Old Home Lunch for a

hundred bucks. I was going to travel swell, riding the cushions. But Pete Swanson wanted me to go down to the Cities first, and we run into some pretty swift travelers in Minneapolis, and a couple of girls—saaaaaaay, kid, some class!"

Bill winked, and Milt—Milt was rather sick. He knew Bill's conception of class in young women. Was this the fellow he had liked so well? These the ideas which a few months ago he had taken as natural and extremely amusing?

"And I got held up in an alley off Washington Avenue, and they got the last twenty bones off'n me, and I was flatter 'n a pancake. So I says 'ish kabibble,' and I sneaks onto the blind baggage, and bums my way West. You'd 'a' died laughing to seen me throwin₀ my feet for grub. Oh, I'm some panhandler! There was one *Frau* sicked her dog onto me, and I kicked him in the jaw and—— Oh, it was one swell hike."

Milt was trying to ignore the voice that was raging, "And now he expects to live on me, after throwing his own money away. The waster! The hobo! He'll expect to meet Claire—— I'd kill him before I'd let him soil her by looking at her. Him and his classy girls!" Milt tried to hear only the other inner voice, which informed him, "He looks at you so trustingly. He'd give you his shirt, if you needed it—and he wouldn't make you ask for it!"

Milt tried to be hearty: "What're you going to do, old kid?"

"Well, the first thing I'm going to do is to borrow ten iron-men and a pair of pants."

"You bet! Here she is. Haven't got any extra pants. Tell you: Here's another five, and you can get the pants at the store in the next block, this side of the street. Hustle along now and get 'em!" He chuckled at Bill; he patted his arm; he sought to hurry him out. . . . He had to be alone, to think.

But Bill kissed the fifteen dollars, carelessly rammed it into his pocket, crawled back on the bed, yawned, "What's the rush? Gosh, I'm sleepy. Say, Milt, whadyuh think of me and you starting a lunch-room here together? You got enough money out of the garage——"

"Oh no, noooo, gee, I'd like to, Bill, but you see, well, I've got to hold onto what little I've got so I can get through engineering school."

"Sure, but you could cash in on a restaurant—you could work evenings in the dump, and there'd be a lot of city sports hanging around, and we'd have the time of our lives."

"No, I—— I study, evenings. And I—— The fact is, Bill, I've met a lot of nice fellows at the university and I kind of go around with them."

"Aw, how d'you get that way? Rats, you don't want to go tagging after them Willy-boys. Damn dirty snobs. And the girls are worse. I tell you, Milt, these hoop-te-doodle society Janes may look all right to hicks like us, but on the side they raise more hell than any milliner's trimmer from Chi that ever vamped a rube burg."

"What do you know about them?"

"Now don't get sore. I'm telling you. I don't like to see any friend of mine make a fool of himself hanging around with a bunch that despises him because he ain't rich, that's all. Met any of the high-toned skirts?"

"Yes—I—*have!*"

"Trot 'em up and lemme give 'em the once-over."

"We—we'll see about it. Now I got to go to a mathematics recitation, Bill. You make yourself comfortable, and I'll be back at five."

Milt did not have to go to a recitation. He marched out with briskness in his step, and a book under his arm; but when he reached the corner, the briskness proved to be spurious, and the mathematics book proved to be William Rose Benét's *Merchants of Cathay,* which Claire had given him in the Yellowstone, and which he had rescued from the wrecked bug.

He stood staring at it. He opened it with unhappy tenderness. He had been snatched from the world of beautiful words and serene dignity, of soaring mountains and companionship with Claire in the radiant morning, back to the mud and dust of Schoenstrom, from the opera to "city sports" in a lunch-room! He hated Bill McGolwey and his sneering assumption that Milt belonged in the filth with him. And he hated himself for not being enough of a genius to combine Bill McGolwey and Claire Boltwood. But not once, in his maelstrom of worry on that street corner, did he expect Claire to like Bill. Through all his youthful agonizing, he had enough common sense to know that though Claire might conquer a mountain pass, she could never be equal to the social demands of Schoenstrom and Bill McGolwey.

He wandered for an hour and came back to find that, in a " dry " city which he had never seen before, the crafty Bill had obtained a quart of Bourbon, and was in a state of unsteady beatitude. He wanted, he announced, to dance.

Milt got him into the community bathtub, and soused him under, but Bill's wet body was slippery, and Bill's merry soul was all for frolicsome gamboling, and he slid out of Milt's grasp, he sloshed around in the tub, he sprinkled Milt's sacred good suit with soapy water, and escaped, and in the costume of Adam he danced orientally in Milt's room, till he was seized with sleepiness and cosmic grief, and retired to Milt's bed in tears and nothing else.

The room dimmed, grew dark. The street lamps outside sent a wan, wavery gleam into the room.

Evening crowds went by, and in a motion-picture theater a banging piano struck up. Bill breathed in choking snorts. Milt sat unmoving, feeling very old, very tired, too dumbly unhappy to be frightened of the dreadful coming hour when Claire and Jeff should hear of Bill, and discover Milt's real world.

He was not so romantically loyal, not so inhumanly heroic, that it can truthfully be reported that he never thought of getting rid of Bill. He did think of it, again and again. But always he was touched by Bill's unsuspecting trust, and shook his head, and sank again into the fog.

What was the use of trying to go ahead? Wasn't he, after all, merely a Bill McGolwey himself?

If he was, he wouldn't inflict himself on Claire.

For several minutes he gave up forever the zest of climbing.

When Bill awoke, brightly solicitous about the rest of the quart of Bourbon, and bouncingly ready to " go out and have a time," Milt loafed about the streets with him, showing him the city. He dully cut his classes, next morning, and took Bill to the wharves.

It was late in the afternoon, when they were lounging in the room, and Bill was admiring his new pants —he boasted of having bought them for three dollars, and pointed out that Milt had been a " galoot " to spend ten dollars for shoes—that some one knocked at the door. Sleepily expectant of his landlady, Milt opened it on Miss Claire Boltwood, Mr. and Mrs. Eugene Gilson, and Mr. Geoffrey Saxton.

Saxton calmly looked past him, at Bill, smiled slightly, and condescended, " I thought we ought to call on you, so we've dropped in to beg for tea."

Bill had stopped midway in scratching his head to gape at Claire. Claire returned the look, stared at Bill's frowsy hair, his red wrists, his wrinkled, grease-stained coat, his expression of impertinent stupidity. Then she glanced questioningly at Milt, who choked:

" Oh yes, yes, sure, glad see you, come in, get some tea, so glad see you, come in——"

CHAPTER XXXIII

TOOTH-MUG TEA

"MY friend Mr. McGolwey—I knew him in Schoenstrom—come on to Seattle for a while. Bill, these are some people I met along the road," Milt grumbled.

"Glad to meet 'em. Have a chair. Have two chairs! Say, Milt, y'ought to have more chairs if you're going to have a bunch of swells coming to call on you. Ha, ha, ha! Say, I guess I better pike out and give the folks a chance to chin with you," Bill fondly offered.

"Oh, sit down," Milt snapped at him.

They all sat down, four on the bed; and Milt's inner ear heard a mute snicker from the Gilsons and Saxton. He tried to talk. He couldn't. Bill looked at him and, perceiving the dumbness, gallantly helped out:

"So you met the kid on the road, eh? Good scout, Milt is. We always used to say at Schoenstrom that he was the best darn hand at fixing a flivver in seven townships."

"So you knew Mr. Daggett at home? Now isn't that nice," said Mrs. Gilson.

"*Knew* him? Saaaaay, Milt and I was brung up

345

together. Why, him and I have bummed around together, and worked on farms, summers, and fished for
bull-heads—— Ever catch a bull-head? Damnedest
slipperiest fish you ever saw, and got horns that sting
the stuffin's out of you and—— Say, I wonder if
Milt's told you about the time we had at a barn-
dance once? There was a bunch of hicks there, and I
says, ' Say, kid, lez puncture their tires, and hide back
of the manure pile, and watch the fun when they come
out.' I guess maybe I was kind of stewed a little, tell
the truth, but course Milt he don't drink much, hardly
at all, nice straight kid if I do say so——"

"Bill!" Milt ordered. "We must have some tea.
Here's six-bits. You run down to the corner grocery
and get some tea and a little cream. Oh, you better
buy three-four cups, too. Hustle now, son!"

"Attaboy! Yours to command, ladies and gents,
like the fellow says!" Bill boomed delightedly. He
winked at Jeff Saxton, airily spun his broken hat on
his dirty forefinger, and sauntered out.

"Charming fellow. A real original," crooned Mrs.
Gilson.

"Did he know your friend Mr. Pinky?" asked
Saxton.

Before Milt could answer, Claire rose from the
bed, inspected the Gilsons and Jeff with cold dislike,
and said quietly to Milt, "The poor dear thing—he
was dreadfully embarrassed. It's so good of you to

be nice to him. I believe in being loyal to your old friends."

"Oh, so do I!" babbled Mrs. Gilson. "It's just too splendid. And *we* must do something for him. I'm going to invite Mr. Daggett and Mr.—Mr. McGollups, was it?—to dinner this evening. I do want to hear him tell about your boyhood. It must have been so interesting."

"It was," mused Milt. "It was poor and miserable. We had to work hard—we had to fight for whatever education we got—we had no one to teach us courtesy."

"Oh now, with your fine old doctor father? Surely he was an inspiration?" Jeff didn't, this time, trouble to hide the sneer.

"Yes. He was. He gave up the chance to be a rich loafer in order to save farmers' babies for fees that he never got."

"I'm sure he did. I wish I'd known him. We need to know men like that in this pink-frosting playing at living we have in cities," Claire said sweetly—not to Milt but to Jeff.

Mrs. Gilson had ignored them, waiting with the patience of a cat at a mouse-hole, and she went on, "But you haven't said you'd come, this evening. Do say you will. I don't suppose Mr. McGollups will care to dress for dinner?"

With saccharin devotion Milt yearned back, "No,

Mrs. Gilson. No. Mr. McGolwey won't care to dress. He's eccentric."

"But you'll make him come?"

Milt was tactfully beginning to refuse when Gene Gilson at last exploded, turned purple, covered his dripping, too-red lips with his handkerchief.

Then, abruptly, Milt hurled at Mrs. Gilson, "All right. We'll come. Bill'll be awfully funny. He's never been out of a jerkwater burg in his life, hardly. He's an amusing cuss. He thinks I'm smart! He loves me like a dog. Oh, he's rich! Ha, ha, ha!"

Milt might have gone on . . . if he had, Mr. and Mrs. Gilson would have gone away, much displeased. But Bill arrived, with some of the worst tea in the world, and four cups tastefully done in cupids' heads and much gilt.

Milt made tea, ignoring them, while Bill entertained the Gilsons and Saxtons with Rabelaisian stories of threshing-time when shirts prickly with chaff and gritty with dust stuck to sweat-dripping backs; of the "funny thing" of Milt and Bill being hired to move a garbage-pile and "swiping" their employer's "mushmelons"; of knotting shirts at the swimming-hole so that the bawling youngsters had to "chaw beef"; of drinking beer in the livery-stable at Melrose; of dropping the water-pitcher from a St. Klopstock hotel window upon the head of the "constabule" and escaping from him across the lean-to roof.

Mrs. Gilson encouraged him; Bill sat with almost closed eyes, glorying in the saga of small-town life; Saxton and Gilson did not conceal their contemptuous grins.

But Claire—— After nervously rubbing the tips of her thumbs with flickering agitated fingers, she had paid no attention to Bill and the revelation of Milt's rustic life; she had quietly gone to Milt, to help him prepare the scanty tea.

She whispered, " Never mind, dear. I don't care. It was all twice as much fun as being wheeled in lacy prams by cranky nurses, as Jeff and I were. But I know how you feel. Are you ashamed of having been a prairie pirate? "

" No, I'm not! We were wild kids—we raised a lot of Cain—but I'm glad we did."

" So am I. I couldn't stand it if you were ashamed. Listen to me, and remember little Claire's words of wisdom. These fools are trying—oh, they're so obvious!—they're trying to make me feel that the prim Miss Boltwood of Brooklyn Heights is a stranger to you. Well, they're succeeding in making me a stranger—to them! "

" Claire! Dear! You don't mind Bill? "

" Yes. I do. And so do you. You've grown away from him."

" I don't know but—— Today has been quite a test."

"Yes. It has. Because if I can stand your friend Mr. McGolwey——"

"Then you do care!"

"Perhaps. And if I think that he's, oh, not much good, and I remember that for a long time you just had him to play with, then I'm all the more anxious to make it up to you."

"Don't be sorry for me! I can't stand that! After all, it was a good town, and good folks——"

"No! No! I'm not sorry for you! I just mean, you couldn't have had so terribly much fun, after you were eighteen or so. Schoenstrom must have been a little dull, after very many years there. This stuff about the charm of backwoods villages—the people that write it seem to take jolly good care to stay in Long Island suburbs!"

"Claire!" He was whispering desperately, "The tea's most done. Oh, my dear. I'm crazy with this puttering around, trying to woo you and having to woo the entire Gilson tribe. Let's run away!"

"No; first I'm going to convince them that you are—what I know you are."

"But you can't."

"Huh! You wait! I've thought of the most beautiful, beastly cruel plan for the reduction of social obesity——"

Then she was jauntily announcing, "Tea, my dears. Jeff, you get the tooth-mug. Isn't this jolly!"

"Yes. Oh yes. Very jolly!" Jeff was thoroughly patronizing, but she didn't look offended. She made them drink the acid tea, and taste the chalk-like bread and butter sandwiches. She coaxed Bill to go on with his stories, and when the persistent Mrs. Gilson again asked the pariahs to come to dinner, Claire astonished Milt, and still more astonished Mrs. Gilson, by begging, "Oh yes, please do come, Milt."

He consented, savagely.

"But first," Claire added to Mrs. Gilson, "I want us to take the boys to—— Oh, I have the bulliest idea. Come, everybody. We're going riding."

"Uh, where——?" hinted Mr. Gilson.

"That's my secret. Come!"

Claire pranced to the door, herded all of them down to the limousine, whispered an address to the chauffeur.

Milt didn't care much for that ride. Bill was somewhat too evidently not accustomed to limousines. He wiped his shoes, caked with red mud, upon the seat-cushions, and apologized perspiringly. He said, "Gee whillikens, that's a dandy idee, telephone to bawl the shuffer out with," and "Are them flowers real, the bokay in the vase?"

But the Gilsons and Jeff Saxton were happy about it all—till the car turned from a main thoroughfare upon a muddy street of shacks that clung like goats to the sides of a high cut, a street unchanged from the pioneer days of Seattle.

"Good heavens, Claire, you aren't taking us to see Aunt Hatty, are you?" wailed Mrs. Gilson.

"Oh yes, indeed. I knew the boys would like to meet her."

"No, really, I don't think——"

"Eva, my soul, Jeff and you planned our tea-party today, and assured me I'd be so interested in Milt's bachelor apartment—— By the way, I'd been up there already, so it wasn't entirely a surprise. It's my turn to lead." She confided to Milt, "Dear old Aunt Hatty is related to all of us. She's Gene's aunt, and my fourth cousin, and I think she's distantly related to Jeff. She came West early, and had a hard time, but she's real Brooklyn Heights—and she belongs to Gramercy Park and North Washington Square and Rittenhouse Square and Back Bay, too, though she has got out of touch a little. So I wanted you to meet her."

Milt wondered what unperceived bag of cement had hardened the faces of Saxton and the Gilsons.

Silent save for polite observations of Claire upon tight skirts and lumbering, the merry company reached the foot of a lurching flight of steps that scrambled up a clay bank to a cottage like a hen that has set too long. Milt noticed that Mrs. Gilson made efforts to remain in the limousine when it stopped, and he caught Gilson's mutter to his wife, "No, it's Claire's turn. Be a sport, Eva."

Claire led them up the badly listed steps to an unpainted porch on which sat a little old lady, very neat, very respectable, very interested, and reflectively holding in one ivory hand a dainty handkerchief and a black clay pipe.

"Hello, Claire, my dear. You've broken the relatives' record—you've called twice in less than a year," said the little old lady.

"How do you do, Aunt Harriet," remarked Mrs. Gilson, with great lack of warmth.

"Hello, Eva. Sit down on the edge of the porch. Those chickens have made it awful dirty, though, haven't they? Bring out some chairs. There's two chairs that don't go down under you—often." Aunt Harriet was very cheerful.

The group lugubriously settled in a circle upon an assemblage of wind-broken red velvet chairs and wooden stools. They resembled the aftermath of a funeral on a damp day.

Claire was the cheerful undertaker, Mrs. Gilson the grief-stricken widow.

Claire waved at Milt and conversed with Aunt Hatty in a high brisk voice: "This is the nice boy I met on the road that I think I told you about, Cousin Hatty."

The little old lady screwed up the delicate skin about her eyes, examined Milt, and cackled, "Boy, there's something wrong here. You don't belong with my family. Why, you look like an American. You haven't got an imitation monocle, and I bet you can't talk with a New York-London accent. Why, Claire, I'm ashamed of you for bringing a human being into the Boltwood-Gilson-Saxton tomb and expecting——"

Then was the smile of Mrs. Gilson lost forever. It was simultaneously torpedoed, mined, scuttled, and bombed. It went to the bottom without a ripple, while Mrs. Gilson snapped, "Aunt Hatty, please don't be vulgar."

"Me?" croaked the little old lady. She puffed at her pipe, and dropped her elbows on her knees. "My, ain't it hard to please some folks."

"Cousin Hatty, I want Milt to know about our families. I love the dear old stories," Claire begged prettily.

Mrs. Gilson snarled. "Claire, really——"

"Oh, do shut up, Eva, and don't be so bossy!" yelped the dear little old lady, in sudden and dismaying rage. "I'll talk if I want to. Have they been bullying you, Claire? Or your boy? I tell you, boy, these families are fierce. I was brought up in Brooklyn—went through all the schools—used to be able to misplay the piano and mispronounce French with the best of 'em. Then Gene's pa and I came West together—he had an idea he'd get rich robbing the Injuns of their land. And we went broke. I took in washing. I learned a lot. I learned a Gilson was

just the same common stuff as a red-shirt miner, when
he was up against it.   But Gene's pa succeeded—there
was something about practically stealing a fur schooner
—but I never was one to tattle on my kin.   Anyway,
by the time Gene come along, his pa was rich, and that
means aristocratic.

" This aristocracy west of Pittsburgh is just twice
as bad as the snobbery in Boston or New York, because back there, the families have had their wealth
long enough—some of 'em got it by stealing real
estate in 1820, and some by selling Jamaica rum and
niggers way back before the Revolutionary War—
they've been respectable so long that they know mighty
well and good that nobody except a Britisher is going
to question their blue blood—and oh my, what good
blueing third-generation money does make.   But out
here in God's Country, the marquises of milling and
the barons of beef are still uneasy.   Even their pretty
women, after going to the best hair-dressers and
patronizing the best charities, sometimes get scared
lest somebody think they haven't either brains or
breeding.

" So they're nasty to all low pussons like you and
me, to make sure we understand how important they
are.   But lands, I know 'em, boy.   I'm kept pensioned
up here, out of the way, but I read the social notes in
the papers and I chuckle—— When there's a big re-
ception and I read about Mrs. Vogeland's pearls, and

her beautiful daughter-in-law, I remember how she used to run a boarding-house for miners——

"Well, I guess it's just as shoddy in the East if you go far enough back. Claire, you're a nice comforting body, and I hate to say it, but the truth is, your great-grandfather was an hostler, and made his first money betting on horses. Now, my, I oughtn't to tell that. Do you mind, dearie?"

"Not a bit. Isn't it delightful that this is such a democratic country, with no castes," said Claire.

At this, the first break in the little old lady's un-dammable flood, Mrs. Gilson sprang up, yammering, "The rest of you may stay as long as you like, but if I'm to be home in time to dress for dinner——"

"Yes, and I must be going," babbled Saxton.

Milt noted that his lower lip showed white tooth-marks.

It must be admitted that all of them rather ignored the little old lady for a moment. Milt was apologetically hinting, "I don't really think Bill and I'd better come to dinner this evening, Mrs. Gilson. Thanks a lot but—— It's kind of sudden."

Claire again took charge. "Not at all, Milt. Of course you're coming. It was Eva herself who invited you. I'm sure she'll be delighted."

"Charmed," said Mrs. Gilson, with the expression of one who has swallowed castor oil and doubts the unity of the universe.

There was a lack of ease about the farewells to Aunt
Harriet. As they all turned away she beckoned Milt
and murmured, "Did I raise the dickens? I tried to.
It's the only solace besides smoking that a moral old
lady can allow herself, after she gets to be eighty-two
and begins to doubt everything they used to teach her.
Come and see me, boy. Now get out, and, boy, beat
up Gene Gilson. Don't be scared of his wife's hoity-
toity ways. Just sail in."

"I will," said Milt.

He had one more surprise before he reached the
limousine.

Bill McGolwey, who had sat listening to everything
and scratching his cheek in a puzzled way, seized Milt's
sleeve and rumbled:

"Good-by, old hoss. I'm not going to butt in on
your game and get you in Dutch. Gosh, I never supposed you had enough class to mingle with elittys like
this gang, but I know when I'm in wrong. You were
too darn decent to kick me out. Do it myself. You're
best friend I ever had and—— Good luck, old man!
God bless you!"

Bill was gone, running, stumbling, fleeing past Aunt
Harriet's cottage, off into a sandy hilltop vacancy.
The last Milt saw of him was when, on the skyline,
Bill stopped for a glance back, and seemed to be dig-
ging his knuckles into his eyes.

Then Milt turned resolutely, marched down the

stairs, said to his hosts with a curious quietness, "Thank you for asking me to dinner, but I'm afraid I can't come. Claire, will you walk a few blocks with me?"

During the half minute it had taken to descend the steps, Milt had reflected, with an intensity which forgot Bill, that he had been selfish; that he had thought only of the opinion of these "nice people" regarding himself, instead of understanding that it was his duty to save Claire from their enervating niceness. Not that he phrased it quite in this way. What he had been muttering was:

"Rotten shame—me so scared of folks' clothes that I don't stand up to 'em and keep 'em from smothering Claire. Lord, it would be awful if she settled down to being a Mrs. Jeff Saxton. Got to save her—not for myself—for her."

It may have been Aunt Harriet, it may have been Milt's resolution, but Mrs. Gilson answered almost meekly, "Well, if you think—— Would you like to walk, Claire?"

As he tramped off with Claire, Milt demanded, "Glad to escape?"

"Yes, and I'm glad you refused dinner. It really has been wearing, this trial by food."

"This is the last time I'll dare to meet the Gilsons."

"And I'll have to be going back East. I hope the Gilsons will forgive me, some day."

"I'm afraid you didn't win them over by Aunt Hatty!"

"No. They're probably off me for life. Oh, these horrible social complications—worse than any real danger—fire or earthquake——"

"Oh, these complications—they don't exist! We just make 'em, like we make rules for a card game. What the deuce do we care about the opinions of people we don't like? And who appointed these people to a fixed social position? Did the president make Saxton High Cockalorum of Dress-Suits or something? Why, these are just folks, the same as kings and coal-heavers. There's no army we've got to fight. There's just you and me—you and I—and if we stick together, then we have all society, we *are* all society!"

"Ye-es, but, Milt dear, I don't want to be an outcast."

"You won't be. In the long run, if you don't take these aristocrats seriously, they'll be all the more impressed by you."

"No. That sounds cheering, in stories and these optimistic editorials in the magazines, but it isn't true. And you don't know how pleasant it is to be In. I've always been more or less on the inside, and thought outsiders dreadful. But—— Oh, I don't care! I don't care! With you—I'm happy. That's all I know and all I want to know. I've just grown up. I've just learned the greatest wisdom—to know when I'm

happy. But, Milt dear—— I say this because I love
you. Yes, I do love you. No, don't kiss me. Yes,
it is too—— It's *far* too public. And I want to talk
seriously. You can't have any idea how strong social
distinctions are. Don't despise them just because you
don't know them."

"No. I won't. I'll learn. Probably America will
get into the war. I'll be an engineering officer. I'll
learn this social dope from the college-boy officers.
And I'll come to Brooklyn with shoulder-straps and
bells on and—— Will you be waiting?"

"Oh—yes—— But, Milt! If the war comes, you
must be very careful not to get shot!"

"All right, if you insist. Good Lord, Claire. I
don't know what put it into my head but—— Do you
realize that a miracle has happened? We're no longer
Miss Boltwood and a fellow named Daggett. We
have been, even when we've liked each other, up to
today. Always there's been a kind of fence between
us. We had to explain and defend ourselves and
scrap—— But now—we're *us,* and the rest of the
world has disappeared, and——"

"And nothing else matters," said Claire.

CHAPTER XXXIV

THE BEGINNING OF A STORY

IT was the farewell to Claire and Jeff Saxton, a picnic in the Cascades, near Snoqualmie Falls—a decent and decidedly Milt-less fiesta. Mrs. Gilson was going to show Claire that they were just as hardy adventurers as that horrid Daggett person. So she didn't take the limousine, but merely the seven-passenger Locomobile with the special body.

They were ever so rough and wild. They had no maid. The chauffeur was absolutely the only help to the Gilsons, Claire, Jeff, and the temporarily and ejaculatorily nature-loving Mrs. Betz in the daring task of setting out two folding camp-tables, covering them with a linen cloth, and opening the picnic basket. Claire had to admit that she wished that she could steal the picnic basket for Milt. There were vacuum bottles of hot coffee. There were sandwiches of anchovy and *paté de foie gras.* There were cream cakes with almonds hidden in the suave cream, and there was a chicken salad with huge chunks of pure white meat wallowing in a sea of mayonnaise.

When the gorging was done and the cigarettes brought out (the chauffeur passed a spirit lamp), they stretched on rubber blankets, and groaned a little, and spoke well of nature and the delights of roughing it.

"What is it? What's wrong? They're so—oh, so polite. They don't mean what they say and they don't dare to say what they mean. Is that it?" worried Claire.

She started. She discovered that she was looking at a bristle of rope-colored hair and a grin projected from the shelter of a manzanita bush.

"For the——" she gasped. She was too startled to be able to decide what was for-the. She spoke judiciously to Jeff Saxton about Upper Montclair, the subway, and tennis. She rose to examine the mountains, strolled away, darted down a gully, and pounced on Milt Daggett with:

"How in heaven's name——"

"Found out where you-all were going. Look! Got a bug! Rented it. Come on! Let's duck! Drive back with me!" At the end of the gully was a new Teal bug, shinier than the ancient lost chariot, but equally gay and uncomfortable.

"Can't. Like to, but—— Be awfully rude to them. Won't do that—not more than is good for their souls —even for you. Now don't be sulky."

"I won't. Nev' be sulky again, because you're crazy about me, and I don't have to be sulky."

"Oh, I am, am I! Good heavens, the inconceivable conceit of the child!"

She turned her back. He darted to her, caught her hands behind her, kissed her hair, and whispered, "You are!"

"I am not!"

"Well then, you're not. Lord, you're sweet! Your hair smells like cinnamon and clean kittens. You'd rather go bumping off in my flivver than sailing in that big Loco they've got there."

"Yes," defiantly, "I would, and I'm ashamed of myself. I'm a throw-back to my horrid ancestor, the betting hostler."

"Probably. I'm a throw-back to my ancestor the judge. I'll train you to meet my fine friends."

"Well—upon—my—word—I—— Oh, do stop being idiotic. We talk like children. You reduce me to the rank of a gibbering schoolgirl. And I like it! It's so—oh, I don't know—so darn human, I suppose. Now hurry—kiss me, and get out, before they suspect."

"Listen."

"Yes?"

"I'll accidentally meet your car along the road. Invite you to ride. All right?"

"Yes. Do. Oh, we *are* two forlorn babes in the woods! G'-by."

She sauntered back to the picnic, and observed, "What is that purple flower up on the mountain side?"

The big car was sedately purring back when it was

insulted by an intermediate host of a machine that came jumping out of a side road. The vulgar driver hailed them with uncouth howling. The Gilsons' chauffeur stopped, annoyed.

"Why, hello folks," bawled the social bandit.

"Oh. How do you do," refuted Mrs. Gilson.

Jeff Saxton turned a ripe purple.

"How do you like my new bug, Claire? Awful little object. But I can make fifty an hour. Come and try it, Claire, can't you?"

"Why——" Claire was obviously shocked by the impropriety of the suggestion. She looked at Mrs. Gilson, who was breathing as though she was just going under the ether. Claire said doubtfully, "Well—— If you can get me right back to the house——"

"Sure," agreed Milt.

When the Loco was gone, Milt drove the bug to the side of the road, yanked up the emergency brake, and carefully kissed the girl who was snuggled down into the absurd low tin-sided seat.

"Do we have to get back soon?" he begged.

"Oh, I don't care if we never get back. Let's shoot up into the mountains. Side road. Let's pretend we're driving across the continent again."

Firs dashing by—rocks in the sunshine—clouds jaunty beyond the inviting mouth of a mountain pass —even the ruts and bumps and culverts—she seemed a part of them all. In the Gilsons' huge cars she had been shut off from the road, but in this tiny bug, so close to earth, she recovered the feeling of struggle, of triumph over difficulties, of freedom unbounded. And she could be herself, good or bad, ignorant or wise, with this boy beside her. All of which she expressed in the most eloquent speech she had ever uttered, namely:

"Oh, *Milt*——!"

And, to herself, "Golly, it's such a relief not to have to try to be gracious and aphoristic and repartistic and everything with Jeff."

And, "But I wonder if I am aphoristic and subtle? I wonder if when she gets the rice-powder off, Claire isn't a lot more like Milt than she thought?"

And, aloud again, "Oh, this is——"

"Yump. It sure is," Milt agreed.

They had turned from a side-road into a side-side-road. They crossed an upland valley. The fall rains had flooded a creek till it had cut across the road, washed through the thin gravel, left across the road a shallow violent stream. Milt stopped abruptly at its margin.

"Here's where we turn back, I guess," he sighed.

"Oh no! Can't we get across? It's only a couple of feet deep, and gravel bottom," insisted the re-stored adventurer.

"Yes, but look at the steep bank. Never get up it."

"I don't care. Let's try it! We can woggle around and dig it out somehow. I bet you two-bits we can," said the delicate young woman whom Mrs. Gilson was protecting.

"All right. In she goes!"

The bug went in—shot over the bank, dipped down till the little hood sloped below them as though they were looping the loop, struck the rushing water with a splash which hurled yellow drops over Claire's rose jersey suit, lumbered ahead, struck the farther bank, pawed at it feebly, rose two inches, slipped back, and sat there with the gurgling water all around it, turned into a motor-boat.

"No can do," grunted Milt. "Scared?"

"Nope. Love it! This is a real camp—the brush on the bank, and the stream—listen to it chuckle under the running-board."

"Do you like to camp with me?"

"Love it."

"Say! Gee! Never thought—— Claire! Got your transportation back East?"

"My ticket? Yes. Why?"

"Well, I'm sure you can turn it in and get a refund. So that's all right."

"Are you going to let me in on the secret?"

"Oh yes, might's well. I was just wondering—— I don't think much of wasting all our youth wait-ing—— Two-three years in engineering school, and

maybe going to war, and starting in on an engineering job, and me lonely as a turkey in a chicken yard,
and you doing the faithful young lady in Brooklyn——
I think perhaps we might get married tomorrow
and——"

"Good heavens, what do you——?"

"Do you want to go back to Brooklyn Gilsonses?"

"No, but——"

"Dear, can't we be crazy once, while we're youngsters?"

"Don't bombard me so! Let me think. One must
be practical, even in craziness."

"I am. I have over a thousand dollars from
the garage, and I can work evenings—as dear
Jeff suggested! We'd have a two-by-four flat——
Claire——"

"Oh, let me think. I suppose I could go to the
university, too, and learn a little about food and babies
and building houses and government. I need to go
to school a lot more than you do. Besides auction
and the piano—which I play very badly—and clothes
and how to get hold of tickets for successful plays, I
don't know one single thing."

"Will you marry me, tomorrow?"

"Well, uh——"

"Think of Mrs. Gilson's face when she learns it!
And Saxton, and that Mrs. Betz!"

It was to no spoken sentence but to her kiss that she

added, " Providing we ever get the car out of this river, that is! "

" Oh, my dear, my dear, and all the romantic ways I was going to propose! I had the best line about roses and stars and angels and everything——"

" They always use those, but nobody ever proposed to me in a bug in a flood before! Oh! Milt! Life is fun! I never knew it till you kidnapped me. If you kiss me again like that, we'll both topple overboard. By the way, *can* we get the car out? "

"I think so, if we put on the chains. We'll have to take off our shoes and stockings."

Shyly, turning from him a little, she stripped off her stockings and pumps, while he changed from a flivver-driver into a young viking, with bare white neck, pale hair ruffled about his head, trousers rolled up above his straight knees—a young seaman of the crew of Eric the Red.

They swung out on the running-board, now awash. With slight squeals they dropped into the cold stream. Dripping, laughing, his clothes clinging to him, he ducked down behind the car to get the jack under the back axle, and with the water gurgling about her and splashing its exhilarating coldness into her face, she stooped beside him to yank the stiff new chains over the rear wheels.

They climbed back into the car, joyously raffish as a pair of gipsies. She wiped a dab of mud from her cheek, and remarked with an earnestness and a naturalness which that Jeff Saxton who knew her so well would never have recognized as hers:

"Gee, I hope the old bird crawls out now."

Milt let in the reverse, raced the engine, started backward with a burst of muddy water churned up by the whirling wheels. They struck the bank, sickeningly hung there for two seconds, began to crawl up, up, with a feeling that at any second they would drop back again.

Then, instantly, they were out on the shore and it was absurd to think that they had ever been boating down there in the stream. They washed each other's muddy faces, and laughed a great deal, and rubbed their legs with their stockings, and resumed something of a dull and civilized aspect and, singing sentimental ballads, turned back, found another road, and started toward a peak.

"I wonder what lies beyond the top of this climb?" said Claire.

"More mountains, and more, and more, and we're going to keep on climbing them forever. At dawn, we'll still be going on. And that's our life."

"Ye-es, providing we can still buy gas."

"Lord, that's so."

"Speaking of which, did you know that I have a tiny bit of money—it's about five thousand dollars —of my own?"

"But—— That makes it impossible. Young tramp marrying lady of huge wealth——"

"No, you don't! I've accepted you. Do you think I'm going to lose the one real playmate I've ever had? It was so lonely on the Boltwoods' brown stoop till Milt came along and whistled impertinently and made the solemn little girl in frills play marbles and—— Watch out for that turn! Heavens, how I have to look after you! Is there a class in cooking at your university? No—do—not—kiss—me—on—a—turn!"

This is the beginning of the story of Milt and Claire Daggett.

The prelude over and the curtain risen on the actual play, they face the anxieties and glories of a changing world. Not without quarrels and barren hours, not free from ignorance and the discomfort of finding that between the mountain peaks they must for long gray periods dwell in the dusty valleys, they yet start their drama with the distinction of being able to laugh together, with the advantage of having discovered that neither Schoenstrom nor Brooklyn Heights is quite all of life, with the cosmic importance to the tedious world of believing in the romance that makes youth unquenchable.

THE END.